Occupied Heaven

The Story of Kashmir

a novel

ALEXANDRE MALLORIE

Mallorie, Alexandre
Occupied Heaven / Alexandre Mallorie
ISBN: 978-0-578-85848-7 Paperback
ISBN: 978-1-7366725-0-1 Hardback
ISBN: 978-1-7366725-1-8 Ebook
ISBN: 978-1-7366725-2-5 Audio

This novel is a work of fiction based on actual events that occurred in Kashmir. But it is a work of fiction, nonetheless. Names, incidents, locations, characters, and the timing of events are based on my imagination and are used fictitiously. Any resemblance is merely coincidental.

The publisher does not have any control over and does not assume any responsibility for author or third-party websites or their content.

This book is dedicated to the people of Kashmir.

Chapter 1

THE BEGINNING OF THE END

July 20, 1993

This dust will demolish

The illusion of day and night,

Though now it lies enchained

In the grip of fate.

-Allama Iqbal

TWO O'CLOCK IN the morning. A high shriek cut through the air. A moment later, a thunderous, debilitating crash shook my bedroom. A second loud shriek, a second crash, a second upheaval of the earth beneath me.

Terror propelled me into the hallway. Tamer was still asleep in his room — he'd always been the soundest of sleepers. Running toward his bed, I screamed, "Tamer, wake up! Wake up now!"

His eyes shot open in alarm. "What is it?" he asked as our parents appeared in the doorway.

Dad looked at us firmly. "Follow me, let's go." A belt of bullets encircled his waist, and he held a rifle firmly in his hand. I hadn't known we had a gun in the house, and the sight of the weapon frightened me. He seized my arm hard and yanked me forward. My mother shouted panicked instructions as the four of us ran.

Chaos greeted us outside. In the valley below, the hospital where my father worked was ablaze, and explosions erupted around the main market. The smell of smoke tinged Kashmir's usually fresh air. Eerie orange glows penetrated the night's darkness.

We fled to the back of our home, where my father sped Tamer and I down a short flight of stairs. He flung open the door to the emergency shelter, which he had built in the small space beneath our house. A generator, a few chairs, a bed, and stores of water and dried fruit lined the dim, cramped room.

He locked the door behind us.

We huddled together holding hands. After a few tense minutes, my father placed his gun against the wall before looking over at us. "Everything is going to be okay," he began, "but for the next few hours, we must be silent. I don't want to hear a single sound from either of you until morning. No one leaves this room, and no one leaves my sight." Tears ran down my mother's cheeks.

Dad was calm. He was wearing a traditional Kashmiri *shalwar kameez*, what he always wore when he wanted to relax, even after nearly 30 years in America. After a few moments, it started again. I could swear that the piercing shrieks and explosions were louder, and the earth shook even more than before. The ground was shaking constantly. It felt as if the house were crumbling on top of us, like our night could end at any moment. My father watched our faces, trying to maintain some sense of calm. I watched my family silently and wondered, "Is this really happening?" Ever since arriving in Kashmir, we had been hearing about destruction, but I had never expected to actually experience it.

In the cool damp basement, my mother and father whispered prayers throughout the night. I could only see their lips moving, and the lines of their faces firm with concentration. Tamer couldn't stop shaking and clutched my parents' hands, scared enough to be dead serious. We had to survive this. I had to make it out to ask Imani's hand. Thoughts of running to the car and driving far away gave me some sense of control over the situation, as hopeless of an endeavor that it would be.

There was an hour of silence. No bombs, no sounds, nothing. My brother and I shared uncertain glances.

"I know there hasn't been a bomb for a while, but everyone is staying right here, together," said my father. "We are not moving until I say so."

Mom's eyes were bloodshot. Tamer stared at the ceiling. We did what came naturally and held onto one another.

My father stood up. He placed a blanket over my mom and Tamer, huddled together on the small bed and said, "Go to sleep. Everything is going to be fine." Then he grabbed his rifle, brought a chair, and sat down in front of them. I grabbed the other chair and joined him. For the first time I noticed a small crevice the shape of a finger, between the top of the foundation and the ground floor. The crevice allowed a ray of moonlight into our basement bunker. I focused my eyes on the silver light, hoping that it wouldn't turn dark. While Mom and Tamer tried to sleep. Dad and I sat next to each other for what felt like an eternity. Another hour passed. We could hear the sound of a helicopter in the distance. We heard some shots fired, but they were faint. They could have been from the other valley.

The night turned into dawn, and the moonlight sneaking in through the crevice became a shadowy gray light in our basement bunker. Perhaps the worst was over. Even in the bunker, I imagined that I could feel the peace of morning settling in.

We heard several helicopters nearby. They sounded as though they were hovering right above the valley. My father stood and peered through the crevice. He shook his head in disappointment and said, "I can't see anything."

"Do you want me to go outside and see if it is safe?" I asked.

He shook his head and said, "No."

My mother and Tamer snuck a peek out of the blanket. I knew that they hadn't slept a wink.

As we waited, my patience began wearing thin. I stood and gazed through the crevice. The sun was right on top of us; all that I could see was a sharp light. I sat back down I felt suspended in time, with no way of knowing the hour because the morning call to prayer did not bellow out as it normally did.

My father took out some bottled water and dried fruit. He gave each of us water, and we handed around the fruit. I had no desire to eat, I doubt that anyone did, but we forced ourselves to take a few bites. The dried apricot felt like sand between my teeth.

Quietly I asked my father "Is there something we're waiting for?"

My father sternly answered, "No, son. The bombs have stopped, but it may be that the armed forces which bombed the village are now here in the village. If we step out, they will know we are here. We will wait. If we must wait a few days inside this basement, then that's what we will do. The bombing could be a prelude to the start of an invasion. We don't know. The best thing to do is patiently wait."

"Come on, Dad," I said, "They probably bombed the village because the *mujahideen* are at your hospital."

My father's face turned ridden with guilt, and I instantly regretted speaking. "I should have kicked them out of the hospital," Dad said helplessly.

"You did the right thing." I said hurriedly. "They would have bombed us anyway. They probably aren't even looking for the mujahideen."

My mother and brother overheard our conversation. "Do you know why these bombings happened?" My mother asked. "Who bombed us? Was it the Indians?"

"Both of you please calm down and relax! We will get out of here, but only when I say so."

The sound of helicopters became louder and now we could hear ground vehicles, then men walking. My father grabbed his rifle and pointed it at the door. Through the crevice I could see shoes. My mother gripped Tamer and he clenched his eyes shut.

My father took out a small pistol, loaded it and handed it to me. "This button is the safety," he said. "Release the safety and then pull on the lever to shoot. Don't shoot unless I shoot." He looked at me. "If I don't shoot, then you don't shoot. Do you understand?"

I had never held a gun before, had never really wanted to.

"Dad, I can't use this thing," I said shakily.

Seeing I was scared, he took back the gun. Gently, he said, "It's easy to use; there's a lot of kickback on the gun, so you have to clutch it and keep it stable. Then you point and shoot."

I didn't want anything to do with that gun, but I took it from him and said,

"Okay, I understand."

Eventually, the men departed. We could hear vehicles moving away from the neighborhood and toward *Keran's* main street, the refugee camps, and the hospital. I took a deep breath. My father tightened his lips and said, "They are gone."

Tamer and my mom lifted their heads from the blankets. I whispered, "Who were they?"

My father whispered back, "It could be the Indians, it could be the mujahideen, or it could be the Pakistani army. I don't know."

My father and I slumped back in our respective chairs and waited. We had been up all night, yet I was still wide awake.

Not for the first time, my thoughts turned towards Imani, who lived in a neighborhood close to ours. "Oh please God don't let anything happen to her," I silently prayed. "Please let her be okay. Please let her family be okay."

An image came to me of one of my visits with her the previous summer, one of my precious moments alone with her when she was trying to show me how to make Kashmiri tea in the kitchen. She had looked down at my soupy mixture of nuts and leaves in amusement.

"Hanzilah, the key to Kashmiri tea is the ingredients," she said. "You need to make sure you know when to put in the ingredients. You don't dump them all in together."

I smiled as I recalled that happy moment, and caught Tamer watching me questioningly. I shook my head at him.

It was at that moment that we heard the trucks return. Men screamed, "*Assalamu-alaikum* brothers and sisters! It is safe, it is safe!"

My father walked up and peered through the crevice. He sighed in relief. "It is the Pakistani military. But don't get up just yet."

Before my father let us leave, he stared out for several more minutes, waiting until some of our neighbors came out and were greeted by the soldiers.

"We are safe for now," he said calmly. "I'll go outside first. You all stay here."

He took his rifle with him and, before stepping out, he said to me, "Hanzilah, if I don't come back or something happens to me, be ready to protect your mother and your brother." He walked up the stairs and left, firmly closing the door behind him. I went to the crevice and surveyed our surroundings. I could see my father's legs. He came into view as he walked towards the soldiers and said "*Biaho*, I live in this neighborhood, what happened last night?" Then suddenly I heard a scream: "Dr. *Sahib*! Dr. *Sahib*! You are alive! Is your family alive? Is everyone okay?" It was the Governor running toward my father. I couldn't hear what they said to each other, but after a few minutes, my father fell to the floor and put his head down. The Governor put his hand on his shoulder. My father composed himself, and they walked to the front of the house, where I could no longer see them. I clenched my hand around the pistol.

"What do you see?" My mother and brother asked anxiously. "What is going on?"

"The Governor is here," I said tersely. "I saw Dad meet with him, and then they both walked toward the front of the house."

A few minutes later, I saw my father and the Governor *Sahib* again.

I couldn't make their words out initially, but once they got close enough I could hear my father shout, "Hanzilah, please come out now! Bring your mother and brother out with you!"

Dad and the governor greeted us at the opened basement door, and as we approached them I could smell something burning. When we got outside, my father hugged each of us and told us to go inside the house. As we walked forward, I could see the damage done to *Keran*. The main street was gone. The hospital, the market, and the refugee camp had been reduced into a jumbled concrete mass. Within our small neighborhood, the houses were untouched. But in the neighborhood next to ours, the neighborhood of Imani and her brother Jawad, smoke rose from houses.

My mother, Tamer, and I stood in shock as we gazed on our beloved village. It was gone. The refugees were dead. They had been living in tents; how could they have survived the bombing? The hospital was destroyed. The patients must have died. I thought angrily to myself what kind of awful person it would take to bomb a civilian hospital. Even the market was destroyed, with bodies littered everywhere.

Hundreds of Pakistani soldiers were scattered about *Keran*. Helicopters hovered overhead, tanks surrounded the valley on hilltops, and there were many military vehicles inside the valley. The village had been enveloped by chaos.

My body began to shiver and my mind was pushed in a hundred directions. I wanted to scream, and I wanted to cry. I wanted to find the men who had did this and take my vengeance. But first I wanted to run to Imani's house. Seething with anger and sadness, I fell to the floor. My mother and Tamer wept loudly. My father took hold of us and forced us back inside the house. We sat down in the living room. I put my hands against my face and openly cried. My father did his best to console us, holding each of us while repeating words of prayer and mercy. After getting us under control, he went back outside to speak with the Governor. Somehow, I found the courage and resiliency to get up. I opened the main house door and leaned against it while I surveyed *Keran*. I saw my dad and a large group of men standing in a circle, listening to the Governor.

I couldn't see Imani's house, only smoke in the distance. I couldn't wait. I ran. My father saw me running, tried to catch up, screamed, "Hanzilah, don't go! Don't go! Wait! We can go together!"

It was a ten-minute run to her house. As I approached, I could see that it had crumbled. At first I thought I was hallucinating, overwhelmed by confusion and bewilderment. My eyes had to be deceiving me. I screamed out, "Jawad! Jawad! Jawad!" I couldn't see anything but burnt and crumbled cement blocks. "Jawad! Jawad! Jawad! Imani! Imani! Imani! *Bahabi*! Anyone! Please!"

My father, the Governor, and a handful of soldiers arrived soon after. My father grabbed me. "It's okay! Everything is going to be okay! We will get them out safe and sound. *Inshallah*, everything will be okay."

I brushed my father away and began frantically pulling at the broken cement.

My father and some soldiers joined me, accompanied by a search dog. The dog started sniffing around the destroyed home before making its way to the center of the house and barking urgently. The soldiers followed him and began pulling blocks of burnt cement out straight from the very center of the home. I could hear a voice! It was faint but discernible. It was Jawad screaming: "Help! Help! We are stuck underneath! My whole family is hurt! Please help! Hurry! Hurry!"

I ran to the center of the house and joined the soldiers pulling out debris, large stones, and burnt cement with our bare hands. My palms grew dirty, burned and cut, but I ignored the sharp pain. Eventually we hit one piece that simply wasn't coming out. It was too large to move with our bare hands. We didn't have time to wait for any earth-moving equipment. I found an undamaged steel rod and wedged it under the cement, but no matter how hard I strained, I wasn't strong enough to leverage it. A tall Pakistani soldier with a thick mustache grabbed the steel rod from me. He looked like a Pathan from the frontier. He raised the slab up straight, and I joined two other soldiers in tying it with a rope. Together, we pulled the rope while the Pathan pushed into the slab with the steel rod and with a slow horrible grinding sound the slab was removed. We uncovered a narrow hole big enough to see through. I could see a body, but I couldn't make out who it was. Jawad's voice became stronger, screaming, "Help! Get us out! Please hurry!" I yelled down through the hole: "Jawad! It's me Hanzilah! We're coming! I have soldiers with me! We'll get you and your family out! We're coming!"

"Hanzilah," Jawad gasped. "Please hurry! My wife is dead! My parents are dead! Everyone is dead! They killed my beautiful wife! They killed my sister, they killed my family! My whole family is gone!"

My heart convulsed, but somehow I refused to believe it was over. No, Imani is not dead, I told myself. She is alive. Jawad's family is still alive. He's in shock. He doesn't know.

It must have taken another half an hour, but finally I could clearly see Jawad. There were four bodies around him: his wife, his parents, and Imani all lying there very still. My father saw through the hole too. He pushed me aside. "Get out of here, your work is done."

"No, I'm not leaving," I said firmly, "I have to help my friend and his family. I have to get Imani out of there."

"I know son, I know you do. But you are not going to like what you see. I don't think you will ever be able to handle what you are about to see. Take it from me. You should leave, for your own sake. I had to bury my friends; I know you don't want to bury yours."

I stood firm. With a clenched face I said, "No, Dad, I'm getting them out. She's alive. Imani is still alive."

We had created enough space for a person to fit through the hole. A soldier brought a rope and lowered it through the hole.

My dad called down to him, "We're going to pull your family up one by one. Place the rope around their waists so that if the rope slides, their arms will stop the rope, and they won't get hurt when they're being pulled!"

"I understand!" said Jawad.

After a few minutes, he hollered, "Go ahead and pull!" He had a body in his arms, his wife. When she came up I grabbed her by the shoulders, and we pulled her out and I gently placed her on the ground. Her body was broken; her face was bruised. She didn't look like the same person. Once she'd been a lively, smiling woman. Now she looked more like a ruined doll. My father placed his hand over her wrists and after a few moments said, "She's dead. To God we belong, and to him we shall return." He placed a white cloth over her body, and we carried her into a military vehicle. My father noticed the wetness in my eyes and pleaded with me again, "Hanzilah, just leave. You are not going to like what you see. I know you want to be a hero, but it might be too late to be Imani's hero."

"Dad, stop it. I'm not a kid anymore. I can handle it. *Keran* is my village too. Kashmir is my country too. This family is my family too."

When we returned, another body was coming up. It was Jawad's father. His body was dismembered. His hair and face were full of dirt. My dad checked his pulse and said, "To God we belong, and to him we shall return." We put another white cloth over him and moved his body.

I could hear my heart thumping loudly. My hands were sweating profusely, and I felt a sharp pain in my neck as if someone had stabbed me with a knife. All I could think was, "Please God, don't take her away from me." I didn't want to see the next person coming up; I had seen enough. My right thigh started shaking uncontrollably. I put a hand on it but it wouldn't stop.

My father looked at me and said, "Take a deep breath." I took a deep breath. He said, "Take another deep breath." I did. He grabbed me, gave me a hug, and said, "You need to be strong. Your friend Jawad is coming up soon and he will need you. Now, take another deep breath." I took a third deep breath. My father grabbed me by my arm and we walked back towards the hole.

Jawad had attached a third body to the rope, and the soldiers were lifting it up. It was his mother. Her hands and arms were burnt as if she had been on fire. Her face was almost beyond recognition. We placed her on the ground. Her body had already tightened up in rigor mortis. She was dead, probably had been for hours. My father didn't even check her for a pulse. He simply said, "To God we belong, and to him we shall return."

At that point, I had lost hope. In my heart, I knew Imani was gone. She would be the next one up, and then Jawad. Tears started rolling down my face. I wasn't crying, or at least my breath and face hadn't changed. I simply had tears coming down my cheeks uncontrollably. I put my hand beneath my shirt and brought it to my face and wiped away the tears. I did that a couple of times, but the tears wouldn't stop, and all I accomplished was a large wet circle on my shirt.

I sat down and thought to myself that I didn't want to see her this way, have my image of Imani tainted. I didn't want my last memory of the beautiful woman I loved to be her burnt and lifeless face. So I said to my dad, "You go help Jawad with the last body. When Jawad is coming up, I will be there for him." My father nodded and went back to the hole in which Jawad had been surrounded by his dead family for who knew how many hours. I couldn't look. I could hear her body coming up, and I heard it being placed on the ground. A pause, and my father shouted, "She is alive! She is alive!"

I immediately stood to see my father and a military medic injecting a needle into her. I ran towards them. Imani's face was dirty and there were some cuts above her eye. Dirt covered her clothes and bruises painted her arms. But her heart was beating.

My father was still hunched over her." We injected her with morphine, which should help with the pain."

I sat there and knelt next to Imani, ignoring the chaos around me. Her eyes were closed, her thick lashes dusted with soot, her warm brown skin turning purple and blotchy. I desperately wanted her to wake up, but I didn't know what I would say. Finally, the Governor came and put his hand on my shoulder. "

"We need to move her son."

As she was taken away, I thought that if she had opened her eyes I would have just kissed her.

My father looked at me and said, "I don't know if she will live, son, but at least there is hope." I nodded, swallowing the lump in my throat.

"It's not over," he added. "Your friend is still underneath the house. You have to be a good friend to him; he needs you now more than ever."

We went back to the hole, where Jawad was being pulled up by the Pakistani soldiers. They picked him out and placed him on the ground as I watched. His eyes were bloodshot, and his breath ragged, but unlike the others, he was still Jawad, with his short hair and goatee, all mangled. I grabbed him by the hand and pulled him up. I reached to wrap my arms around him but he pushed me out of the way and asked angrily, "Where is my family? Where is my wife, my mother?"

As I stared at his dirty feet I said softly, "Jawad, I am sorry, I am so sorry." I nodded toward my father, who was standing next to the military vehicle that held their bodies. He stared at them, then after a few moments, calmly said, "There are only three bodies. Where is the fourth?"

My father approached Jawad and said, "Imani is alive and has been moved to a temporary clinic in the next valley. I am profoundly sorry son, but your wife and parents didn't make it."

Jawad walked up to the bodies. He was about to open the white shroud to the body on the very right when my father gently blocked Jawad's hand. "Son, you don't want to do that."

Jawad calmly said, "Dr. Ali, you have been very good to me and my family. But with all due respect, please move your hands."

My father stepped back. "You are right. Forgive me."

Jawad's tears had dried up. His face was pained but steady.

He opened the first shroud and looked down at his mother's face. A white cloth was wrapped around her head and jaw, so that her mouth would remain closed. Her face was burned beyond seeming human. I don't think Jawad had seen the extent of the damage down in the dark. He put his hand against her forehead and said some words that I couldn't make out, then rewrapped his mother's shroud.

He opened the shroud of the body in the middle, his father. There was another white cloth wrapped around his head and jaw. His father's face wasn't burnt, but it was dirty. I had always found Jawad's father intimidating, but in death I realized how physically small of a man he was. Jawad touched the top of his father's forehead as he had his mother's, whispered a few words, and rewrapped his shroud.

He moved to the last body and opened the shroud. It was his wife. She too had a white cloth wrapped around her head. Jawad stood there for a long time and stared at her badly bruised face. I tried not to look at Jawad, thinking how I would feel if it were Imani in his wife's place. He shook his head. He put his head against her body for a few moments. He kissed her forehead, said a few words, and then rewrapped the shroud.

"Leave these bodies here," he said harshly, "I am taking them out of the vehicle." He started pulling his wife's body out of the vehicle. "I will bury them myself. They are martyrs. They can be buried in the clothes they died in and their bodies don't need to be cleaned."

My father said, "Yes, you are right Jawad. They are martyrs." He moved forward to help Jawad take the bodies out of the vehicles. But he added in a solemn voice, "Jawad, I know martyrs are buried in the spot where they died. But they cannot be buried here. There are hundreds, maybe thousands more bodies that we need to bury today. We will bury them together at the graveyard. Those people are martyrs too."

Jawad had the look of a man who had been beaten. Grudgingly he nodded and moved away from the military truck.

One of the soldiers who had been helping us said, "We have already started digging the funeral plots. They will be buried after sunrise tomorrow morning."

Jawad took a step back and silently conceded. He turned his gaze to my father and quietly asked, "Where is my sister? I want to go to her."

At that moment, the Governor had returned in his military vehicle. My father pointed to him and said, "The Governor will take you." He walked up to the Governor as he was getting out of the car and whispered something in his ear. The Governor looked over at Jawad and said, "Come here, son."

As Jawad walked toward the vehicle I ran to him, hugged him, and said, "Jawad, I am so sorry." This time, he hugged me back. We held each other very closely, and tears came down his face. He wept against my shoulder. Then he pulled away and said, "Why am I still alive? I was going to die soon anyway. They should have lived, not me."

I didn't know what to say. I stood there and stared at his grief-stricken face. I spoke the words I had heard my father say: "To God we belong, and to him we shall all return." Jawad turned away and sat in the vehicle with the Governor. The car drove away from us and headed toward the neighboring valley. I knew I hadn't done enough.

My father approached me and said, "You should have gone with him. He needs you."

"I know," I replied guiltily.

Dad placed his hand on my shoulder. "Since you are here, let's go help as much as we can."

I looked out through the valley and saw death. Hundreds of bodies lay littered about. Debris and devastation were everywhere. My father noticed me looking into the valley and remarked, "They destroyed everything on the main street. The hospital has been destroyed. The ER doctor was killed, and the Internist who was on call also died. We lost four nurses as well. The refugees, most of them if not all, are probably dead. At last count they numbered about five hundred people, many of them women and children." He paused. "Only Keran was bombed. They didn't attack any of the neighboring valleys and villages. According to the Governor, the target for the Indian army was our hospital. They were after the mujahideen. Several of the bombs strayed and hit homes."

I was silent as my father spoke. With anger and hurt in his voice, he said, "I can't believe they would target a hospital. Don't they know it's a civilian hospital? Why?"

My chest felt hot with anger: "Because they want to destroy all hope. You were wrong, and *Chacha Riaz* was right. Peace can only come from the rifle."

My dad stared at me for a moment and hugged me. "I know you are hurt. We are all hurting now."

We walked back to our house. My father's Toyota was still working, so we drove toward the center of *Keran*. The village was surreal. Parts of it had not been touched. Others were thoroughly destroyed. It looked like the scene we had witnessed in Alabama a few years back when tornados had ripped through entire sections of the town but left other parts entirely untouched. About half a kilometer before the main market, we stopped near a small neighborhood that had been hit by several stray bombs. Villagers and soldiers were picking up bodies and placing them in military vehicles. My dad and I joined them. The bodies were dismembered; some lacked limbs; some had unrecognizable faces. Once I stepped aside to vomit from the sickly sweet smell. We would put a shroud over a body, wrap it up, and place it in the truck, and it sickened me to realize how easily I got into the routine. After we were done, we got back in our Toyota and continued driving toward the village center.

Three hundred yards beyond the main street, my father pulled over, parked the car, and said, "We will walk from here." At least two hundred Pakistani emergency military personnel were scouring the main street of *Keran*. There were numerous military vehicles and several large-earth moving construction vehicles, search dogs with their handlers probing through the debris. They had cleared a sizable portion of the main street. My father approached one of the emergency workers and asked, "Are you identifying the bodies first or are you just putting them in the vehicles?"

Pointing toward a group of men in uniform the man answered, "I don't know. Go talk to the major over there. I am only doing what he says."

I recognized him immediately as the major who had escorted us when we first came to *Keran*. I couldn't remember his name, but it was him. My dad on the other hand, had an uncanny ability to remember the name of every person he met. If he had a conversation with you for more than five minutes, he would know your name for life. My father looked at me and said, "It's Major Jamal. Let's go talk to him."

Four men surrounded him, talking among themselves. My father waited for them to leave. As they dispersed, he went up to the major and said, "*Assalamu-alaikum*, Major Jamal." The Major shook my father's hand and said solemnly, "*Walaikumasalam* Dr. Ali." Before, the major had been all business. This time, he wasn't like that.

He looked at me and my father and somberly said, "Dr. Ali, I am sorry about your village. The events of last night are a tragedy. The Indian army bombarded your village for over two hours. I don't know why. It appears as though they targeted the hospital and the refugees. That is the main place where the shelling and bombings occurred. Some other homes were hit in the valley, but those appear to be strays. I can't imagine why they would bomb a hospital and the refugee camp surrounding it."

My father interrupted him and explained that a group of severely injured mujahideen had been admitted to the hospital. The Major shook his head and said, "There must have been Indian agents among the refugees. How else would they have found out? Would one of the doctors or employees have told them?"

"No, it couldn't have been a hospital worker," my father said sharply. "But why would a refugee be an agent for the Indian army?"

"Maybe the Indian army had something over the agent, like a family member in custody," the major answered. "Look, it doesn't matter anyway. There will be an investigation and a report. We will find out soon enough. We are going to keep searching for bodies. We have yet to find a single survivor. We haven't even found a complete body. We have found limbs, arms, torsos, heads, but not a single whole body." He took a breath. "Do you have any idea how many refugees there were? Do you know how many patients and workers were at the hospital last night?"

"There were approximately five hundred refugees," my father said. "I think maybe there were six hospital employees working last night, two physicians and four nurses. I don't know how many patients were in the hospital."

"Do you know the names of the people who were working last night?"

"Yes, I think so."

Major Jamal explained how they were conducting their search. "We have divided the area into four quadrants. Each quadrant has its own soldiers, dogs, and personnel searching for survivors. If they are still alive, we will find them."

"How can my son and I help?"

"You can help by working with the soldiers searching through the debris."

My father and I walked toward a group of soldiers, and they handed us shovels and hoes. One of them told us, "We will pick around the debris in an area the size of a small car. If we don't find anything, then we will use a small bulldozer to clear the space. If you find anything, let us know."

The work was hard, but our earlier experience digging through the debris at Jawad's home helped us. After about twenty minutes, I sat down on a large slab of damaged concrete to survey out progress. Looking out toward the end of the main street, I saw a lanky young man with wavy hair accompanied by a stockier one — Daniyal and Isa. I ran to them and we embraced each other quietly. They were both a little dirty, but they had survived. A small blessing. After Isa gave me a hug, he asked, "Is your family okay Hanzilah?"

"Yes, we're okay. How about you two? Are your families okay? Did anyone get hurt?"

"No one was hurt," Daniyal answered quietly.

"What about your neighbors? Did anyone's house get hit?"

"In my neighborhood, not a single house was hit. But one was in Isa's neighborhood."

"Did they live? Did they survive the shelling?"

With sorrow in his voice Isa answered, "No one survived. There were two families living in that house. Two brothers with their wives and children living together. I knew them well."

After a few moments of silence, Isa angrily blurted, "The Indian army will pay. Do they think they can shell us in Keran and get away with it?"

"Where is Jawad?" Daniyal asked. "Is his family okay?"

I didn't want to retell it, to relive the pain and fear of describing what I had witnessed. I looked at Daniyal and Isa, shook my head, and turned away. Isa ran in front of me and asked, "Are they alive, Hanzilah? Tell us *yaar*, he is our friend!"

I pushed Isa out of the way and kept walking. Daniyal came in front of me, took my hand, and quietly said, "Hanzilah, please sit down and talk to us."

I sat down where one of our favorite restaurants had been. No one said anything for several minutes. I kept looking away from them. Finally, Isa asked me, "Hanzilah, is our friend Jawad okay?"

I shook my head. Suddenly, the tears started flowing again. I was sick of crying, tired of shedding tears. My eyelids hurt. I bit my lip and told them everything. Daniyal and Isa sat and listened intently.

As I told the story, Daniyal began to tear up. Isa didn't. His face turned cold. He stood up when I was done and began to pace, cursing the Indian army. Daniyal and I didn't say a word. I was too sad to vent. I wanted to go home, lie down on my bed, and go to sleep. I kept thinking that if I went home and went to sleep, when I woke up maybe this would all have been a bad dream.

The afternoon sun was upon us and I desperately needed some water. I went toward the tent that the Pakistani army had set up with supplies, and grabbed a bottle of water, then returned and sat down with my friends. After a few sips I said to Isa and Daniyal, "My friends, our community needs us. Keran needs us. We will rebuild our village, our marketplace, and our hospital."

I realized that I sounded exactly like my father. The words of patience, of rebuilding, of creating a new Kashmir were his words. But I didn't know if I believed them anymore.

The three of us helped the soldiers sift through the debris. As the day progressed, more and more villagers joined in. Zahid, the doctors, business owners, hospital workers, and many others came forward to help.

In the late afternoon, a large caravan entered Keran. It was eerily similar to the scene a few weeks earlier, when we had entered with our supply trucks. But instead of seeing the beauty of Keran, the people in these trucks saw the horror of war.

A small truck pulled up and the Governor stepped out of the vehicle. The volunteers and residents gathered around him, looking for answers. He had one of those old megaphones, and he announced to the small crowd, "The Pakistani Corps of Engineers have arrived. The Pakistani government has agreed to rebuild the entire village: the marketplace, the hospital, the school, the mosque, and the homes that were destroyed. Over the next few months, Keran will become just like it was before. The Army will never allow this to happen again. They will set up several permanent outposts above the valley. We will rebuild our lives, we will rebuild Keran, and Keran will be stronger than before."

When the Governor finished, the small crowd of people began shouting and screaming. My father took the Governor by the hand and led him away from the crowd. They spoke privately to one another, and as they were speaking, the Pakistani Army Corps of Engineers entered the main street in trucks, bulldozers, and compactors.

As the Army Corps was setting up, five red Toyota 4 X 4 trucks entered the main street. There were about two dozen men in the trucks, wearing the thick hats called *pakol* that are common in northern Kashmir, and wielding AK-47s and rocket launchers. Neither the Pakistani army nor the engineers acknowledged their presence. It was as if these men weren't even there. Daniyal, Isa, and I recognized one of them, our childhood friend Ali, who had left Keran to join the mujahideen earlier in the summer. I hadn't seen Ali since last year. All I knew was that something terrible had happened to his family in Jammu and Kashmir, causing him to join the mujahideen. Daniyal, Isa, and Jawad collectively refused to tell me the real story of what happened. Ali now had a thin beard and his curly hair was much longer than it had been. He saw us from afar and ran towards us screaming, "Daniyal, Isa, Hanzilah! You're alive! We heard what happened and came immediately," he said as we embraced.

He looked around as we told him all that had happened, that his hometown was as good as gone, and it was shocking to him as it had been to us. "These types of attacks will never stop, not until we have our freedom," he said. "I will fight for Kashmir and for our people. We will have freedom one day, but we need more help. He looked at us each with a brightness in his eyes. Hanzilah, Daniyal, Isa, why don't you join us? The mujahideen will train us. We will create a guerilla campaign that will result in our freedom. It worked in Afghanistan; the Russians were defeated this way. We can use these same tactics against the Indian army. They will leave Kashmir, *inshallah*."

Headstrong, passionate, Isa didn't hesitate. He held his hand out to Ali and said, "I am with you, Ali. You're right. We need to fight for our freedom; it won't be given to us. I want to join the freedom movement and join the mujahideen."

I was taken aback, too tired and devastated to make any decision. I hadn't had a moment to myself all day. When giving me the book of poetry, the Governor had said to me, "If you only have a moment to think, take that moment to pause and reflect, because the decisions you make now will change your life forever."

I calmly said to Ali, "You are my friend, but I can't answer you right now. My *Chachaa Riaz* always said that the rifle is the only way to win our freedom, but my father doesn't believe that war will bring peace. I don't know what I want to do"

Ali turned to Daniyal, the most gentle and practical of us, who said levelly, "I can't join you, Ali. I want a normal life. I want to go to college, have a career, get married, and have children."

"Daniyal, these things won't happen if they randomly bomb our village for no good reason," Ali insisted. "What if your house had been hit? You and your family wouldn't be alive. You can't live this normal life that you want without freedom." He paused briefly, then added, "Hanzilah, I don't need your answer now. Today, we are here to help. But I want you at least to consider it."

When Ali left Daniyal and Isa alone with me, I implored them to not make any rash decisions. "We have the rest of our lives ahead of us," I said. "Don't make a choice you will regret. We are angry and emotional right now. Isa, you want to join now, but at least hold off for a few days until things are more settled. Daniyal, I understand you don't want to join and I respect your decision. It's not the life for you. Me, I don't know. Before, I had wanted what you wanted. But now, what's the point? Imani probably isn't going to make it. Maybe I can't have that life anymore."

They both stood there silently. Isa shook his head, lowered his lip, and said with conviction, "Don't preach to me Hanzilah, my mind is made up. I am going to join the fight. I hope you do too, but this decision is one we must make for ourselves.

As we spoke, I watched Ali and the mujahideen working with the village volunteers. We walked back together and rejoined them. We didn't say another word as we searched through the debris. Whenever someone found a dismembered human body, the volunteers would surround the body and try to figure out who it was, taking turns looking at the face, and searching their pockets if the face was too damaged to recognize. It was harder for those who didn't find their dead friend or relative, and had nothing they could say goodbye to.

By ten o'clock that evening, there were no more bodies or remains to be found. We had cleared the main street and placed the bodies and remains into a fleet of twenty large military trucks. The trucks slowly drove the bodies to the village graveyard, as the entire village walked behind them solemnly reciting prayers and weeping. It was a parade of tears.

When we arrived at the graveyard, we pulled the bodies out from the military vehicles, laid them out one by one before the graveyard, and removed the white shrouds. The dead had been declared martyrs, so they were to be buried unwashed and in the clothes they died in. The Governor stood before the villagers and said a few words. He told us that we would bury the bodies immediately after the noon prayer tomorrow. Under Islamic law, we had to bury the dead within twenty-four hours of their death. He asked the entire village to identify anyone they could out of the rows upon rows of bodies.

Candles were lit around the bodies so that the villagers could identify their dead relatives and friends throughout the night. People wept and prayed as they walked through the rows of dead bodies of men, women, and children.

At the graveyard I approached my father and asked him if we could go to the next valley to visit Jawad. He was in no position to say anything but yes. Daniyal, Isa, Ali, and I got into my father's Toyota with him. The next valley was only four kilometers away, but it took us half an hour to get there.

The village was called *Abbaspur*, and it looked like any other valley in Kashmir. There was a large tent set up on the outskirts of the village, surrounded by several ambulances and cars. My body began shaking again. I couldn't bear to see my Imani hurt, or to face Jawad alone again. This time my friends and my father were with me. I hoped that their presence would give me the strength I needed.

As we approached the tent we could hear a whirring sound like a small helicopter coming from a large gas generator used to provide power to the medical equipment.

We entered the tent and saw several rows of medical beds occupied by debilitated villagers. My father left us and went to speak to the person in charge of the makeshift clinic. As we walked through the dark tent, amidst drips, and machines, and people in pain, I found Jawad sitting in a chair, holding his sister's hand. My Imani. Her face had gotten frighteningly pale, as though being sapped of life. My heart felt on the verge of collapse and my stomach was light.

Jawad saw us, and we tried awkwardly to say words of condolence. We were too young and lucky to know what to say to a person in Jawad's situation. We stood silently as he described to us what had happened.

He didn't look at us. He stared into the distance as he spoke in a low voice and said, "We were sleeping when the bombing started. My father and I got the family together, and we made our way to the basement. We could hear the bombs falling around us. Out of nowhere, our house was directly hit. The shock and strength of the bomb caused the entire house to collapse on us. There was a fire running through the house, and it stopped right before it got to me. I don't know why it stopped. But it did. I couldn't see anything down there. We were stuck under these massive bricks of cement. I started moving the cement away. I was able to get my family free, but I couldn't tell if they were alive or not. It was too dark. I waited until I heard some sounds and, when I did, I screamed as loud as I could. Then Hanzilah and the Pakistani soldiers came and got us out."

He put his hands to his face and silently wept. "My wife and my family are dead. The doctors have told me that

Imani has serious internal injuries, that she won't make it through the night. She is dying as we speak."

Hearing this, my mind went temporarily blank with rage. I could feel a hotness spreading throughout my body. It was the same anger I had felt when I left my home this morning and saw for the first time what they had done to Keran and my people. What did the enemy expect? Did they expect that they could murder, kill, maim, and bomb without fueling visceral hate and vengeance? They murder us in the name of occupation, they rape our women, and they commit unspeakable evil acts of hatred, and they deserved to face the consequences. My rage was beyond practical thinking, from some primitive place that human beings had never been able to evolve away from.

I went up to Jawad and forced him to stand up straight. My decision had been made. With great emotion I told him, "Your family didn't die in vain. There will be justice, and I will make sure of it." I looked at Ali, Isa, and Daniyal and said, "I am joining the mujahideen. My father is wrong. What is the point of living if our people can't live without freedom?"

Ali held out his hand and said, "You join us too, brother. We will show them that we won't stand down to their occupation, that we Kashmiris are free people."

Jawad held out his hand to Ali and said, in a forceful tone, "I will."

My father arrived soon after and politely asked Jawad if he could examine Imani. He asked us to leave and used a curtain to shield her. After completing the examination, he left us and went to speak to the doctors in charge of the makeshift hospital.

Jawad, Ali, Isa, and Daniyal decided to leave. Jawad had to return to Keran to prepare for the burial of his mother, father, and wife. He asked my father to take him to Keran and requested that I stay behind with his sister until he returned. I agreed and tried my best to hide my fury.

Before they left, Dad took me aside and spoke to me privately in the tone that doctors use when they're giving bad news to a patient's family. "Son, I know you care for Imani," he said quietly. "I hope you can forgive me for what I am about to tell you. She is not going to make it. Her injuries are too severe. She is hanging on by a thread at this point. I say this to you because I know you have feelings for her. If you don't want to stay, then just tell me. I'll talk to Jawad and someone else can stay with her."

I shook my head and calmly said, "No, Dad, I am okay. I'll stay. I understand that she won't make it. I have spent enough time at the hospital to be able to see death coming. I will say some prayers and say my goodbyes."

My father hugged me and said, "I never thought something like this would ever happen. When I was your age, many of my friends and family members died. I went on. Why I went on and they didn't, I don't know. But you have to trust the fate that God has bestowed upon you."

My anger dissipated. I could hear my heartbeat, and I felt a depressive calmness come over me. I didn't have any more tears to shed. I had wept enough. I responded to my father with the simplest answer: "Okay."

When they were gone, I sat down in the chair next to Imani. I stared at her pallid face. She had lost a large amount of blood. Her face was patchy with scratches and burns. They had placed small bandages on her wounds.

Somehow, her reddish-brown hair was still silky. Even with the bruises, she still looked beautiful. I pushed some hair away from her face. I am touching her face for the first time, I thought, and it's when she is dying.

I recited some prayers that I knew. I asked God repeatedly to let her live. I tried to bargain with God, as if he could be bargained with. I was emotionally spent and physically exhausted. Without even knowing it, I fell asleep right in front of her in that small chair.

I slept that entire night by Imani's side. Just after five o'clock, the morning call to prayer could be heard ringing through the valley of *Abbaspur*. I awoke, sat up straight, and saw Imani lying there still alive. I grabbed some water, washed myself, and did the morning prayer next to her bed. The sunrise was starting, and light streamed into the makeshift hospital tent. A bright ray landed on Imani's face. Her face glowed in the natural light. As I stood next to her bed, tears streamed down my face. I don't know why I did what I did next.

I went to her feet and knelt on the floor. I put my hands on her feet, caressed them gently, and kissed them both, as the tears kept flowing. I put my head against her feet for several minutes. I got up and went back to the chair. I held her hand and told her, "Imani, it has always been you. All these years coming in the summers to Kashmir, I came for you. I have been dreaming about sharing a life with you. I want to marry you. I still want to marry you. Please live, so that we can share a life together. Please, my love, stay alive."

It was after I said those words that I realized the hopelessness that I felt, the hopelessness in everything that had happened. These events occurred entirely beyond anyone's control. I felt the desperateness of forty years of unrequited struggle in Kashmir. The Kashmiris of Indian-occupied Kashmir had begun this revolution for freedom. In a moment of intense anger, I had made a pledge with my friends to join the fight. But as I thought about the rest of my life, I realized that it had become meaningless without Imani. I would likely die fighting with the mujahideen, but I would rather die for a good cause than lead a meaningless life.

I slumped back in the chair and my exhaustion took over. Several hours passed, and I jerked suddenly in the chair after hearing a sudden sound. It was my father, standing over Imani. He had returned, alone. I rubbed my eyes as he sat down next to me. "Son, in a few hours she will be gone. There is no hope for Imani. I am sorry."

I looked over with tears in my eyes and said, "I know." I paused for a brief moment and said, "Dad, I want you to know something. You are my hero. I strive to be like you in so many ways. The way that you carry yourself, the way you treat others, and the way you care about our people is amazing. In these past few weeks, I've learned so much from you. The last twenty-four hours have only confirmed how honorable you are. But I have made a decision. I am going to join the mujahideen and join the fight for freedom."

My father was stunned. He sat quietly and reflected carefully on the words he was going to say to me. Anger and fear in his voice, he said: "No, son, you are not joining the mujahideen. Your life is in the United States."

"I have made my decision," I responded unwaveringly.

"What decision have you made? I know you are angry about what happened. I know you are sad about Imani. But this time shall pass. You have your whole life ahead of you and I forbid you to do anything of the sort. We are going back to the States together, and that is the end of it."

I got up from my chair and tried to put it in a perspective he would understand. "No, Dad. You can leave, but I am not leaving. You've been treating the symptoms of the disease, Dad. I am going to kill the disease. I am going to win the freedom of Kashmir. Chacha Riaz was right; only the rifle will bring peace in our land."

My father stood up from his chair, he was about to say something, but then he sat back down. For several minutes he said nothing.

He pushed his hand through his wavy white hair and lurched back. He gathered himself and spoke in a calm, neutral tone. "Son, you may be right. The ultimate solution may only come about through violence and war. But you just turned eighteen. You have your whole life ahead of you. What about your mother, your sister, and your younger brother Tamer? You are making a selfish decision. This war isn't your war. No matter what you may think, a few thousand mujahideen cannot defeat an army of occupation numbered at seven hundred thousand soldiers. It's impossible. Please come back to the States with me and prepare for college at Stanford in the fall."

I shook my head. I embraced my dad and said, "All my life, I wanted to be just like you. The way you behaved, the way you carried yourself, the way you cared about your faith, cared about your family, and the way you cared about Kashmir. People love and respect you, Dad. But look at all the hard work, resources, and dedication you put into creating and running the hospital. In just a few moments it was destroyed, and not for anything you or I did, but because the Indians chose to bomb our village indiscriminately. No matter what we do, we won't live in peace until we have our freedom. I won't sit idly by and let our people suffer any longer. You took your path, and now I have to take mine."

My dad closed his eyes, took a deep breath, and murmured, "Let's go to Keran. The martyrs are going to be buried immediately after the noon prayer. Imani will be safe here. It is getting late and we need to leave."

With the knowledge that I would never see her again, I took one last look at Imani's still face and said to my dad, "Let's go."

We drove to Keran without exchanging a word. The silence was palpable. It was a beautiful day in Kashmir. The sun was high and bright. There was greenery everywhere in the valleys, the flowers were in bloom, and we saw several majestic waterfalls. As I stared out of the truck, I thought to myself: These valleys and mountains are full of majesty and beauty. The natural splendor is a rebuke to the ugly history of the people who live in these valleys, these valleys of hopelessness.

As we entered Keran, our vantage from the top of the mountain allowed us to see the entire village. With the sun out, the destruction and devastation of the village was clearly visible. Its heart was gone.

The main street with the hospital, the market, and the school had been obliterated. The small houses around the main street were also destroyed. The inside of a house, where people used to live, was a strange and intimate sight to see. In one house I could see the bathroom, no walls, just a toilet surrounded by broken glass.

The village was empty. The refugees whose tents had surrounded the marketplace were dead. Innocent women and children dead, entire families wiped out. Five hundred refugees had been murdered, dying from the very destruction they had fled. Azad Kashmir was supposed to be their haven, but it had become their graveyard. We gave them food, we provided them education, we even treated their illnesses, but we didn't defend them.

We drove through the entire village to get to the graveyard. The graveyard in Keran is right outside the village, but it can't be seen from any point in the village because it is hidden by a small forest of enormous chinar trees. We parked at the entrance to the chinar forest. A small dirt road led between the trees into the graveyard. As we walked along it, a breeze ran through the trees, soothing my worn down skin. After a fifteen-minute walk through the shade of the chinars, we entered the graveyard. The entire village was there.

The bodies of the dead were surrounded by their male friends and relatives. The women of the village, clothed in black, stood at a distance, shaded by the chinar trees. I saw Jawad standing with Isa, Daniyal, and Ali, beside the bodies of Jawad's parents and wife, their blood and injuries in full view. They weren't to be washed, nor buried in traditional white funeral shrouds. They died as heroes and were to be buried accordingly. I walked over to my friends. I gave each of them a somber hug. Jawad looked sick. My friend with the easy smile was no more. He looked as if he had aged ten years in one night, his eyes looking sullen behind dark circles. I whispered in his ear that Imani was still alive. He nodded his head in acknowledgment.

The Governor was there and announced to the villagers, "The maulana is here and will lead the funeral prayer."

We stood in straight lines before the rows of hundreds of dead bodies. As the maulana began to lead the funeral prayer, many of the grown men around me wept as they prayed. My heart stung and I read the one prayer that I was familiar with:

> O God, forgive our living and our dead, those who are present among us and those who are absent, our young and our old, our males and our females. O God, whoever you keep alive, keep him alive in faith, and whoever you cause to die, cause him to die with faith. O God, do not deprive us of the reward and do not cause us to go astray after this. O God, forgive him and have mercy on him, keep him safe and sound and forgive him, honor his rest and ease his entrance; wash him with water, snow, and hail, and cleanse him of sin as a white garment is cleansed of dirt. O God, give him a home better than his home and a family better than his family. O God, admit him to Paradise and protect him from the torment of the grave and the torment of Hell-fire; make his grave spacious and fill it with light.

As I finished the funeral prayer, I realized that something about the despair I was feeling had changed. I mourned the loss of my neighbors and the innocent dead, but my heart had turned to vengeance. I found strength and confidence in it. It felt wrong, to be at a funeral and thinking this way. But at least I now knew what I had to do.

When the prayer ended, the village men walked toward the individual gravesites that they and the Pakistani soldiers had dug throughout the night. While we were placing Jawad's family into their graves, the entire village was doing the same for the rest of the dead refugees and villagers. Jawad and I entered into one of the graves that he, Daniyal, Isa, and Ali had dug for his family the night before. When I entered the grave that was to be his mother's, I was struck suddenly by an unwanted reminder of my own mortality, which seemed more imminent now than ever. This earthly soil is the final place for all of us. We return to the clay that we were formed from. Daniyal and Ali lowered Jawad's mother's body, and I helped Jawad set his mother into her grave with her head facing east. As I placed her feet down, I thought to myself, "How is Jawad capable of doing this? Where is he finding the strength?" I couldn't imagine being in his situation.

Isa and Ali helped Jawad and I out of the grave, and lowered his father into the earth, taking each other's hands both for physical and moral support. It was time to place Jawad's wife into the grave. Jawad paused for a few moments. He knelt on the floor and removed her veil. He looked at his wife one last time. He said some words quietly, placed his hand over her cheek, and put the veil back over her face. Before I could help him lower his wife into the grave, he pushed my hand back. He picked up his wife, jumped in the grave, and placed her in there by himself. Then he set her head facing east and stood over her body. He stood there, not moving, for minutes, with no one saying a word. I extended my hand to him, but he remained motionless. I had always known that Jawad loved his wife, but seeing him standing over her that way, his grief and vulnerability plain on his face, made me realize the depths of what she meant to him, and what Imani meant to me. I knew that he had never expected that it would be him losing her, but the other way around. Finally he turned his head, grabbed my hand, and allowed me to pull him out of his wife's grave.

Jawad started shoveling dirt into his family's graves, and we followed his lead, shoveling until each grave was completely filled. My arms and hands ached from the digging, really had been aching for hours, but I went as efficiently as possible. When we came to his wife's grave, we placed the dirt over her grave as hurriedly as we had done for his parents. Then we helped as many others as we could to bury the remaining dead. A little over two hours later, the bodies of all the martyrs had been buried. There were rows upon rows of mounded dirt marking their graves. People crying became a natural part of the background as we worked.

The villagers began to leave the graveyard and return to their homes, heads bowed. My father drove us all back to my house, and I asked Jawad to stay as long as he liked. He didn't look at me, or even move his face. He just stared at the floor of the car and nodded in agreement.

At home I told everyone to come inside for food. We sat down in the living room and my mother brought snacks, water, and Coke. We sat quietly together, no one saying a word, all of us hoping Jawad would speak. But he only sat there staring, not looking at anything or anyone in particular.

Evening had arrived, and my mother brought dinner. Still, no one spoke, and barely ate. I realized that there was no point in saying anything. There was nothing to discuss. We all understood the atrocity of what had happened. No matter what any of us said to Jawad, it would be meaningless. After dinner, I prepared everyone a place to sleep. Jawad got up, gazed out the window for a few moments, and finally turned to Ali and spoke his first words since the funeral: "When can we start our training with the mujahideen?"

I was happy finally to hear my friend's voice again, despite the pain that it carried.

"We can go tomorrow afternoon to the training camps together," said Ali.

Jawad nodded. "I am ready."

Isa said, "I am ready."

I looked at my friends, at their dirty hands and grieving faces. "I am ready," I said.

May 22, 1993

My younger brother and I were playing Nintendo on the living room TV when our father came running down the stairs. He nearly tripped and tumbled down them in his haste.

"Your sister is engaged!" He said exuberantly.

Aliyah had recently graduated from the University of Alabama with a degree in biology, and a few days after graduation she and my mother had traveled to our second home in Kashmir for the summer. My brother and I looked at each other, dumbfounded. To us, Aliyah was still a kid.

My father wrapped us in a hug, laughing at out stunned expressions. I had never seen him so openly excited.

"Aliyah met a boy," he announced. "His name is Khalid, and he recently graduated from King Edward Medical College in Lahore. She and your mother have been meeting with him and his family for the past few weeks. They visited and proposed yesterday. They will be married at the end of July, and he will come to the States to do his residency in Internal Medicine in New York City."

My dad himself had also attended King Edward, then the leading medical college in Pakistan, thirty-five years earlier. My siblings and I had been born and raised in Birmingham, but spent most summers of my childhood in my parents' homeland, Kashmir. My father's family lived in a village in the disputed region, just a few miles from the Line of Control, the militarized de facto border with India.

My father had built a hospital that served the poor in his village Keran and the surrounding area. It was fairly busy because it was the only hospital around for miles. People injured by the constant bombing and fighting in the area sought treatment there. Local villagers also sought treatment there for different ailments, as well as women in nearby villages who went there for childbirth. The thirty-bed hospital served nearly 15,000 people. The Pakistani government had built very little infrastructure in the area because they were focused on creating fortifications, securing the Line of Control, and positioning themselves to defend Pakistan from the Indian army.

Another summer in Kashmir, this time for my elder sister's wedding. I was excited. I enjoyed going to my family's ancestral village, Keran. Many of my cousins and closest friends lived there. In Keran, my friends and I played cricket, went to the market, ate barbecue chicken, drank Kashmiri tea, and hung around as any young people would. Also, the only girl I had ever really liked, Imani, was Kashmiri. I looked forward to hanging around with my friend, her brother, and hoping to catch sight of her.

My father went to Kashmir every summer, but he spent most of his time at the hospital, and visiting the *muhajirs*, or migrants, in the refugee camps, who had made the arduous journey across the Line of Control from the Indian-controlled portion of the disputed region. He took food, medical and educational supplies, and anything else he could to help. I suspected that he felt guilty for leaving his native land for the easy life in the United States. He did not suffer the way many of his childhood friends had. Most of his friends had never left the village, and many of them had died in bombings or defending the village against Indian soldiers, but we knew this only by word of the villagers — our father had never confided in us about his losses.

Tamer, only thirteen years old at the time, jumped with joy when our father told us we were going to Kashmir. "When are we leaving?" he asked.

"In three weeks, so start packing your bags. We have to help your mother and sister prepare for the wedding! There are so many things to do" said my father. "Hanzilah, this could be your last trip to Kashmir for quite a while. You will be starting college in the fall, and your next few summers will be spent completing internships, studying for the MCAT, and preparing for medical school. You may not get back to Kashmir for eight or nine years."

That thought had not crossed my mind. I'd been accepted at Stanford and I was going to be starting my freshman year in the fall. My parents wanted me to become a physician like my dad. I'd never felt called to the profession, but I didn't want to disappoint my family. All my life they had been telling me that I was destined to be a doctor, and that was the end of it. In school, I always did well in science, so I knew I had the ability to make my parents happy by becoming a physician. But my real passion was the social sciences: religion, history, economics, and government. The two people I admired the most were attorneys. Mahatma Gandhi and Mohammed Ali Jinnah, both British trained lawyers who brought peace and helped create the countries of India and Pakistan. Still, my father had found his life's purpose in being a physician, and although the job did not have draw for me, I wanted to honor his work. Still, the thought of being stuck in the States for the next eight years studying a field I didn't connect with depressed me. I decided not to think about it until the summer was over.

June 24, 1993

Traveling to Kashmir was a long and cumbersome journey. First, we had to fly from Birmingham to John F. Kennedy International Airport in New York City, then from JFK to

London Heathrow Airport. Still not done, we flew from London to Lahore, Pakistan, where we had to trek through a combination of buses, taxis, and trucks until we reached *Muzzafarabad*, the capital of Azad Kashmir. Even once we reached Muzzafarabad, proceeding to Keran was no simple task. In the Himalayan Mountains, and especially in a poor country like Pakistan, just finding transportation to our village was difficult.

In part to break up the journey, we decided to spend a few days in New York City with one of our father's friends. A car pulled up and a man stuck his face out the window: "*Assalamu-alaikum*, Dr. *Sahib*!"

"*Walaikumasalam!*" Said my dad. I knew that it made my dad happy to see his Kashmiri friends partially because it allowed him to speak Kashmiri outside of the family. My siblings and I had all been raised in Kashmiri and English to honor our heritage and better connect with the people back home in Keran.

Uncle Yasir opened the car door, walked around, and gave my father a big hug. "How are you? How was the flight from Birmingham? Congratulations on your daughter's engagement! *Oyeh*, Hanzilah, you got so big, I can't believe you will be beginning college soon, how time flies! Tamer, you are so tall for only thirteen. Welcome! Welcome! Let's go, quickly go ahead and sit in the car. I'll take care of the bags, you guys relax. Dr. *Sahib*, we are happy that you decided to spend a few days with us before you head out to Kashmir."

Uncle Yasir was also from Kashmir. He had moved to New York in the early 1980s and owned a grocery store in Queens. He was a slightly pudgy man with a thin beard and smile lines around his eyes. It had been three years since I'd last seen him.

"How are things in New York?" my father asked him. "How is the family? How is business?"

"Oh, everything is great!" said Uncle Yasir. I'd forgotten how booming his voice was.

Uncle Yasir lived in a nice two-story home with a basement in Queens. His wife, Aunty Riffat, opened the door and invited us in. She had cooked a traditional Kashmiri dinner, rice with raisins and a dish of grilled pieces of chicken kabobs.

After the meal, per their tradition, my Uncle Yasir and my father headed to the living room to eat dessert and drink Kashmiri tea. The topic inevitably shifted from gentle pleasantries to politics and conditions in Kashmir. "The Indians will never let us join Pakistan," Uncle Yasir muttered. "We will never be free. The war is going badly. The *mujahideen* are not making any inroads with their fight against the Indian soldiers. The Pakistani government can't do anything. The Indians have the nuclear bomb. They have more soldiers, a larger army, and support from the Russians. We cannot win."

My dad nodded his head as he listened. "Yasir, we need to forget about this war," he said. "We need to build schools, hospitals, orphanages, and roads. War will never end. War has been going on for nearly forty years. All my life, all we have ever known is war. We need to focus on peace."

"Dr. *Sahib*, you are right," replied Uncle Yasir, "but every time we build anything substantial in Azad Kashmir, the Indians blow it up. On the other side of the Line of

Control, the Pakistanis hail down artillery fire. How can we make our country without freedom? We must win our freedom, and we must be reunited with our families in Jammu and Kashmir. I have never seen my grandfather or grandmother. I have not even met my father's brothers and sisters, my very own aunts and uncles! My father was not able to attend his own father's funeral. He has not even visited his grave. The situation of our homeland and our people is depressing. We must support the mujahideen. We must defeat the Indians and kick them out of our land. They don't belong there."

I was sitting with my father and Uncle Yasir. I always enjoyed listening to the older people talk. Tamer was in the family room, playing video games with Uncle Yasir's son Adeel.

While the men spoke about Kashmir, Aunty Riffat entered the living room and sat next to me. "Congratulations Hanzilah on your sister's engagement," she said. "Are you happy? Do you like your future brother-in-law?"

"He seems nice," I responded, somewhat surprised. "I talked to him on the phone only once. I will get to know him better when I finally meet him in person."

"Are you excited about college? Your father has told us you plan to go to medical school."

Not uncommon in Kashmiri women, Aunty Riffat was a bit nosy.

"Yes, I think so," I said politely.

"That is great," she said, endearingly. "We need more doctors like your dad.

My dad looked over at us from across the table and smiled. I mumbled something in assent and changed the subject.

June 25, 1993

Uncle Yasir dropped us off at the airport. He helped us get in line at the Pakistan International Airlines counter and check in our baggage. He wished us a safe trip. "Hanzilah, have a fun time at the wedding and be careful in Kashmir," he said to me with a kind smile.

I nodded my head, hugged him, and said goodbye. "I wish you and your family was coming too," I said.

The long journey to Lahore was exhausting. On the bright side, my father was good friends with the airport manager in Lahore, and we always received VIP treatment. After we disembarked from the airplane, the other passengers were escorted to the main terminal on a bus, but a luxury car was waiting to take us to the VIP lounge. There, we sank our tired bones into plush chairs and ordered a heaping hot meal. When we finished, *Chachaa* Riaz, our paternal uncle, would be waiting to pick us up.

Upon exiting the airport the aromas of dry gravel, spices, and animal waste welcomed me to Pakistan. *Chachaa* Riaz shouted and waved from his car, and in our excitement, Tamer and I ran to him like young children. He hugged us.

"*Assalamu-alaikum bachay*! How are you doing? It is so good to see you guys. Your sister is getting married! Can you believe it? Ahh, you must be happy to be rid of her!"

Tamer replied with a big goofy smile, "*Chachaa*, we are thrilled to be rid of her!"

Chachaa Riaz was a medium-sized man, with black hair streaked with grey. He dressed like a proper Englishman, in trousers and a twill sports jacket despite the summer heat.

My father walked up behind us and said, "Don't listen to a word *Chachaa* Riaz has to say. He is not a serious person." He embraced his brother.

"Big brother, you are not headed home yet," said *Chachaa* Riaz assertively. "You and the boys stay with me. After a few days of rest, you can continue to Keran."

"We cannot stay for a few days," said my father. "But we will stay the night at your place. We will begin our journey to Keran after a night's rest. We have to help with this big wedding."

"Listen," persisted *Chachaa* Riaz, "You are not going anywhere for a few days at least. Every time, you come and stop by for one, maybe two days and leave. Let me show you this city."

"Little brother, you are forgetting I spent seven years in this city at Government College and King Edward Medical College. I have seen this entire city!"

Chachaa Riaz frowned. "Not you," he said loudly. "Your kids! You need to show your sons Lahore. This city is beautiful, and they have yet to see it."

He turned to us, "Hanzilah, Tamer, do you boys want to see Lahore, or do you want to go to Keran and help with silly wedding stuff? Tamer, there is even a beautiful new park with a basketball court in our neighborhood of *Defence*."

"Riaz, stop trying to bribe these kids," Dad said shortly. "Tamer can play basketball in America. Okay, listen, we won't go first thing tomorrow, we will stay the day"

"One day is not enough."

"After the wedding, we will come back, and we will stay with you before we head back to the States," said my father. "I promise."

"Alright," said Uncle Riaz. "But I will hold you to that promise."

June 27, 1993

Chachaa Riaz had never wanted to immigrate to the United States or England. In jest, he would say that he was not a traitor to the country that gave him everything (like my father). Even so, he may not have left Pakistan, but, he had left Kashmir. He was chair of the economics department at Government College the premier public college in the Punjab. Government College had been established by the British in the 1860s. When my father and uncle had been there in the 1950s, many of their Professors were Englishmen who had remained after independence.

Many people complained that Pakistan was failing as a country because the British had exploited the subcontinent over two centuries of colonialism. That may have been true, but everywhere I looked, the institutions that still thrived had been created by the British. My dad went to a high school taught by Christian missionaries, a college that was created by the British, and a medical college founded by the British and named after a British king.

My father would taunt *Chachaa* Riaz: "You are the one teaching economics to the politicians of this country, and this country is showing no economic growth!"

My uncle did teach many of Pakistan's well-known politicians, and they were infamously corrupt. His most famous student was Nawaz Sharif, who at that time was the country's prime minister.

Lahore is a city of contradictions. It is a city full of beautiful and impressive buildings constructed by the Mughals and the British. Many of its residents are enormously wealthy. The bazaars are loud and plentiful. The city is famous for its restaurants and extravagant food.

At the same time, Lahore can be extremely ugly. The air you breathe is toxic, because there are no environmental controls. Diesel engines are the most popular, cars lack catalytic converters, there is no formal trash pickup system, there is no safe way to handle toxic chemicals, factories throughout the city pollute freely. Poverty is endemic, the economy is weak, and the working class is exploited by the middle and upper classes because there is no minimum wage.

Chachaa Riaz loved the city of Lahore because he was an upper-class Pakistani. For him, Pakistan was a beautiful place to live. He had a driver, a cook, a gardener, and a cleaning lady. He lived in a five-thousand-square-foot home in one of Lahore's most prestigious neighborhoods. His kids went to the best private schools. His neighborhood was surrounded by beautiful parks and modern shopping centers. In his eyes, he had nothing to complain about, but I doubted that those who worked for him felt the same way.

That evening after dinner, Dad and *Chachaa* Riaz went to the living room to relax over Kashmiri tea. I decided to join them as they started talking about Kashmir.

"Riaz, how much longer will this war last?" Dad asked.

"Big brother, this most recent rebellion has been going on since 1989," *Chachaa* Riaz replied "It will end when Kashmir is free." He corrected himself. "But this is not a rebellion, this is a war of independence. We are fighting for our country, for freedom, and for Kashmiris to be free to make a political decision on whether to join Pakistan, remain with India, or become independent."

"We don't want to be with India," said my father. "Why else are we Kashmiris fighting the Indians?"

"That is a good point," said my uncle. "Remember that when this war began, it did not start in Pakistan-controlled Kashmir; it started in the Indian-controlled region. Pakistani Kashmiris have never rebelled or asked for independence from Pakistan. The Kashmiris of Jammu and Kashmir started this war for independence. They don't want to be part of India.

Chachaa Riaz turned to me. "India has been taking advantage of Kashmiris. They build no schools, highways, or hospitals. Our economy is struggling because the Indians don't invest in Kashmir. The local economy is surviving only because people throughout the world come to see our beautiful mountains, valleys, rivers, and waterfalls."

"Growing up in our village," said my dad nostalgically. "We had Buddhists, Shiites, and Hindus. We were all together in harmony. Now things are different. The Indians and Pakistanis don't care about Kashmir; they are only using our situation for their political agendas."

"You are right about our past brother," Said my Uncle sternly, "but those times are long gone. Kashmiris are 95 percent Muslim. We belong with Pakistan. Pakistan was created for the Muslims of India. We have always fully expected to be part of Pakistan, Pakistan expected us to be part of Pakistan, and even India expected us to be part of Pakistan.

This fight is not a nationalist agenda for Kashmir. We are fighting for our human rights, our right to freedom, but most importantly for our right to self-determination. We have to decide for ourselves what future we want." He paused briefly in thought. "We can't live normal lives. Did you know that the Indians have a law where they can hold a Kashmiri for two years without even alleging what his criminal act or wrongdoing is? They put people in jail whenever they please. This law does not apply anywhere else in India, only Kashmir."

I couldn't help but see my uncle's point of view, although I kept my face neutral.

My dad took a breath. "Riaz, I understand and I see your point. I want our people to live in peace so that the families of Kashmir will stop suffering. Look at how many of us have fled our lands. You live in Lahore and I live in America, for God's sake. When will there be peace, Riaz?"

"There will be peace and Kashmir will be reunited," said Chacha Riaz. "One day this war will end, but it will be the rifle and only the rifle that will end our hopelessness."

Dad pointed his finger at my Uncle. "Too many will suffer if we take this route. Too many will die. I have lost many of my childhood friends, and so have you. It is time for peace. I fundamentally disagree with you. We need to come to the table. We need to have the plebiscite the UN ordered."

"That plebiscite will never happen," said my uncle. "For 40 years we have been waiting for this plebiscite. Listen, with the Indian army on one side of the Line of Control, and the Pakistan army on the other side, the Line of Control will be our border forever unless we as Kashmiris destroy it ourselves."

"I think we Kashmiris should have our own independent nation," I said. "We should not belong to either Pakistan or India. We are our own nation."

My father smiled at me. "Son, this is a good notion," he said "But we are caught between two warring countries and their political agendas. They will never let us be free. They will always remain involved in our lands even if we have independence. They will play us against each other, create warring tribes, just like they do in Afghanistan. In fact, they are doing it already. We will never have peace if we as Kashmiris continue to use weapons to win our independence. We should start a peaceful civil disobedience movement in Kashmir, like Gandhi did to win India its freedom from the British Empire. The world will see us suffering because we espouse non-violence and civil disobedience, and then there will be peace. We need a leader to see that vision through. Remember what Gandhi famously said: There are many causes I would die for, none that I would kill for."

Are you kidding big brother?" *Chachaa* Riaz scoffed, "We tried to live in peace for so many years! This strategy has failed us. The world does not care about Kashmir. They have never cared about the people of Kashmir. How many Amnesty International reports have there been? How many international organizations have written about the atrocities committed against us in our lands? No, we must win this fight on our own, and only with the rifle."

"If we go about things the way you are saying, Riaz, then our people will suffer forever, and there will never be peace. I am going to sleep. This conversation isn't going to solve our problems. We have a lot of travel ahead of us. Hanzilah, let's get ready for bed."

I looked at my father and my uncle, at their stubborn, angular aces and set jaws. I respected both of them. I knew that they both loved their homeland, but their ways of doing so were irreconcilable with one another. I wasn't sure which one I believed. I wished my uncle goodnight and followed my father upstairs.

June 28, 1993

We awoke early, feeling the jetlag from our journey like a weight on our backs, and Chacha Riaz took us to the Daewoo bus station. We sat together at the very back of the bus.

"How long before we get to Islamabad?" Tamer asked.

"At least four, maybe five hours," my father told him.

Tamer growled. "Then I am going to sleep!"

I had always had difficulty sleeping on the bus. Instead, I looked out the window at the scenery along the new motorway. The plains of the Punjab reminded me of the Midwestern plains of the United States, dotted with farms and villages.

My father was drinking Earl Grey, eating biscuits, and reading a Pakistani newspaper. Every now and then he would stop reading, stare out the window, and sigh. After reflecting on his inner thoughts, he would then return to his newspaper. Watching him contemplate was a familiar sight.

As the bus continued towards Islamabad, and the grassy plains turned into hills he looked at me and pointed towards the window. "Look over there, Hanzilah," he said "We are coming close to the Khewra Salt Mines, the second-largest salt mines in the world. Those mines have been producing salt since the times of Alexander the Great, and they are still producing. Amazing, huh?" He gazed at me thoughtfully, "Pakistan is a rich country, son, full of natural resources. If we had real leadership, things would really change around here."

My father's friend Zahid was waiting for us at the bus station in Islamabad, waving his hands through the crowd and loudly calling, "Dr. *Sahib*, *assalamu-alaikum*!" We walked through the crowd and he came to meet us. "Congratulations on the wedding! How is everything? How is *Amreeka*? Are you going to be spending time at the hospital, or will you be preparing for your daughter's wedding? You will probably be doing both."

My father hugged Zahid. "All praise due to Allah, we are well," he told him "Don't you worry; I will be doing my rounds at the hospital. I am here for the wedding, but I am also coming to help."

Zahid was the manager of my father's hospital, my dad's right-hand man. He also took care of our house in Keran when we were away.

"Zahid, did the shipment arrive?" my father asked, "Is it here?"

"Absolutely, Dr. *Sahib*," Zahid reassured him "Everything is here. The donors in America are kindhearted and generous. I can't believe they sent such a large quantity of medical supplies. They even sent us an X-Ray machine!"

My dad knew many doctors in the States. He had been gathering donated medical supplies for the past six months and in advance of his arrival he had set things up so they would be delivered to Islamabad and stored in a secure place until he arrived to take them directly to his small hospital in Keran.

He did not trust anyone else to do this job. These supplies were critical to the Kashmiri community in and around Keran and had to last a full year.

Zahid had brought four large trucks with him. It was midday on a blistering, steamy day in Islamabad, and sweat was already beading on my forehead.

Volunteers from the village awaited us at the storage facility to drive the moving trucks.

It took us only fifteen minutes to get there from the airport. We all worked together to put the medical supplies into the trucks as quickly as possible so we could get on the road to Keran. Tamer was full of energy doing the work of two grown men.

"How come you're working so hard?" I asked him.

"Dude, once we finish here, we get to eat, and I am starving," he said.

My brother always liked to make a joke wherever he could. "I thought you were working hard because you cared about the hospital," I laughed.

Three and a half hours later the trucks were filled with the medical supplies. And we were exhausted.

Zahid pulled out a rug, and set out chicken biryani and several bottles of Pepsi. We sat in a circle and ate the food. I was starving. It was 4p.m., we were eating for the first time that day, and we still had a long journey remaining. It was going to take five hours to travel to *Muzzafarabad*, and from *Muzzafarabad* another four hours through the high mountains and deep valleys of Kashmir *to Keran*.

"How are things at the hospital?" Dad asked Zahid as we ate.

"Dr. *Sahib*, we are busy and the staff is overwhelmed," Zahid replied candidly. "We desperately need more physicians, nurses, and medical supplies. The problem is that not only are we taking care of our village and the surrounding villages, but now we have so many refugees that we are responsible for. Throngs of refugees from Jammu Kashmir are flowing across the Line of Control, and when they arrive many of them have various traumas, illnesses, and injuries."

He took a few more bites and added, "We need to add more beds. We can do more. "

My father listened intently. "Zahid, I am running out of funds," he said. "My savings have been put into this hospital. I started a non-profit organization in the United States to raise money from donors in America, telling them of our good work. But the people of America, they don't know about our problems. They are not aware of our situation."

Zahid was astonished. "Dr. *Sahib*, how is that possible? This war has been going on for four years now. Is it not in the news in the USA?"

"No, it is not in the news. The people in the U.S. are not aware of our struggle," my father told him bluntly. He changed the subject. "What are we doing in Pakistan to raise funds for the hospital?"

"Dr. *Sahib*, we are doing what we can. A handful of Pakistani non-profits have donated money. We received a steady amount of cash during the winter refugee crisis from wealthy individual donors. A handful of government hospitals in the Punjab donated medical supplies and equipment."

"Zahid, I understand. It sounds like we need a serious infusion of capital. When I return to the States, I will contact as many Kashmiris as I can in America. I will double my efforts."

I listened silently. It was the first time I realized how much work my father had put into this hospital, and how difficult his job really was. It was true that no one in the United States seemed to know about Kashmir. For me, Kashmir and the U.S. were almost two separate lives of mine.

After our well-earned meal we got into the trucks and drove towards Rawalpindi and onto the Kashmir Highway. When Kashmir Highway was first built in the 1880s, you could travel from Rawalpindi all the way to Srinagar, the capital of Jammu and Kashmir. My dad looked at me and Tamer. "I once took this road to Srinagar back in the mid-fifties with my own father," he told us. "In 1948, when the first war between India and Pakistan over Kashmir ended, my father decided to leave Indian-controlled Kashmir. He assumed he would return soon once the political situation had been resolved. He did not get far into Azad Kashmir; he just passed the Line of Control and settled in Keran. But by the mid-fifties, he no longer thought the political situation would get fixed quickly, so he returned to Jammu and Kashmir to sell our family's lands. I traveled down with him to Srinagar on this same Kashmir Highway. I haven't returned there since. Now, we are permanently settled in Keran."

Tamer smiled at my dad. "I thought we were from Alabama."

My dad looked back at Tamer with a gentle smile and said softly "Yes, you are right, we are proud to be from Alabama. And here I am again, on this same highway exactly forty years later, traveling down this road with my two sons."

Until that moment, I had always presumed that Keran was my family's village. I had not known that we originally came from the Indian-occupied part of Kashmir. My father had never before discussed his family's history, Kashmir's politics, and its past with us. I don't know why he finally chose this day to speak about these things — perhaps because of his conversation with our uncle.

It was dark now and we were nearing Murree, a hill station in the Himalayan foothills built by the British. My father looked at Tamer and me and pointed towards its large western-style church, built in the mid-1800s and still being used by local Christians. "This town was built so that the British soldiers would have a safe haven for their troops who were attacking and trying to capture Afghanistan," he told us "The Russians and the British fought over Afghanistan. They called it the Great Game. A British general named Lawrence even built a college for troops and their families here in Murree called Lawrence College.

Until 1947 the college was only for British soldiers and their families. Then In 1947, Pakistan got its independence and Lawrence started accepting Pakistani students. It is still running. Some of my childhood friends from Keran went there."

He paused. "You know, now that I think about it, British soldiers named Lawrence have a history of being agents in this part of the world. In the Arab world, the British sent T.E Lawrence to create a war between the Arabs and the Turks. In the subcontinent, they used a British general named Lawrence to create a war between the Afghans and the Russians."

I stared out the window of the truck as we passed large dense trees and green valleys. Stars were shining in a clear dark sky. We drove through the city, past the main bazaar and up into the mountains.

As we drove further, we came upon a majestic waterfall falling right past the carved-out road so the water would not hit passing vehicles. Just beneath the waterfall was a small mosque, its loudspeaker blazing the call to prayer. The *muezzin* cried out "God is great, hurry to prayer, hurry to success, there is only one God and Muhammad is his messenger."

Deciding to take a break, we secured the vehicles and went inside the mosque beneath the waterfall. After prayer I walked carefully across the road and looked down at the water dropping straight down the valley. We must have been at least seven thousand feet above sea level. I could not see where the waterfall ended, but watching it spill down from this height was breathtaking. To the northwest

I could see the peaks of the Himalayas touching the sky. Tamer stood right next to me and peered down.

"Don't slip. That fall looks like it would never end."

My father shouted at us from the car, "Hey, you two! Get back in the car, that's dangerous!"

When we turned back, his face was tight, so I let the waterfall go and made my way back to the safety of the car. I had never seen anything like that before and have seen nothing like it since.

As we got closer to Kashmir, the mountains got larger.

I looked at my watch. It was 11:45 p.m. and we were about 35 kilometers from Muzzafarabad. I knew Dad would not risk driving into Keran at night. It was too dangerous so near the Line of Control. Not only might the Indian army shoot at us, but the Pakistan Army would not even allow us into Keran in these trucks without inspecting them, and perhaps taking some of the supplies for themselves.

We entered a large valley surrounded by mountains. At the top of a mountain in the northwest corner was a large, well-lit home with a view of the entire valley below. The civil governor of Azad Kashmir lived in that house. He wasn't a politician, but a government bureaucrat, appointed by the Pakistanis to run the capital and its surrounding valleys. Nothing entered Kashmir without him knowing about it. He was also an old school friend of my father's. Our vehicles made their way slowly up the mountain towards that house. In the streetlights I could see villagers staring at us and our large vans as we steered up the winding mountain road.

The house was surrounded by a high wall, and the only way to enter was through the main gate. Zahid and my father exited the trucks and approached the gate to talk to the security officer. Then gate opened and our small convoy entered and parked within the secure wall. I had been to this house several times before, but this time it felt different, too still somehow. My father and Zahid had been very quiet, speaking only to each other, and too softly for me to understand.

They took me and Tamer aside as we entered. "A few days ago," said my father, "The Governor was informed that his son had been blessed with martyrdom. This house is still in mourning. Don't smile or joke too much, especially you, Tamer. We need the Governor's help to get our trucks into Keran. He will give us the protection we need to get there."

The Governor awaited us at the front door along with several servants. Zahid and my dad went up to him and hugged him in turn. He motioned for us to enter. We went into the high-ceilinged living room. Tamer and I sat quietly beside our father on a beautiful but stiff sofa of deep blue and mahogany.

Our host sat down across from us. "How was the flight from America? Not only do you have a long flight, but then the laborious journey to Keran afterward. Allah rewards the traveler because there is much benefit in traveling."

"Governor *Sahib*, thank you so much for hosting us tonight," said my father.

"Please don't mention it," said the Governor. "You are embarrassing me. It is a blessing to have you and this group with us at our home."

"We are truly sorry to hear about your son Mahmoud's death," my father said, "He is a *shaheed.* You and your family have been blessed with your son's martyrdom. He was an honorable young man, fighting for his family, for his religion, and for his country. To God we belong, from God we come, and to God we shall all return." He paused briefly and asked, "How old was Mahmoud?"

The Governor had a pained look on his face and simply answered, "He was 23. Yes, my family and I have been blessed with his martyrdom. However, I did not want this war for him. The youth of Kashmir, they are all joining the war; they see no hope for their future."

After a brief pause, he continued, "I sent Mahmoud to college in Karachi. I wanted to keep him far away from here, so he would not become involved in the war. I wanted him to come back after his studies and help create a better Kashmir. I wanted him to become a civil engineer."

We sat quietly listening to the soft-spoken governor. "Two years ago, he came to visit us during his spring break. When he left, we thought he was going back to Karachi, but instead he called us from the mujahideen camps, telling us that he had joined the jihad. He said he would either live to see freedom or die fighting for it."

The Governor paused for a few moments to gather himself, for his voice had grown strained with emotion. "I went to the camps and tried talking him out of it. But it was too late; his mind was made up. For the past two years, every day, his mother and I have been praying to see him safe and sound at our doorsteps. The last time we heard from him was three weeks ago. He called us from Indian-occupied Kashmir. His group of mujahideen had infiltrated Srinagar and were attacking Indian soldiers. What can a group of ten or fifteen Mujahideen do against 700,000 Indian soldiers? Yes, Allah has blessed us with his martyrdom, but he could have instead helped Kashmir by building our poor nation. We don't need freedom fighters. We need smart and educated citizens. We need people who can establish businesses, create jobs, and help our economy grow. I told my son about you, Dr. *Sahib*, and how you have built a hospital and helped so many Kashmiris."

The Governor wiped away his tears. "Back when he was born, there were no hospitals. Newborns were delivered at your house. There was always one woman in the village who delivered all the babies. I still remember her bringing my son to me when he was first born. I looked at this pale baby with red rosy cheeks and curly brown hair. I couldn't believe I was a father. My son, my beautiful son." He paused again "My family and I, we can't even visit his grave in Indian-controlled Kashmir. We don't even know where he is buried."

After a few silent agonizing moments the Governor continued, "Mahmoud's life and death will not be in vain. I won't let it. God blessed us with his presence for twenty-three years, and I will be with him again." Quietly, he repeated: "I will be with him again, *inshallah*."

No one knew what to do except listen.

"I am sorry, Dr. *Sahib*," the Governor said finally, "I know you are not here to listen to an old man talk. I know you are doing good work. I can see the large trucks you brought. Are they packed with medical supplies? As usual, you are here to help the people of Kashmir. You are an honorable person, Dr. *Sahib*. If only you could come twice a year, not just once. We need you to build more hospitals. I will help you get these supplies to the hospital in Keran. I will call the Pakistani commander and have a squad of Jeeps and soldiers escort you to the village to protect your cargo and ensure its safe arrival. The Pakistani army will lead your trucks safely through the narrow roads of our mountains."

"Thank you Governor *Sahib*," said my father gently. "We need more Kashmiris like you."

The Governor shook his head and said, "No Dr. *Sahib*. Kashmir needs people like you." He got up to leave. "I know you are all tired. Please stay the night and rest. I have plenty of space for everyone."

June 29, 1993

It was past midnight. I tried to go to sleep, but my head was full of thoughts about Mahmoud. I couldn't stop thinking about how passionately his father had spoken about his future, a future that was no longer going to happen. I wondered if Mahmoud still would have joined the jihad knowing he wouldn't make it out alive. I thought about Kashmir, about our travels, about my sister's wedding and my college plans, how time was moving too fast and I still wasn't even sure where I was going. At around 4:30 am, I got out of bed, went outside to the patio, and looked out into the mountains. It was a beautiful Kashmiri summer night, and I could see the entire valley in the moonlight, with houses buttressing on all the surrounding mountains. There was a full moon and the stars were vivid and plentiful. It was a clear night with only a few small clouds in the sky.

I looked at the end of the patio and to my surprise, the Governor was sitting beneath a tree with a book in his hands, and several others scattered around his feet. I watched him read for a few minutes then stare out into the valley below. Suddenly, he looked over and he saw me. I started feeling sheepish, but he motioned for me to come to him.

"Son, come over here and sit next to me against this tree," he said. "Your name is Hanzilah, yes? I have known your father for many years. He is a good man, and your Uncle Riaz is too. You have a noble family.

I didn't know what to say. "Thank you," I said shyly.

"Kashmir is a beautiful land," he said. "Some even say it is heaven on earth. In America, where you and your family live, is the terrain like Kashmir?"

"No sir," I replied. "It is a flat land with lots of trees, forests, and rivers. We live in the southern part of the United States, in a place called Alabama."

The Governor nodded his head. "I see. Your father is very proud of you. He tells me you graduated at the top of your class. That you were a gold medalist."

I was surprised to hear that my father had told him about school. "Yes, sir, but in the States we call the top student the valedictorian."

"That is wonderful, son. Are you going to become a doctor like your dad or do you wish to do something different?"

I was unprepared for that question. "I will become a doctor because that is what my parents want for me." I said hesitantly "but I really like other things too, like law."

"You want to be a lawyer?"

"I don't know sir."

"You are young, Hanzilah, and this world is what you make of it. You can achieve your dreams, but you should also honor your parents. You know, Allama Iqbal was a lawyer. Do you know who Allama Iqbal was?

"Yes, sir, he was the national poet of Pakistan. He pushed for the creation of an independent state for Muslims in India."

"That is right. But have you ever read his poetry?"

"No," I admitted.

"That is something we must change," he said. "Let me give this book as a gift to you, it is the poetry of Allama Iqbal."

He picked up an old book bound in a maroon cover, with paper that had yellowed with age. He placed the book on my lap and said, "My son Mahmoud loved the poetry of Allama Iqbal. This was his book. I want you to have it now."

"Governor *Sahib*, I can't accept this gift," I said. "It's too much."

He shook his head. "It's your book now. Promise me you will read it."

"Yes, of course I will," I promised.

"You can't just read it once," he insisted. "Every time you read the poetry of Allama Iqbal, even if it is the same poetry you read a hundred times before, you will find more meaning in it. Promise me you will always read it."

"Yes sir, I will always read it."

For the first time, I saw him look happy.

"What were you reading?" I asked him. "Was it some work of Iqbal, Governor *Sahib*?"

"Yes," he said. "Why don't you read the verse I was on?"
I took the book from him and read:

Thou art not for the earth,
Or for the heaven alone;
The world is for thee,
Not thou for the world.

"What does this verse mean?" I asked the Governor.
He was smiling when he replied. "Ahhh, that is a good question. For me, I am finding comfort in this verse right now in my state of loss. But for you, this verse could mean something entirely different. That is the beauty of Iqbal." Then he asked, "Why are you up at this time my son? Have your travels not tired you?"

"I couldn't sleep. My body is tired, but my brain is buzzing. I still can't believe my elder sister is getting married, that I will be attending college two months from now. I've learned so much in a short time during these travels with my father. I've been thinking about my country, my people, my faith, and my future. What if I don't come back to Kashmir for many years once college starts in the States?"

The Governor then gave me some advice that I understand much better now than I did then. "Son, you are becoming a man," he said. "That is it. Life changes quickly. Just remember, the decisions you make now, in your youth, they will affect your life forever. You won't realize it now, but what you do tomorrow could affect your life for the next twenty years. Think about it. Your sister is getting married. This is an enormous step. From this decision she and her husband will begin a life together that will involve children, happiness, and pain. Events will transpire that would not have happened had she and her fiancé not made a decision to marry each other. You are choosing whether to become a doctor or a lawyer, or something entirely different. You are choosing to go to college. You will make friends there that you don't even know exist right now. Those friends you meet, they could change your life. You could meet a girl and she could change your life. Let me give you some advice. Whatever you do from this point forward, whatever decision you make, don't make it in haste. Your friends, your family, your experiences may push you in one direction. But before you do anything, think about it, even if only for a moment. Think about what that decision will involve, not only in the short term, but also think about the long-term effects it may have."

I listened intently. The Governor was talking like a father. Maybe he was telling me the things he had wanted to say to his own son. "You should go back to bed and rest," he now said. "You have to travel to Keran, you have to help your father, you have to meet your future brother-in-law, and you have a big wedding coming up."

"Governor *Sahib*, will you come to the wedding?" I asked him.

"Yes, of course I'll be there," he assured me. "Now get some rest, Hanzilah. Everyone will be waking up in a few hours."

When I got into bed, I placed the book beneath my pillow and fell asleep immediately.

A few hours later Tamer pushed me off the bed, and I crashed onto the cement floor, my nose stinging. He was hovering over me, laughing his head off. The clock on the side table said 8:30 a.m., and I was too sleepy to lunge back at him. "Grow up," I said with a glare.

"Get up," he said. "Everybody is getting breakfast, and then we have to hit the road."

In the dining room, people were drinking British tea and eating eggs. I could hear engine noise outside. A man in a military suit walked in and stood at the door. He was tall with a pronounced chin and a thick mustache. "*Assalamu-alaikum* Major Jamal, welcome to my home," said the Governor. "Please come on in and join us for breakfast."

The major was all business. "Thank you for your hospitality, Governor *Sahib*," he said, "but I am here in a professional capacity to assist you. I was told you needed some help to get some medical supplies into Keran near the Line of Control. Is that correct, sir?"

Yes, Major, that is right. Do you know Dr. Karim Ali? Dr. Ali is a cardiac surgeon who runs the medical hospital in Keran. You will be escorting him and his caravan of medical supplies into Keran. I don't want any trouble for him. I want him to get there safe and sound. His work is critical to the success of our community."

"I understand, Governor," said the major in a formal voice. "I will escort Dr. Ali and his trucks to Keran safely."

The major went outside, and my father addressed the Governor. "Governor *Sahib*, there was no need for this help. We have made this journey many times without the assistance of the Pakistani military."

"Dr. *Sahib*, things have changed since last year," said the governor dryly. "This conflict is spilling into Azad Kashmir. So many refugees have arrived from India. Many

Kashmiri freedom groups from India have set-up bases in Pakistan, and they are a security risk. Your medical supplies are a valuable asset, and they may try to get their hands on them as they pass through the valleys and mountains."

My father was taken aback. "Do we have to worry about the Pakistani military?" he asked. "Will they take our supplies?"

"No, they won't do that, I assure you. However, they have many military checkpoints on the way to Keran, and you will need a military officer and escort to get you through the checkpoints without any hindrance or delay."

The Governor walked us to our trucks and embraced my father. He glanced back at me with a smile and gave me a warm hug. "Remember what we talked about."

"I will," I promised. Tamer looked at me curiously.

The major and his soldiers were in two trucks ahead of and behind ours.

We followed them onto the main road. As we entered the shopping district, I saw five red Toyota 4 X 4 trucks swarming through the roads, stopping for no one and wasting no time. In the back of each truck sat several men with AK-47s and RPGs strapped to their bodies.

"Who are those guys?" I asked my dad. "Mujahideen?"

"Son, don't worry about those men," he said. "They are not important."

I pressed him. "You don't think these guys are important. Why not?"

He shrugged, "Their intentions may be good but Kashmir needs peace not war. They are going about it the wrong way."

"Dad, do you think Mahmoud died in vain?"

"No, I do not," he said sternly. "He died with honor, and our Lord, the most high, will grant him paradise for his sacrifice. Son, you don't understand because you are too young. What we need is a concerted organized effort to bring peace to Kashmir. The problem is that there are so many different groups, each with a different agenda. If all the Kashmiri groups unified under one umbrella, under one strong leader, and then that leader decided that fighting was the only solution, then I would support that. But right now we don't have that leader."

I gazed out the window of the truck. We traveled up mountains, down mountains, around mountains, from one valley to the next.

After about an hour of driving, we came upon a station of Pakistani soldiers. Our convoy stopped and the major got out of the front vehicle. We watched as he approached the soldiers, showed them some papers, talked to them for a few minutes, and then waved us through the station. As we drove by, I looked at the soldiers, who wore green camo fatigues and helmets and carried small arms, each also sporting a tidy mustache.

As we approached the Line of Control, I saw large guns pointed out of the mountains, straight toward the Indians. The nearer we got to Keran the more of these small outposts we saw. I had not seen them on our previous trips to Kashmir. I observed my father noticing them too, his face grim. Every time we entered a new valley or approached a mountaintop, we ran across another Pakistani outpost. Each time, the major got out of the front vehicle and then waved us through.

I opened the book the Governor had given me.

Revealed in these words
Is the secret of life and death;
Love is death with honor,
Life without honor is death.

"What are you reading?" Asked my dad.

I told him.

"Where did you get this book from?"

"The Governor gave it to me."

"The Governor was very nice to give you such a book. Iqbal was an amazing person. I'll take you to visit his grave in Lahore one day. He is buried in a small mausoleum right outside the *Badshahi Mosque*. Your Uncle Riaz was right about Lahore. It is an amazing city. Someday we will spend more time there.

Our convoy came down a large mountain and entered a large valley surrounded by mountains. We were home. It was summer, and the valley was filled with greenery. The tulips were blooming, the sky was light blue, and the river flowed glistening through the valley. My dad poked Tamer. "Wake up sleepy head, we're in Keran," he said.

The *Neelum River* flowed right through Keran, and the valley was dotted with many small homes. The hospital was right on the main road, just before the small bazaar. Throughout the mountains, above the valley were more houses, some large, but most small. There were no Pakistani military outposts here or in the surrounding mountains. As we came down the mountain, I saw something I had never before seen in Keran: hundreds of small black tents surrounding the hospital and the bazaar.

My dad stared at the tents in disbelief. "Zahid told me that many Kashmiris on the Indian side had fled to our valley in the past few months and are staying as refugees," he said in dismay. "But I did not expect it to be so large. We have a lot of work ahead of us."

The villagers stared curiously at our convoy as we entered the town with our military escort, slowly approaching the hospital. We came face to face with hundreds of black tents. Many men with long faces sat in circles, staring at us. Women stared too, through colorful translucent veils. Some were cooking, some holding babies, some sitting on charpoys. Kids ran towards our convoy, surrounding it and slowing us down. I heard one of them screaming: "Do you have any gum? Can you give me some chewing gum?" I tossed the bubble gum in my pocket out my window. He jumped to catch it and showed it to the kids around him. They jumped up and down in excitement. He cut up the gum in four pieces and gave three to his friends. When I saw that, I smiled.

The hospital was a four-story cement building that stood out from the rest of Keran. At the entrance, we quickly began unloading the supplies, helped by the major and his men. My dad and Zahid went inside the hospital and emerged with fifteen more volunteers. What had taken four hours to load in Islamabad took thirty minutes to unload at the hospital.

My father's hospital was managed like a hospital in the States. Each department had its own staff physician and a set of support staff. There was an Internal Medicine Department, a Gynecology and Obstetrics department, a Department of Surgery, a Pediatric Department, a Psychiatric Department, and an Intensive Care Unit, and each department had its own set of supplies and equipment that it would be receiving. As soon as we entered, the staff doctors vied with one another, pleading with my father for a greater share. "Dr. Ali," one man argued, "you must understand my department is laboring under the stress of the new refugees. We need more beds. We need to construct a new floor of beds for the Internal Medicine Department."

Another red-faced doctor literally shoved him out of the way with his broad shoulders.

"Dr. Ali, the Surgery Department needs more beds. He and his staff can visit the camps and provide many of their treatments outside of the hospital. But surgeries can only be performed in the hospital. The surgical department needs its own floor."

My father gave each of them a friendly smile, composed as always, and said, "You are both under a lot of pressure. I know you both are understaffed and undersupplied. I can only promise that I will do my best to get additional supplies and more funding. I'll get on the phone and see what I can do, but right now I need to get home."

He then paused a moment and said to me quietly, "Hanzilah, go get Tamer and let's go home to meet your mother and sister. I don't think I am going to get a chance to enjoy this wedding. Things here are worse than I anticipated."

I found Tamer playing cricket with kids in a field near the refugee camps. They used a damaged tennis ball that flew barely five feet regardless of how hard you hit it. "Tamer, let's go," I called to him. "Dad is waiting for us." Up close, I could see how thin and unkempt the refugee children he played with were. I wondered if they would survive the harsh Himalayan winter.

Our home was located in the northwestern part of the valley. It was getting late, and the sun was setting on Keran, casting a warm orange glow on the lush scenery.

Our house was in a small neighborhood of eight stucco houses surrounded by an exterior wall. Since our last visit, our house had been painted beige and new flowers had been placed throughout the garden. "Wow, there are even Christmas lights in the front!" Said Tamer "Why do we have Christmas lights?"

"Son, we are having a wedding," my father told him. "And these decorations are part of wedding tradition. This is the house of the bride-to-be."

My sister and mother opened the door with big smiles. They were spitting images of one another, my sister a slightly taller version of my mother with my father's nose. Tamer and I ran to them and gave them big hugs. This was our first time seeing them in a month, and it was a relief to have the family all together again. My father was behind us, and he hugged Aliyah and placed his hand on her head. He looked at my mom and smiled. "*Assalamu-alaikum begum*," he said.

My mom told our servant to grab our bags and said to us with a bright happy smile, "My boys must be exhausted. I know you want to relax. I have made a big dinner so you can eat quickly and get some rest."

The interesting thing was that I wasn't tired. I was excited to be back in Kashmir. At the dinner table Tamer said jokingly to Aliyah, "When are we going to meet this boyfriend of yours?"

Dad rolled his eyes. "Son, we don't have this thing in our culture, this boyfriend and girlfriend nonsense."

I cut in. "Yeah, when are we meeting this guy?"

"He and his family are coming tomorrow for dinner to meet Baba and you boys." Aliyah said with composure.

"Begum, when is the wedding?" Dad asked Mom in a serious tone. "When is the *Mendhi*?"

"In two weeks," she replied. "Time is flying, the wedding is nearly here, and we still have so much more to do to get ready for Aliyah's marriage to Khalid."

My father stroked his chin. "I only have three weeks' vacation, and then I have to go back to the States. We have a lot of work to do at the hospital. There are so many refugees, and many of them need medical care, food, and other basic supplies. I'm sorry, but I won't be able to help you with the wedding. First thing tomorrow, I am going to the hospital."

My mom shook her head in frustration "When will you actually take a vacation? You need to spend time with your family. You need to spend time with your daughter before she gets married and leaves our home. You can't save everyone, Karim."

But she knew it was pointless to argue with him. Of course he would attend the wedding, but he would spend most of his time here at the hospital, as he always did. The hospital was his life's work, and his way of giving back to his people.

After dinner I changed clothes, but instead of going straight to bed I went to the living room, where my mother was sitting on the floor with a sewing machine, sewing *shalwar kameez* and untailored suits for men. Her brow was knit and her hair astray.

"Are you going to sew all these clothes?" I asked her gently.

She looked at me tiredly. "I have given a lot of clothes to the tailors, but I need to sew some things myself if everything is going to get done in time."

Aliyah was in the kitchen. "Are you cooking Aliyah?" I asked. "I have never seen you cook."

"Hanzilah, don't make fun of your sister," my mom scolded. "She needs to learn how to cook some dishes before she gets married."

I went into the kitchen, sat at the table and gave Aliyah a friendly smile. "You like this guy?" I asked her.

"Yes, he's very nice and smart," she said. "He comes over with his mother or father at least three or four times a week to visit me. I have talked to him a lot, and we have gotten to know one another. He has a good sense of humor, but he is also serious about his studies. He went to King Edward, just like Baba."

"You think I am going to like him?" I asked her "Is he cool to hang out with?"

"Yes, you will like him. I don't know if Tamer will like him. Tamer is a little wild."

"My Tamer is fine," Mom called from the living room. "He is a teenager. You were just like him, Hanzilah. Aliyah, be nice to your younger brother. He is my little *munna*."

I stuck a spoon into Aliyah's Dum Aloo and savored the tang and turmeric on my tongue. "You know, this tastes pretty good," I said encouragingly.

She gave me a half smile and shrugged. Suddenly, I felt exhausted.

I said goodnight and walked to my room. I sank into the familiarity of my bed and I fell into a deep sleep.

June 30, 1993

I slept until two o'clock in the afternoon. The jet lag, the physical work, and the long journey had taken their toll. I arose and peered out my window at the neighboring houses. My friends would be back from school soon, and I was hoping we could play cricket in the evening. I took a bath, changed into a traditional Kashmiri *shalwar kameez* and went downstairs.

Mom and sister were in the kitchen. "Eh sleepy head, you finally woke up," Aliyah remarked.

"Can I get some coffee?" I asked her. "My brain is telling me to go right back to sleep. I need some caffeine." I looked. "Where is Dad? Is he still sleeping?"

"No, your dad is at the hospital," said my mom with a frown. "He woke up at 5a.m. and left right after completing the morning prayer. He is still there. I called him a few moments ago. He says he will be back in the evening to meet Aliyah's fiancé and his family."

"Oh, are they coming here tonight for dinner? I didn't know that. Do you need my help?"

Aliyah smiled and said, "Just please be nice to Khalid."

"Yeah, yeah, don't worry about it," I teased her. "I promise I'll be nice. Do I have to wear something more formal, or can I wear what I have now?"

"What you are wearing is fine, as long as you don't mess up your clothes playing cricket with your friends."

She handed me toast and a cup of coffee and sat next to me. "Is Tamer awake?" I asked her.

"No, he's still sleeping."

There was a knock on the front door. "It must be one of your friends," Aliyah said. "A couple of them came by a few days ago, asking Mom about when you would be coming."

I ran to the front door. It was Daniyal. "You are finally here, *yaar*," he exclaimed. "Welcome back."

I hugged him, "Thanks for coming over. It's great to see you."

Daniyal was of medium height and skinny with wavy black hair and light brown skin. "Are you tired?" he asked. "Do you want to go out?"

My excitement at the thought of seeing my friends overcame my fatigue. "I'm not tired," I insisted. "Let's take a walk. What's been going on? Are you done with school?"

"I am done for the summer and I begin college in the fall," he said with enthusiasm.

"Where are you going for college?"

"To Lawrence College in Murree."

"What do you plan to study?"

"I think I am going to study Computer Science. Everybody is telling me that computers are the future and that is the best thing to study, because there will be a lot of jobs and opportunities."

The confidence in his voice pleased me. "That's terrific. How has everybody been doing around here? How is Jawad?"

"Jawad is doing real well," Daniyal said with a twinkle in his eye. "You know he got married."

I was stunned. "What? He's our age. That is unbelievable!"

"You know how he is. He's always in a hurry. That guy does everything fast. He finished up his high school at fourteen. He finished his college at eighteen and now he is married."

I was upset that I was only now being told that my good friend had gotten married months ago. "Daniyal, why wasn't I told about his wedding? Someone should have called me. I would have come to the wedding. I would have really liked to see Jawad get married."

"Yeah, like we can just call you in the States. There are only a few phones in the village. You're lucky if you can afford one, and the long distance charges are crazy."

"I guess you're right," I conceded. "How is Ali?"

Daniyal now told me something even more surprising. "Ali has changed a lot since last summer," he said. "His relatives' village in Indian Kashmir was attacked, and then his cousins joined the mujahideen. They wanted him to come help them in the war. I heard that after he finished school, he left to join the mujahideen."

"You've got to be kidding! How is that possible? He was the biggest clown among us. I don't believe it."

"Things have changed a lot since last summer Hanzilah," Daniyal said in a serious tone. "Things have gotten much worse. People don't see any hope or chance for peace. Either people are leaving Kashmir, or they are joining the revolution." He paused. "It's hard to find work. The tourists have stopped coming. On the Indian side it has decreased, and in Azad Kashmir people no longer visit our valleys and mountains. The only people that come anymore are the

Western mountain climbers and all they want to do is climb *K-2* or *Nanga Parbat*. They don't care about what is happening to us either. So many Kashmiris from India have fled to our side that every single valley has throngs of refugees now. They're fleeing the war. Kashmiris are putting up a strong and valiant fight. There are also peaceful protests, but the Indian army responds to them with vicious brutality. They keep people in jail for up to two years, without even charging them. Many of the peaceful protesters end up joining the fighters after experiencing horrific brutality in the detention centers. I think that I will have to leave this place. I love my village, but I can't live a normal life here."

At that moment, I heard the rumble of a motorcycle from behind, and saw our friend Isa ride by. Happy to change the subject, I called out to him.

Isa turned his head and saw me waving. He immediately made a u-turn and drove his motorcycle right up to us. As we embraced, he said loudly, "Hanzilah, what in the world are you doing here? Aren't you supposed to be in college in America?"

Isa was short and stocky but athletic. He was the quickest and fastest among us on the soccer field.

"He is here because his sister's wedding is in two weeks," Daniyal told him.

Isa grinned and patted me on my shoulder. "Congratulations on your sister's wedding! I didn't know *bahabi* was getting married. I didn't even know you were coming this summer. How long are you going to visit?"

"Actually, I don't know how long I'll be here," I confessed. "I am going to try to stay the rest of the summer, though. What's up with you Isa?"

"Not much, really. For now, I'm headed to the bazaar. I try to help out at the refugee camps these days. The good news is that college will be starting soon. Daniyal is headed to Lawrence, but I am going to Lahore to study at UET.

"What is UET?"

This time Daniyal answered for Isa. "University of Engineering and Technology is one of the best engineering schools in Pakistan, and really tough to get into."

"Are you planning to study engineering?"

"Yeah, I think so," said Isa. "Right now I'm thinking about pursuing a degree in mechanical engineering. But who knows. I was thinking that if I don't like engineering I might study textile science."

"Wow, everybody is leaving Kashmir," I remarked.

"We have to leave. There are only a handful of colleges and universities here. The good thing about Pakistan is that there are national entrance exams, and if you score well you have an opportunity to get into a good college anywhere in the country." He changed the subject. "Where are you guys headed?"

"We're walking towards the center of the village," said Daniyal.

"I'm headed there. You guys need a ride?"

"The three of us can't fit on the motorcycle," I said. "Daniyal and I can walk."

"Then I will walk with you," said Isa. He grabbed his motorcycle and pushed it along as we walked together.

As we approached the center of the village, the refugee tents, the bazaar, and my dad's hospital came into sight. Isa shook his head. "The refugee situation is a big problem," he said. "Our small village can't handle all of them. There is not enough food, not enough water, not enough housing."

"Keran has become a gateway for refugees," Daniyal added. "These people will only stay here a few weeks, then their relatives will find them and take them back to their homes. Their extended families will help them find work, and more permanent housing."

Isa nodded and said graciously, "They come here because of your dad's hospital, Hanzilah. They know that they can get treatment, then continue their journey into Azad Kashmir. Your dad's hospital not only treats these people; he feeds them. The residents of Keran and the surrounding villages help by donating money, food, and supplies."

I had not been aware of the extent and importance of my father's work. I looked at Isa and Daniyal. "When the wedding is over I think I'll volunteer at the hospital. It would be a good experience. I'm old enough now; I think my dad can trust me to help."

"Our Kashmiri brothers and sisters need our help," Isa said. "We each have to do something." Daniyal nodded in agreement.

We entered the area of the main bazaar, the hospital, and the refugee camps. Everything and everybody was packed into a small area. On the main market street Isa said, "I'm volunteering with this group that helps the refugees locate their extended family members in Azad Kashmir. I have to go meet up with them. I'll see you around, Hanzilah."

But I put my hand on Isa's shoulder to hold him back. I wanted to make sure I would see him again soon. "I would really like it if you came to my sister's wedding,"

I told him. "I don't have a formal invitation card to give you, but I want you to come."

Isa nodded. "I wouldn't miss it, my friend. *Inshallah* I'll be there."

Daniyal and I walked around the refugee camps. Some small children huddled around a makeshift play area, running around and giggling. Their parents sat watching them play, not with joy and pride, but with a deep sadness.

There was one family in particular, a family of five, that caught my attention. The wife, husband, and two older kids were sitting on a thin carpet watching their youngest child play. I went up to them and said, "*Assalamu-alaikum biahsaab*, which kid is yours?" The father pointed to a boy with wavy brown hair wearing a light blue *shalwar kameez* and said, "That is my son. His name is Arif. Would you like a place to sit, son?" The man asked. "We must all help each other. Right now, the only thing I can offer is a place to sit."

I didn't want to be rude, so I sat next to him. He was dark-skinned with a thick mustache and many scars and sores on his feet. He caught me looking at them and said, "The travel here was difficult, but the burden and hardships we faced were worth it. We are now free."

I didn't know what to say. "Which part of Kashmir are you coming from?" I asked.

"We lived in the outskirts of Srinagar, in an area called *Hari Parbat*. My family and I had a small restaurant there. For years business was good, because many tourists came to see the holy shrines and the Mughal fort. Hindus, Sikhs, Muslims, they all came. There was a beautiful gurdwara that the Sikhs built that they would visit, and Hindu temple in our area that was popular also. But the main reason people came was to visit *Makhdoom Sahib*, a famous Sufi sheikh buried in our area. Hindus, Sikhs, and Muslims all would visit his shrine. Now, with this war and violence, no one comes to *Hari Parbat* anymore. Our business was destroyed by a fire that was ignited by a stray mortar. I have waited for this war to end and for things to get better. But the war is taking too long. It has been four very long and hard years. I could not keep my family there anymore. It is not safe. We used to live in peace. Those days are over. My brother told me to come to Azad Kashmir; he migrated several years ago. He told me that my children can grow up here in peace. I am waiting here for him to take us to his home and host us until I find work. Where are you coming from? Which part of Kashmir are you fleeing?"

"My family lives right here in Keran," I told him. "Well, actually we live in America. I come to Keran every summer because our family home is here."

"Are you related to the man who runs the hospital? They say the doctor who runs the hospital is from America."

"Yes, he is my father."

"Your father is a good man. I took my eldest daughter to the hospital a few days ago. She was vomiting and had a fever. The hospital gave her medicine, and she is much better now. The hospital even gave our family free food and supplies." He looked at me intently. "Why does America not help us? They are the most powerful nation in the world. Why don't they stop this war? Why don't they pressure India to let Kashmir be free?"

"The American people do not know what is going on in Kashmir," I told him.

"How is that possible?"

I didn't know what to tell him, so I sat quietly and listened. I remembered when my father had told Zahid the same thing. Truthfully, many of my American friends had never even heard of Kashmir before they met me.

He pointed his finger at me, "When you get back to America, please tell them what is going on here. You have to let them know. The Americans are good people. If the American people knew what we were going through, they would help us."

More gently, he added, "We are being occupied. The only thing we want is freedom. Tell the Americans, tell the world, that we want freedom so that our children can grow and live in peace."

I listened intently to this man. He was clearly upset, and any words I could say would be meaningless.

"When I get back to the States I promise I will do my best to let people know," I said finally.

I saw my father standing at the entryway of his hospital, looking out into the refugee camp. "Forgive me, *biahsaab*," I said respectfully, "but I must leave. It was nice meeting you. I wish you and your family the best."

I waved to my father. He was surprised to see me and waved back. "What are you doing here son?" He asked.

"I came with Daniyal. We walked here from the house."

"It is good that you came. Stay close to me, because we both have to be back at the house soon. Khalid and his family are coming soon for dinner, and your mother will be unhappy with both of us if we don't show up ready and on time."

"Sure Dad. I was thinking that before we return to the States, I should stick around here at the refugee camp and volunteer at the hospital until the wedding."

It was the first time in days that I had seen my father smile. "That is a good idea, son. You can work in a hospital setting, gain experience in the medical profession, and most importantly help your brothers and sisters in Kashmir. Times are not good. I have never seen it like this before."

As we entered the hospital, a man in scrubs ran up to my father and screamed out, "Dr. Ali, hurry come quick! Ms. Nazia's organs are failing. I don't think she will last the night."

"Stay close, so we can return home together." My father told me. "Okay Dr. Khan, let's go."

Together they walked quickly toward the stairwell.

I went back outside and sat on the stairs of the main gate. And as I sat there, I realized that maybe I did want to be a doctor. At least, I wanted to be like my father.

Fifteen minutes later he came out with a resigned face and said, "Let's go home."

"So is there any hope for Ms. Nazia?" I asked him. "Can you treat her?"

"I don't think she will live much longer," he told me. "It is likely she will pass from this world tonight. We tried to save her with surgery, but she got an infection and it has spread quickly. Her situation is deteriorating."

"What happened to her, Dad? Is she dying of old age?"

"No, son. She was fleeing Indian-held Kashmir with her family. A stray mortar hit the caravan she was traveling in. They didn't see it coming. We don't know if it was a stray Indian army mortar or from the mujahedeen. But what does it matter? Her children won't have a mother much longer, and her husband will soon be a widower. She is only 33. It is the story of the past four years in Kashmir."

We sat in our family's Toyota Land Cruiser, one of the small Jeeps built in the mid to late seventies, and the most popular car in Azad Kashmir. It was good on gas, small but large enough to fit four people comfortably, and could travel up and down the mountain valleys with ease because of its four-wheel drive.

At home the aroma of rice, chicken, and skewered beef filled the air. My mother saw us and said sarcastically, "My boys are always helping me and always on time!"

My dad was exhausted. He hadn't rested for a moment since he had arrived. He slumped and said to my mom, "I have had a long day. I am going to get ready quickly." To deflect any blame from himself, he added loudly so my mother could hear, "Hanzilah, you get ready quickly and help your mother."

I went upstairs, washed my face, combed my hair, changed my clothes, and came downstairs as quickly as I could, but Mom didn't need my help, everything was set.

As I was about to sit down, the doorbell rang and she cried, "Is your father still upstairs getting ready? The guests are here. This night is the first time he is meeting his future son-in-law, and he is upstairs getting ready!"

Mom was falling apart. Whenever she had a dinner party, she would get nervous, and tonight was more than a dinner party. "Go upstairs," she said tensely. "Tell your brother and father to come down quickly. Then go open the door and greet our guests, Hanzilah."

I did as she asked. Mom stood behind me in the foyer, as I went to open the door.

There standing before me were a man my parent's age, a young man and two girls who looked between nine and twelve years old. “Welcome!” I said to them. “Come inside! I am Aliyah’s younger brother, Hanzilah. It is an honor to finally meet you.”

“*Assalamu-alaikum*,” said my mother with a gracious smile, polished and projecting calm. “Please come inside.”

I walked the guests to the living room and everybody sat down. Not knowing what to say or how this worked, I sat quietly.

After a few tense minutes, my father came down and greeted our guests. I sat in the corner of the room as he talked to his future son-in-law and his family. Khalid nervously watched our fathers talk. My dad always talked to people as if they had been his friends his entire life. My mother brought in some appetizers as we sat and chatted. Tamer looked bored, but behaved, smiling like an angel and only speaking when spoken to.

To break the ice, I walked over to sit next to Khalid. I told him it was nice to finally meet him and that my sister had said very nice things about him.

He smiled back. “Thank you,” he said, “I am honored to finally meet your father. As a young boy I heard about his work, and it inspired me to become a doctor. He is well-known and respected in Azad Kashmir.”

I asked him about medical school at King Edward Medical College in Lahore. He talked about the difficult coursework, but also about what an amazing experience it was to learn and work with the best doctors in Pakistan. He told me about diseases that occurred in Pakistan but not in America, that I had never even heard of. As we talked, I noticed how every time my sister walked in the room he would glance at her and she would look back and smile.

They were like kids in a classroom flirting with each other and thinking that no one noticed.

He excused himself and went into the kitchen at the same time my sister went in to make tea for everyone, and I smiled to myself. It did not seem that my father's tardiness could do anything to sway Khalid's affection for my sister, and their fondness for each other left me excited for the wedding. It left me excited, even, for the prospect of my own wedding one day.

July 3, 1993

Over the next few days, I divided my time between my mother and father. Some days I would help mom with wedding preparations, and other days I went with my dad to the hospital. I preferred going to the hospital. For the first few days, he had me help out with fairly easy tasks. He wanted to introduce me to how a hospital worked before he had me do anything else. I was the lowly unpaid intern. He first had me work in the kitchen. I took food directly to patients and refugees, which gave me an opportunity to meet with many of them.

On this summer day, I was sitting outside the hospital entrance, taking a short break, having a cup of tea and biscuits. I saw a group of young men and recognized one of them immediately. I waved and called out, "Jawad!"

Jawad was my closest friend in Kashmir. Daniyal and Isa had told me that he had gotten married, and I hadn't had an opportunity to congratulate him. He and his group walked towards me. There he was with his short hair and goatee, walking tall and strong. Jawad was only about five feet nine inches tall, but he walked on his tiptoes, with his chest sticking out and his head held high. He always had a smile on his face. I gave him a big hug and said, "Congratulations! I heard you got married!"

"Yeah, can you believe it?"

"I can't imagine a girl actually wanting to marry you. What lies you must have told her!"

He laughed. "I told her the truth, that I am a good-looking genius with a large inheritance."

"How is married life?"

"It is really nice. I have a great wife. Where are my manners? These are my friends from work." He introduced them and said, "I started a business making furniture, and these are my workers. I make the furniture and wholesale it to retailers in Lahore, Peshawar, Hyderabad, and Karachi."

I was impressed with Jawad. He was nineteen years old, and already a college graduate with a wife and a business. It was remarkable that he had accomplished so much so quickly. I said, "Jawad, my sister is getting married; you and your wife should come."

"I am coming," he said, "Your mother sent us the wedding invitations a couple of weeks back. We won't miss it."

He sat down with me and we chatted for more than an hour like old times. Jawad was only a year and a half older than me but he had always been a friend who gave me good advice. He asked me about school, about life in America, about how my family was doing. He was clearly happily married. He gushed about his wife and couldn't stop talking about her. My childhood friend had become a man.

The funny thing about Jawad was that, unlike our other friends, he never talked about the political situation in Kashmir. I didn't know if it was because he didn't care, or he was willfully ignoring it.

As he was about to leave, he said, "You should come over to the house. My wife and I are still living with my parents. Feel free to come over any night before the wedding."

Just then, Isa and Daniyal stopped by. Jawad greeted them and said, "Hanzilah is coming over to our house soon. You two come with him. It will be like old times."

After he left Daniyal said with a smirk, "*Yaar*, that is a dangerous invitation. Isn't your girl Jawad's sister?"

"Yeah *yaar*, make sure you wear your best clothes when you go over to see Imani," Isa teased.

"You guys need to stop that," I said, feeling the blood rush to my face. "She's Jawad's sister and she's not my girl."

"Have you not seen her since you got back?" Asked Daniyal.

"Come on everybody knows you like her," Isa said. "We see how you look at her. Last summer you were hanging out at their house every day."

"Imani is good friends with my sister," I said staunchly. "I would go there to hang out with Jawad, and Aliyah would hang out with Imani. That's it. You guys need to stop this nonsense."

Of course, I was crazy about Imani, and not good at hiding it. I'd been waiting to run into her ever since coming back, but my sister had been busy with wedding planning and I felt weird going by without her.

I told Isa and Daniyal, "Let's go visit Jawad at his home together like he suggested." They shook their heads and grinned.

July 4, 1993

The picture that this world presents

From woman gets its tints and scents'

She is the lyre that can impart

Pathos and warmth to human heart.

- Allama Iqbal

Jawad's family were a traditional Kashmiri family, pious and strict, and they kept a watchful eye on their daughter. Most likely, my only chance to see Imani would be if she opened the door. I ran late on purpose hoping Jawad would be entertaining Daniyal and Isa in the living room.

I rang the bell, and to my happy surprise Imani answered it smiling brightly in a black *shalwar kameez*. "*Assalamu-alaikum*, Hanzilah," she said. "So you are finally back from America. How are you?"

She had green eyes, olive skin, and light brown hair parted in the middle that flowed down to her shoulders. I looked into her eyes for too long, trying to take in every detail of her.

"I am well, Imani. How are you?"

"I am okay. Jawad is with Daniyal and Isa in the living room. I'll take you there." I looked down at the floor and said, "Yes, thank you."

As we walked, she looked me over "You know, this is Kashmir, not America," she said. "You always dress like an American teenager in the movies we see, with your jeans, tennis shoes, and t-shirt. Then you put on that American baseball hat backwards." She shook her head. "You don't even put the hat on right."

Caught off guard, I laughed.

"This is what we wear in Alabama." I changed the subject. "Congratulations on your brother's marriage! Is he happy? Do you like your sister-in-law?"

"Yes, he is happy, and I like *Bahabi* very much. Congratulations to you also — Aliyah is getting married soon."

"Yes, her fiancé is a nice guy. I like him a lot." I paused. "Isn't this year going to be your last year of high school?"

"Yes, I am getting ready for the college entrance exams. I am hoping to go to college in Lahore. Either I will try to attend Lahore College for Women or Kinnaird, *inshallah*."

I glanced at her unhappily.

"Oh, you also want to leave Kashmir for college," I said, "It seems everyone is leaving Keran to continue their studies."

As we spoke, I kept glancing at her, trying to see if there was a spark in her eyes for me. She was warm and elegant. I didn't want to walk to the living room; I wanted to stay and catch up. But I knew we couldn't do that.

As we got closer to the living room, I held her gaze.

"Will I see you at Aliyah's wedding?"

She smiled back. "Of course. How can I miss Aliyah's wedding? She's my good friend."

My heart skipping, I nodded and said, "*Khudafiz*," and walked through the doors into the living room.

Jawad got up and greeted me. I gave him a wedding gift. I had brought golden earrings for his wife that Aliyah had picked out for me. Jawad's wife came in with a tray of Kashmiri tea. She was short and pretty with long dark hair and a round face. Jawad introduced me and said, "This is Hanzilah, my friend from America."

She looked at me curiously. "Are you Aliyah's brother?"

"Yes, she is my sister," I muttered.

"Jawad has told me all about you. Congratulations on Aliyah's wedding. Her fiancé Khalid is a friend of our family. He is a very nice boy and he comes from a good family."

"I think he and my sister are a good match." I said. "Will you attend the *shadi*?"

"Of course we will all be there, including Imani," she said with a smirk, then left.

Jawad asked, "So Hanzilah, how is everything in America? We have been telling you everything that is going on in our lives, but we haven't heard a single thing about your plans."

I thought about it for a moment. "There isn't much to tell, actually. I'm looking forward to college. I'm leaving home just like Daniyal and Isa to attend. I'm actually going quite far from home to this college on the West Coast called Stanford."

"What are you going to study at this college?" Asked Isa. "Are going to be a doctor like your father?"

"Maybe. I'm not totally sure yet."

"That is one of the many great things about America," remarked Daniyal. "A person doesn't need to make a decision about what they want to do with the rest of their life at age eighteen. You can take some time to think about it. Here in Pakistan, you need to decide what you plan to do for the rest of your life before you finish high school and take your college entrance exams."

"It's a lot of pressure," I agreed.

After about half an hour, Imani and Jawad's wife came in and placed before us dishes of Kashmiri rice, barbecue chicken, and sweet yogurt. I glanced at Imani and our eyes briefly met, making my insides melt.

I tried to shake her from my thoughts so that my friends wouldn't notice. I looked over towards Jawad. "Jawad, what is up with Ali? I haven't seen him since I got here and Daniyal said to me that he is leaving to fight with the mujahideen by the end of the summer. Is that true?"

Isa cut in. "No no, Ali left already. He told everybody he was leaving at the end of the summer so no one would try to stop him. I don't blame him. What the Indian army did to his family was evil."

Ali was our good childhood friend. Every summer for the past 10 years, the five of us had played sports, hung out in the market, gone fishing in the *Neelum River*, and kept each other company. He had been a big part of my life in Keran. "What happened to his family?" I asked.

"Look Hanzilah, the Indian side of Kashmir is worse than you think," replied Isa in a serious tone. "When villages are attacked, some of the Indian soldiers don't behave well with our families. He looked at me meaningfully. "Especially the women. His family's honor is at stake. Talking about it won't do any good, but let's just say if I were Ali, I would be doing the same thing he is."

After dinner, Jawad's wife brought us dessert. I was hoping Imani would come back, but she didn't. It was the last I would see of her that night.

That night was like summers past, only now we had grown up. Jawad was married. Ali had left to join the fight. Daniyal, Isa, and I were about to start college and soon thereafter enter the real world. We were young adults, our futures were before us, and all we had to do was grab it, or, at least, so it seemed.

July 8, 1993

Kashmiri weddings are typically three-day affairs. The first night is the mehndi, when the bride has henna in decorative patterns affixed to her hands, arms, legs, and feet. This is entirely a women's event in Kashmiri culture. My father, Tamer, Khalid, and I were the only males at Aliyah's mehndi. We sat outside of the wedding tent as the women of Keran went in and out in droves, in their brightest, and most glamorous clothes. Khalid seemed nervous. I wasn't sure whether he was nervous about getting married, or because he was about to be surrounded and stared at by over two hundred women. He would have to go inside at some point and sit next to Aliyah at the podium of the tent, while the women gave both of them blessings and force-fed both of them with different Kashmiri sweets.

Sitting outside, I watched Imani and Jawad's wife as they walked into the wedding tent. Imani was wearing a beautiful off-white *shalwar kameez* that made her large green eyes shine. She glanced over at me and smiled. I was behind my father, Khalid, and Tamer, so they didn't see me wave hello to her. I hoped that an opportunity to talk to her would present itself at some point during the mehndi. I excused myself and went to the back of the tent and peered in. Women were socializing and loud music was playing over speakers. It was an all-women gathering and conservative Kashmiri women who would not dance in front of men let out all their inhibitions and danced feverishly, their eyes wild and free. I felt guilty for looking and turned away.

I walked back to where Khalid, Tamer, and my dad were sitting. Khalid asked, "What is going on in there?"

I shook my head. "You're in for a surprise."

Suddenly the music stopped. Food and soda were being brought in by a group of men. They spent about twenty minutes inside setting up the food then left as quietly as they had come in. After they left, the loud music came back on.

My mother came out, bringing us food and soda. "Are you boys having fun outside?" She asked. "Khalid, get ready, you will be coming in soon."

Khalid quietly nodded and smiled nervously at my mother.

Tamer was getting impatient; he was too young to care much about the ceremony. He asked Dad if he could go back inside the house and before Dad could even answer, Tamer was on his way. A few minutes later, my mother came outside to bring Khalid in. Now it was only my dad and me sitting outside the wedding tent.

I pondered taking another peek inside, but then I saw Imani coming out of the tent, bringing Kashmiri tea for my dad and me. "Thank you so much, Imani," My father said to her. "*Mashallah*, you have grown up so much. I have not seen you in a long time. How are you?"

"I am doing well, thank you." she said respectfully.

"Are you in college yet?"

"No, not yet, I have one more year of high school."

As she made small talk with my father, I looked at her and pointed towards the back of the tent. I couldn't stop staring at her. She had changed her hairstyle since the night before. Tonight, her brown hair had wavy bangs in front and curled down below her shoulders.

I could only hope that she taken my hint. After about five minutes, I told my dad that I had to use the restroom and would be right back. I walked to the back of the tent, and waited for what seemed an eternity. I could see Khalid and Aliyah sitting together, as women lined up to plop Kashmiri sweets into their mouths. At that moment I felt a tap on my shoulder. I turned around and it was Imani.

My face felt tight from smiling. "So," I asked, "do you always meet boys in secret?"

"Do you always meet girls in secret?"

"Only you," I said

I stared at her for a few moments. Finally, with as much finesse as I could muster said, "You are the prettiest girl at this *mendhi*, did you know that?"

She smiled back and whispered, "Thank you." I could have stared at her forever. "How do you like the mehndi so far?" I asked.

She was smiling the entire time, her dimples prominent. I couldn't stop gazing into her large green eyes.

"Oh these things are always fun," she replied. "The whole community comes out to meet one another. Everyone wears their expensive jewelry and best clothes. Then there is the dancing. Some of the girls can really dance."

"Have you been dancing?"

"Not yet. *Bahabi* and I are going to do a choreographed dance together once Khalid leaves."

"Really? I will have to see that."

She smiled back and shook her head. "But you can't," she said coyly, "That is only for women to see."

I blushed, but held her gaze.

Hastily she said, "I have to go back inside before anyone sees me talking to you." and rushed back inside.

My dad was still drinking his Kashmiri tea at the entrance. My father always drank his tea slowly.

He took a sip and said, "Son, thank you for coming to the hospital and helping out. I want you to stay in Keran and help out at the hospital for the rest of the summer. It will be a good experience for you. You have learned how a hospital works and gained some basic medical training these past few days. You can learn more. You should spend as much time here as possible before college begins."

"Yeah, I want to stay and help, Dad. "I want to learn more." I assured him.

After about twenty more minutes, Khalid emerged from the tent and sat back down with us. "How was it?" I asked him.

He shook his head. "I need a large cup of water. My mouth is dry from the sweets the women fed me. And my stomach hurts."

Khalid left and the tent started booming again with music. I excused myself and went to the back. I stared inside through a small crevice and there was Imani in the middle of the tent, dancing with Jawad's wife!

She was graceful and enchanting. Her long brown hair swung in the air while her feet and body moved to the beat of the music. Sometimes she closed her eyes, as if losing herself in another world. All the women stood and watched. When the music ended, a new group of girls went up and started dancing. I returned to my father, thinking how badly I wanted to dance with Imani myself one day. He looked at me and asked, "Is everything okay? You look like you just saw a ghost."

"I am definitely okay," I said.

July 9, 1993

Chachaa Riaz and his family arrived sometime after the *mendhi* was finished. I was sound asleep when he, his wife, and their four sons arrived at our home in the early morning hours. I woke up later than normal that day, and when I went to grab breakfast, I found my jovial uncle sitting on the couch, drinking coffee and reading the latest issue of *Newsweek*.

I greeted him with a warm hug and sat next to him. He put his magazine down. "Your only sister is leaving the family home in just a few short hours. It shall never be the same again. Are you ready for that?"

My sister's wedding day had finally arrived. Amongst the dizzying preparations, I had become preoccupied with volunteering at the hospital and meeting up with my old friends. At that moment, it finally dawned on me that my sister was no longer going to be a part of our family's daily life. Aliyah and Khalid were leaving immediately after the wedding festivities for their honeymoon in southern Spain, then off to New York City, where he would embark on his medical career. "I hadn't thought about that," I answered honestly.

Jokingly my uncle said, "You're next."

Thinking of Imani, I replied "Really, right now? I can get married before I finish college?"

"No, no, you are too young to think about marriage and things like that," he said with a laugh. "First, you have to complete your education. Once you have completed your studies and are starting a career, the girl will follow. You are young. Go live your life first." My heart sank. I knew who I wanted to marry, and I didn't see the point of waiting.

The wedding night was finally upon us, as guests began trickling into the wedding tent outside our home. I stood at the front along with my father and Chacha Riaz as we greeted them. I observed the deep respect everyone showed my father and uncle. My uncle had established a school in Keran, the only primary school other than a local government establishment. At least half of the kids in Keran were educated at my uncle's school, and more importantly, the children of the refugee camp were provided a free education while they stayed in Keran.

To our happy surprise, the Governor had traveled from *Muzzafarabad* to attend Aliyah's wedding. The Governor cordially greeted them and placed his hand on my father's shoulder as they spoke. I overheard him say, "I want to talk to you and Professor Riaz later on tonight. Please make time during the wedding to come and sit with me."

"Of course," my father answered him. "Thank you for coming and being a part of this happy occasion for our family."

The Governor then approached me and said politely, "Hanzilah, it is good to see you. How do you like the book so far? Have you finished it?"

"Yes sir," I replied. "Iqbal's poetry is amazing, but I have been really impressed with his writings on Indian Muslim society and government."

The Governor's eyes lit up. "You have to remember the time at which Iqbal was writing these monumental works," he told me. "The British ruled India, the independence movement was at its zenith, but the idea of a separate Muslim nation was at its beginning. Iqbal was speaking to the Muslims of India and selling them the idea of Pakistan. He was describing what an independent Muslim state could look like, what kinds of freedoms they could expect, what we could achieve." He paused and laughed at himself. "We will talk about this later. Tonight is a celebration. Enjoy your sister's wedding."

I watched him go, happy to see him in a good mood.

Imani, Jawad, their parents, and Jawad's wife approached the wedding tent. As I was hugging Jawad I briefly glanced at Imani, standing a few feet away. She wore a light blue *shalwar kameez* with silver lining and a thin diamond necklace with a small emerald in the middle and two small diamond emerald earrings. The emeralds matched her eyes. I stared at her and raised both my eyebrows, hoping that in some small way she would acknowledge me, but she just stared at the floor and said something to her mother. After Jawad let me out of the bear hug I said,

"Thanks for coming, I hope the food is good. I know how picky you are about your food."

"The food will be good, and we wouldn't miss tonight," he replied. "It has been the talk of Keran. The Kashmiri doctor who went to America and whose daughter is marrying another Kashmiri doctor going to America!"

I laughed. "Try to stay close to the wedding stage. That way I might have time to talk to you."

Daniyal and Isa approached the wedding tent next. I had never seen them dressed up before. "So which girl are you trying to impress here?" I said jokingly to Isa.

He responded with a wink. "All of them."

Droves of people came into the wedding tent and my father and uncle and I patiently greeted them one by one. My mother was inside, nervously hoping that things would go smoothly for her one and only daughter's wedding. My father, meanwhile, had a grand old time greeting guests and friends he had not seen in twenty years.

A loud drumbeat commenced. Khalid and his family began walking towards the wedding tent. Some of his young male relatives and friends were dancing around him as they walked towards us accompanied by the loud beat. Khalid smiled and joked with them. My father and uncle and I greeted them as they entered in traditional fashion, placing a necklace of rose petals on the groom. We also honored his parents and esteemed guests by placing necklaces of tulip petals on them. Khalid and his family slowly made their way up to the wedding stage and sat down.

After about fifteen minutes, my mother went to fetch my sister. My father, Chacha Riaz, and I huddled together and organized ourselves into a wedding procession with the rest of our relatives and Aliyah's friends. This time it was our turn to walk the bride to the wedding stage, where she too would be surrounded by her friends and family as we strode to the loud rolling drumbeat. I looked for Imani, and found her standing close to my sister. I positioned myself between them, in what I hoped was a subtle manner. My sister wore a crimson wedding dress and exotic gold jewelry. She looked glittering and beautiful, but her face was obscured. She kept her head down as we slowly walked towards the wedding tent. I looked at Imani, and she looked at me. I inadvertently stepped on her foot, and cursed myself inwardly. She giggled and softly whispered, "It's okay."

Our procession stopped at the front of the wedding stage and sat down. My parents, Tamer, and I walked Aliyah up to the wedding stage and guided her to sit down with Khalid. A wooden chair separated them. We sat on the wedding stage beside Aliyah. After a flurry of picture taking, a man with a thick black beard sat down between them. It was the *Maulana,* and he was holding papers. Everybody in the tent quieted down and the Maulana began the marriage vows. He recited some verses from the Quran then began the marriage sermon, composed of verses from the Quran and sayings of the noble Prophet. "All praise is due to God," he said.

We thank him, glorify him, and beseech him for help. We ask for his forgiveness and protection, and seek refuge in him from the temptation of ourselves and the evil of our deeds.

Whomever God guides, there is none that can lead him astray; and whomsoever God leaves in error there is none to guide him. We bear witness that there is none worthy of worship except God. He is one, no associate has he. And we bear witness that Muhammad is his servant and messenger.

God has told us in the Quran "O Mankind keep your duty to your lord, who created you from a single soul and the same created its mate, and spread from these two countless men and women. And keep your duty to your lord, by whom you demand one of another your rights, and be heedful of the ties of relationship, for God is ever watching over you."

O ye who believe, keep your duty to your lord, and die not but in a state of faith. And among God's sign is this, that he created for you mates from among yourselves that you may dwell in tranquility with them. And he placed love and mercy between your hearts. Verily, in that are signs for those who reflect."

I watched Imani, whose eyes were on the Maulana. Suddenly she turned and looked at me. I flushed with embarrassment at being caught, but she kept her gaze on mine and smiled.

Our noble prophet said, "The world and all things in it are enjoyment, but the most enjoyable thing in the world is a virtuous woman."

The Maulana asked Khalid if he wanted to marry Aliyah, and he calmly said, "Yes."

The Maulana turned to face Aliyah and asked whether she wanted to marry Khalid, and she said, "Yes."

I thought to myself, "Was that the marriage ceremony?" It took only a few simple words for two people to be forever betrothed.

After that there was celebration. Khalid's friends rose up and started dancing, waving their hands and arms as high as they could around Khalid. We danced in a collective flurry for some half an hour, and then it was time to eat.

There is nothing else like Kashmiri food. The grilled meats, the rice with raisins, and spices like turmeric give it its culinary uniqueness. At weddings the food is even more elaborate, and it is served in a specific Kashmiri tradition known as the *wazwan*.

The wedding guests were grouped into fours for the serving of the *wazwan*. The staff of the catering company first placed a large silver serving dish piled high with heaps of rice decorated and surrounded by a variety of meats and vegetables. There were four *seekh kababs*, four pieces of *meth maaz*, two *tabak maaz*, sides of barbecued ribs, one *safed kokur*, and one *zafrani kokur*, all placed magnificently around the rice in a rich array. They brought out yoghurt garnished with Kashmiri saffron, different salads, and Kashmiri pickles and dips as sides.

Eating in this traditional manner, with upwards of twelve courses, takes time. The *wazwan* meal can take an hour and a half, sometimes two hours to complete. It is a meal designed to be, eaten at a slow pace, with much conversation and merriment.

The men sat together in one area for the *wazwan* and the women sat together in another area. The only mixed-gender group was a group of two instead of the traditional group of four at the *wazwan* meal: the bride and groom.

Daniyal, Jawad, Isa, and I sat together in one group and ate together. Across the wedding hall I saw my father, *Chachaa* Riaz, the Governor, and another man seated together.

Daniyal joked, "Has Jawad ever told you about the time he caught a dolphin while fishing on the Indus River?"

Jawad shook his head, grinned, pointed his fork at Daniyal and said, "Look, I really caught a dolphin, and it was amazing."

Daniyal, Isa, and I looked at each other and laughed hysterically. I said to Jawad in disbelief, "Dolphins live in the oceans and seas, not in rivers."

Jawad emphatically said, "Listen, I really caught a dolphin. I am telling you there are dolphins in the Indus River!"

Isa said, "Jawad, you really have some crazy stories, but this one is simply impossible."

Jawad told the story hoping we would believe him. "It was a couple of years ago, and there was this great fishing location at an Indus River basin about 35 kilometers outside of *Muzzafarabad*," he said. "I had gone there fishing before many times. Every time I went out there, I would always catch a large number of fish. I expected to catch a few fish that day, but I didn't expect to catch a dolphin. I threw my fishing line out and waited patiently for a strong bite. After a few minutes, there was a crazy tug. It wasn't a slight tug, like a small fish would cause on the line. This was something different; it nearly pulled me face-first into the water. I knew immediately that it was a big fish, was stronger than anything I had experienced before. Before I knew it, I was knee deep in the river, trying to pull this fish in. I fought it for what seemed like hours. I knew he bit into my line and hook real strong because no matter what he did, he couldn't get away from my line. Finally, he got tired and I started reeling him in. As I was pulling it in, I could see that it was no ordinary fish. It was a dolphin. It was big and smooth with black eyes."

As he finished, I thought to myself how Jawad made up the most ridiculous stories. "How did the dolphin taste?" I asked him.

Jawad shrugged. "I don't know. I let it go."

"You let it go!" Cried Daniyal. "Why?"

"I couldn't kill a dolphin. I untied the hook and let him go."

"Jawad, you should have kept the dolphin," said Isa. "If you had kept the dolphin as proof, then we would believe you."

Jawad shook his head. He knew we didn't believe him and probably never would, no matter what he said. "I don't care if you believe me. I know I caught a dolphin."

Daniyal, Isa, and I laughed as we ate the *wazwan*. Jawad sat there smiling and shaking his head. "There are dolphins in the rivers, and I really caught one while fishing."

After the formal dinner was finished it was time for tea and dessert. Kashmiri tea has a real kick to it. It doesn't taste or look like the traditional British tea, or the *chai* that you see throughout the rest of the subcontinent. Kashmiri tea is pinkish in color and has a slight salty taste to it. It is composed of black tea and even has a bicarbonate of soda as part of its recipe. It was unlike the tea from anywhere else, and I loved it.

The wedding caterer and his staff brought out two types of dessert and placed them before us. One was *phirni*, my favorite, a creamy rice dessert topped off with almonds.

I ate it with my eyes closed to feel the refreshing sweetness melt into my mouth.

After the meal was over, the music started blaring and Khalid's friends began to dance in a circle, clapping, waving their hands in the air, shaking their shoulders, and pointing to the groom. Daniyal, Isa, Jawad, and I jumped in. I had no clue what I was doing, just jumping up and down with my arms straight up. It must have looked silly, but we were having fun.

Jawad and I decided to take a break, and we both grabbed a couple of sodas on our way out of the tent. We sat outside on a couple of stranded chairs and stared out into the bright summer night. The wind was breezy and slow, the evening weather perfect.

Jawad looked at me and sighed, "Don't forget about us."

"I'm not going anywhere anytime soon," I told him. "I'll stay at least another four more weeks in Kashmir."

Jawad then said something I will never forget. "I think our time is coming to an end. I want you to remember me as your good friend."

Instinctively I said, "Good friend-you are a great friend, the best of friends. I'll come back soon. When I come back, you better have some little Jawads running around."

Jawad laughed. "Yeah, maybe." He got up and said, "I am going back inside."

"I'll catch up with you later." I said, confused

I stayed outside a few minutes, drinking my soda, listening to the music and cheers emanating from the wedding tent. As I arose to return to the festivities, I noticed Imani walking toward me, smiling. I went up to her and said, "Aren't you looking very pretty? I don't think anyone is supposed to be prettier than the bride."

"Maybe I am trying to impress someone," she said.

I smiled at her and said, "Really? This person that you're trying to impress, does his name start with H?"

She pulled her hand over her mouth, covering her embarrassed smile, and said, "Maybe." She changed the subject. "Kashmiri weddings are so long. These three day affairs are tiring."

"Yeah, I'm exhausted." I agreed.

"I saw you dancing in there. You looked like a crazy person," she said playfully.

I was embarrassed to realize that she had been watching me dance. "Yeah, dancing is definitely not my thing," I said.

"Are you leaving for the States soon after the wedding?" she asked.

"Not if you don't want me to. I can stay longer, but only if you ask," I answered, looking at her earnestly.

She looked at me unfazed, "I think you plan to stay longer anyway and just want me to ask you to stay. I must go. But I will see you soon."

She turned away. I tapped her lightly on the shoulder and said, "I am staying longer, and I will see you before even a few days pass by, but please don't leave the wedding party without saying goodbye."

She turned back to face me and I felt as if I could touch the energy between us. "I'll try." Then she walked back to the wedding tent. As she was about to enter the tent, she glanced back at me and smiled.

I walked slowly back to the wedding tent in the utter bliss and misery of falling deeply for someone.

I saw my father and *Chaacha* Riaz stand with the Governor, discussing something. By the way they were behaving; I could tell by their body language that it was important. I walked over and sat close by. The Governor was saying, "The work you two have done in Keran has been tremendous. The combination of the school that Riaz has built and the small hospital you have built, Dr. *Sahib*, has changed this valley into one of the more successful areas near the Line of Control. We can't wait for the government to set-up more schools and hospitals. We Kashmiris will have to do it on our own and on a local level. We can get private funding, and I can find us land to build more schools and hospitals, but I don't have the expertise to do it. Will you help?"

"I want to help," Chacha Riaz said. "But running and funding the local school here in Keran and serving the educational needs of the refugee children is my most important responsibility. We can create a standard curriculum and hire teachers and administrators to make the teaching uniform in Kashmir."

"Dr. *Sahib*, can I count on you?" Asked the Governor

My father thought for a while and said, "I too want to help, but the hospital is barely solvent financially. If it weren't for a few major donors and local volunteers, it wouldn't run. If you can find the funding, find the land, give us a proper budget, then I will help, but originally my next step was to broaden medical services to other areas. I was thinking of purchasing several large vans. We can transform the vans into mobile clinics. Our physicians and staff can travel to different areas and valleys and serve the communities that way. If they need long-term care or there is an emergency, then they can be admitted to our hospital."

The Governor said, "This idea of creating mobile clinics is a great idea, and I will support it. However, people are already traveling from far and away to come to your hospital for emergency care. Imagine what Azad Kashmir can become if every valley had a hospital and a school!"

Daniyal and Isa walked over to where I was sitting and sat down, sweat glistening on their foreheads. "You guys can't dance but that doesn't stop you from trying," I told them.

"This is a wedding," Isa replied. "We are celebrating and having fun. You are such an uncle Hanzilah."

It was time for the bride and groom to depart. The remaining guests watched as they walked out of the tent together, and their families joined together to walk them to the wedding car, a small car decorated with bright red and white flowers. My sister, the happy bride, suddenly began weeping. This was standard fare in Kashmiri weddings: all brides weep to reflect the sadness of leaving their parents' home. It's a symbolic gesture. But as I watched my sister entering the car and leaving to join her new husband and family, I felt real sadness, knowing that life was forever changing. Little did I truly know, it would change in more ways than I could imagine.

July 17, 1993

After the wedding was over and my sister had left, our home began to settle down. My father's summer vacation was coming to an end in a few days, although I don't think he took a day off the entire time he was in Keran. My mother felt relieved. She was planning to stay in Keran the rest of the summer with me and Tamer.

In the few days before he returned to the States, I would follow my father around at the hospital and do whatever he asked. He planned to put me under the wing of his most trusted physician at his hospital, an Internist named Dr. Khan for the rest of the summer. Dr. Khan was a serious man who was constantly reading medical journals and asking my father questions about the newest technologies and treatments.

This morning, walking with Dr. Khan as he performed his rounds, I snuck a peak into a private hospital bed and saw Jawad lying there. His wife was in a chair by his bedside, holding prayer beads, and there was an IV drip and a machine attached to him. He seemed to be out cold. My friend's face was pale, and he looked to be sedated.

I stopped Dr. Khan when he passed by Jawad's bed and said to him, "I know that patient. He is my good friend. Why is he here?" He replied in a low serious tone, a tone I was familiar with: I had heard doctors use it when giving bad news to patients and their families. "Your friend is not well," he said. "I am not at liberty to discuss his condition. I think you should talk to your father."

I returned to Jawad's private room and stopped outside his door. I saw that he was waking up. I decided to give him a few moments to gather himself. He said something to his wife with a smile, and she grinned and laughed. I knocked on the door. He smiled and waved me into his room.

After some brief pleasantries I said, "I didn't know you had been admitted to the hospital. Is everything okay?"

Without emotion he said, "I had some breathing problems, no big deal. Every now and then I have to get some treatment for it, but it's nothing."

I didn't press the issue, despite my misgivings. I excused myself and told him I would visit again.

I climbed the stairwell and walked hurriedly to my dad's office. His door was open, and he was sitting behind his desk reviewing some documents. I knocked, he lifted his reading glasses above his forehead and asked, "So, are you enjoying the experience of monitoring and watching Dr. Khan work? He is an excellent doctor. I handpicked him myself. He was at the top of his medical class at *Allama Iqbal Medical College.*"

Before he could continue I said, "Yeah, Dad, he's great. But that's not why I am here. I was walking with Dr. Khan on his rounds, and I saw Jawad and his wife in a private room. I talked to them for a while, but they wouldn't tell me anything. What was he admitted for?"

My father removed his reading glasses from his forehead, lay back against his chair, slumped his shoulders, and stared toward the ceiling. After a few moments, he got up and sat next to me. He said, "I didn't know Jawad had been admitted into the hospital. But I suspect he's here for the same reason he has been coming into our hospital for years. He probably has a sinus or lung infection and is getting treatment for it. Your friend Jawad several years ago requested that I never mention his condition to you. But maybe it's time you knew."

He paused briefly. "Jawad doesn't have much time in this world left; he never did. He was born with a rare terminal illness. Son, Jawad has Cystic Fibrosis."

"What do you mean, Dad?" I asked in disbelief.

He gave me a stern look. "Calm down. You are not a little kid anymore. You need to be strong for your friend. Cystic Fibrosis is a genetic disease that affects the pancreas and causes the entire body to suffer. It affects the lungs by causing mucus buildup and inflammation. Typically speaking, people with Cystic Fibrosis don't live past their late twenties, early thirties. Jawad has been a regular patient of our hospital for many years. He has been coming regularly since he was nine years old, in order to receive antibiotic treatment. He knows he won't have a long life, and so do his family and wife. His wife is a wonderful young woman. Her family called me in America asking about Jawad's health, and I told them the truth. She spoke with me directly, and you know what she said? I'll never forget it. She said if I only have one day as his wife, then that one day is enough for the rest of my life. Her parents tried to talk her out of it, but she didn't listen. She wanted to marry him even with the knowledge of his condition."

It now dawned on me why Jawad had always seemed so much more mature than the rest of us. I now understood why he was rushing through life. I had never seen Jawad angry or upset. He was always cheerful and quick with a smile. Now I understood. Jawad didn't have time to be sad or angry.

I felt a great wave of melancholy, but I gathered myself and stood up. My father did his best to calm me down. "Take the rest of the day off, son. Go home," he said gently. "I know that Jawad is your good friend, and you have never lost someone you are close to. But you have already seen death at the hospital, and you will see it for the rest of your life as a physician."

I thought about Imani and the great sadness that hung over her family like a dark cloud. In all my years of visiting their house, I had never gotten any sense that they were going through such an experience together.

"Son, you can't let him know that I told you about his condition," my father warned. "You have to be strong and positive when you talk to Jawad. He doesn't know you're aware of his illness, and he doesn't want you or any of his friends to find out. He doesn't want anyone's pity. Can you blame him?"

I walked into the hallway and knew I didn't want to go home. I walked out of the hospital and sat on the steps outside. Tears started rolling down my cheeks. I watched people going in and out of the hospital. I saw the joy of a husband and wife leaving with their newborn as their families greeting them and their new baby. I saw a family coming to pick up the body of a relative who had passed away. I saw a bald middle-aged man wheeled out to a small truck. As I observed, I realized that there are only three potential outcomes that ultimately occur at a hospital: someone being born, someone being healed, or someone dying. Jawad was getting treatment for his disease, but in the end he would die. No matter what we did, the disease would take his body. That is the essence of the practice of medicine: delaying the inevitable. What a depressing career.

I gathered myself. I decided to follow my father's advice and behave as if everything was normal. I walked right back into the hospital and went into a small area reserved for medical staff. I went into the restroom, washed my face, and returned upstairs to catch up with Dr. Khan as he continued his hospital rounds.

At the end of the day I caught up with my dad as he was leaving. He was organizing the papers on his desk to take home. "Are you still here?" he asked, surprised. "I thought I told you to go home."

"What is the point of going home? To go and sulk? I decided to stay."

"Did you meet with Jawad again after we talked?"

"No, I didn't. But why should I go see him again?"

"So he doesn't think anything is wrong, my father said tersely. "Go and see him for fifteen minutes, and then we will go home together."

As I approached Jawad's room, I tensed up. My mouth went dry, and my legs turned to wax. I don't know how I was able to walk into Jawad's room without falling down. His wife wasn't there. Jawad was lying on his bed, reading. He heard me coming and put down his book. He looked at me with his silly goatee smile. He had his oval glasses on. I sat down beside his bed.

Before I could open my mouth, he asked me, "How do you like working at the hospital?"

I thought for a moment. "It's interesting, but it's an emotional roller coaster. Maybe I take things too personally, because it takes a toll on me. Sometimes our treatment succeeds, and, when it does, I'm happy. But sometimes you get a case and patient where there can be no joy. Dr. Khan says to keep plugging along. He says eventually you stop seeing a person; instead you see a disease that you're trying to beat. I haven't gotten there yet. I still see the person."

Jawad listened intently. "You will be a good doctor, Hanzilah."

I shrugged, then nodded. "How are you feeling?" I asked.

"I'm doing well," he said nonchalantly, "Your dad says they will let me out in the next three or four days. He wants to make sure I go home healthy."

"My dad saw you today?"

"Yeah, he came in an hour or so after you left. He said I was going to be okay." As he talked, Jawad would cough intermittently. I could hear the phlegm in his voice. My mind started to drift. I snapped back and said, "Yeah, of course, you're going to be okay." I stood up. "You need anything, food, drink?"

"I'm okay." He gave me a look as I was leaving. He knew that something had changed. He didn't want my pity, he wanted my friendship, and I no longer knew how to act as if everything was normal. From that point on, there would always be a strange silence between us.

July 18, 1993

The next day, my father gave me the responsibility of sanitizing a handful of beds in the maternity ward. The hospital had a small birthing area comprised of four beds on the third floor. It was enough to serve the village and surrounding valleys. After I finished cleaning up the last of the rooms, a family entered. The expectant mother had a noticeable baby bump, but she looked like a teenager. Her parents were with her looking extremely worried. Everyone else I had seen entering and leaving the maternity ward had been excited and happy.

There was one OB-GYN physician in charge of the maternity ward, a woman named Dr. Fatima. She ran the ward along with two nurse midwives. My father had given Dr. Fatima free reign. The maternity ward was the least of my father's worries. Dr. Fatima was a well-respected physician, and everyone knew her. She was a plump woman who covered her hair with a see-through veil, but the veil only went to the back of her hair and was constantly falling off.

When the girl and her family entered the maternity ward, Dr. Fatima met with them privately, as she always did. After about fifteen minutes, she opened her office door frantically. Seeing me mopping the lobby floor, she ordered me to bring either Dr. Khan or my father to the maternity ward immediately, but they were both with patients. I rushed back to Dr. Fatima and told her. She looked at me in annoyance. "Where is your father? Is he in his office?"

"Yes, but he is with a patient," I repeated.

She ignored me and walked toward the stairwell to my father's office. "I need to talk to him now."

I followed her down the stairwell. She barged right in. "Dr. Ali, I need to talk to you right now, it is an emergency."

"I'll be right there," he answered calmly. "Please wait for me outside." He finished up quickly with his patient and then asked Dr. Fatima, "How can I help you?"

"There is a fifteen-year-old Kashmiri girl who recently arrived from Jammu and Kashmir with her parents. They have asked that I abort the baby. She is six, maybe seven months pregnant. The baby is healthy, and the mother is at no risk."

"Well, under the law we cannot abort a child whose fetus is older than 120 days, unless the mother is in danger," my father said. "We have to follow the law. You cannot abort this baby."

"Please go talk to them, Dr. Ali," Dr. Fatima pleaded, "They are adamant that if I don't abort this baby immediately they will simply kill the baby when it is born."

My father turned toward me with a serious face. "Hanzilah, can you please bring Dr. Ahmad from Psychiatry and tell him to meet me at the maternity ward?" I nodded and left. My father and Dr. Fatima went together back up the stairwell.

About an hour later, Dr. Ahmad and Dr. Fatima entered my father's office. "The girl's name is Yasmin," Dr. Ahmad told him. "She is a decent girl who is in a terribly difficult position. She and her family arrived in Azad Kashmir a month ago from Jammu and Kashmir. Her village was attacked, and only a handful of villagers survived. The Indian soldiers gathered the women of the village into one house. They then rounded as many of the village men as they could find, brought them into the village center, and placed them in a straight line. For twenty minutes, the officer leading the soldiers lectured and shouted at the village men. He was looking for some people, and the village men didn't answer his questions the way he wanted. He told them that he was going to make an example of this village. He ordered them into a house and ordered the soldiers to lock it and put it on fire. As the village men tried to escape the burning house, the Indian soldiers shot them one by one. Yasmin's father is a man named Qadir. Qadir was out on business in a neighboring village an hour's walk away when this tragedy occurred. Yasmin and her mother were not with the rest of the women who were forced into one house together but in their own home. Two soldiers barged into their home, assaulted Yasmin's mother, and bashed her to the floor. While one of the soldiers held down the mother, the other forced himself upon Yasmin and raped her. Yasmin's clothes were torn and her body was shattered.

"When Qadir returned that night, he found the village destroyed. There were bodies littered everywhere. He ran to his home. When he arrived, he found his wife and daughter hiding under the bed, holding each other. When he picked up his daughter's bloody clothes from the floor, they turned their heads away. He didn't discuss what had happened with his wife and daughter; he could tell what terrible events had transpired. He had to pull his wife and daughter from beneath the bed. He gathered a few clothes and what little money he had and the family left the village in the middle of the night and traveled to his mother in law's home in another valley seven kilometers away.

"Before they left the village, they went into the house where the other village women had been forced to gather by the soldiers. They found several women hanging from the ceiling. They found bodies on the floor, beaten to death. One had been decapitated. The house was littered with bullets. Next door was the house where the men had been burned alive and executed as they jumped out the windows. Smoke was still rising from what remained of the structure and you could see the burnt bodies. The whole village reeked of death.

"After spending several months with his mother-in-law, Qadir decided to emigrate to Azad Kashmir. He and his family have been staying in one of the other refugee camps about thirty kilometers from here. They heard about this hospital through one of the social workers there. They didn't find out that Yasmin was pregnant until two weeks ago. The whole family is in a state of shock and despair.

"I explained to them that this baby is innocent. I told them that this baby could be the good from this horrible and tragic event. But they want to forget what has happened and move on with their lives. They want to cut everything out from their life that is associated with the heinous crimes that they were victim to. They don't want to raise this child. They know the baby is innocent, but they want to forget about what happened and move on. Dr. Fatima and Dr. Ali, they want to abort this fetus. I discussed adoption and other options, but they refused to consider any suggestion I made. The only thing they want is an abortion. If we refuse to offer the service, they will simply find another way. They will kill the baby after it is born.

I asked the parents to leave so that Dr. Fatima and I could speak to Yasmin privately. We spoke for twenty minutes about what she wanted to do. She told us unequivocally that she wanted to abort the baby. I asked her if her parents were making her get an abortion, and she said no. She just wants to go to school and have a normal life. Both of her parents affirmed that this is her decision, and neither of them are forcing it upon her."

My father, Dr. Fatima, and I all had tears in our eyes. My father left the room and returned to his office. I followed him. He sat down, and swiveled his chair away from me. He stared at the ceiling quietly for thirty minutes. Every now and then he would take a deep sigh. I was so shocked by the story that I felt an urge to get a gun and head straight for the Line of Control and go after the criminals that had perpetrated these heinous crimes, but I didn't. I sat in my father's office and waited to hear his thoughts.

My father swiveled his chair back to face me and said, "Tell Dr. Ahmad and Dr. Fatima to come into my office."

When I returned with the doctors, my father calmly said to Dr. Fatima, "It is my understanding based on my assessment of the ultrasound that Yasmin's pregnancy is still in its first trimester. Is that correct?"

Everyone in that room knew from that line of questioning what answer my father was seeking. Dr. Fatima looked at him and didn't say anything. My father repeated the question, this time with a stronger tone, "Dr. Fatima, don't you agree that this pregnancy is still in its first trimester?"

Dr. Fatima nodded and said resignedly, "Yes, that is correct, Dr. Ali."

"Well then, we can perform the medical service they have requested. Please prepare a bed for Yasmin and go perform the procedure immediately."

Dr. Fatima and Dr. Ahmad left my father's office together. My father sat down and asked, "Hanzilah, can you please bring me a cup of Earl Grey?" I got up and he added, "While you're at it, bring a cup for yourself as well."

When I returned, he told me to sit down and we drank tea together in silence. After about five minutes of silence he said, "Hanzilah, I don't know if it is right or wrong, but I know that no matter what decision I made, this was going to be bad. I think I chose the lesser evil, I don't know. But that family has had plenty of time to reflect, think, and make a decision for what is best for this girl. I don't know, and I can't imagine, what they have been through. I know that it is not for us to make this decision. It is that little girl's decision."

I had never seen my father helpless before. I didn't know what to say. I sat silently for a few moments, and then whispered, "I understand Dad. We all do." Right and wrong was not so simple when you were living in the presence of great evil.

July 19, 1993

The next morning as my father and I walked into the lobby of the hospital, Dr. Khan was waiting for us. He was in a chair with his right leg crossed over his left, rocking back and forth, his gaze on the floor. When we walked in he raised his face and rushed towards us. He hurriedly said, "Dr. Ali, at 3 o'clock this morning seven strange men were dropped off by a large group of red Toyota jeeps. They dropped the men at the entryway, handed the receptionist a bag of cash, and left. These men were severely injured. They had gunshot wounds and a couple of them were missing body parts. The emergency room physician didn't know what to do and admitted them. He immediately called me and the on-call surgeon, and we did what we could. Three of the men passed away a few hours after arrival. One who suffered a severe head injury appears to be in a coma and is not responding. We believe he is brain dead and are planning to stop the ventilator if he doesn't respond to any of our tests in a few hours. The three remaining men are currently in stable condition, but things could change quickly for them. Sir, they appear to be mujahideen who fled India through the Line of Control. The BBC reported a major attack on an Indian military installation in Jammu and Kashmir a few days back. Maybe these are the men involved with the incident? I don't know. I am guessing, since they have been refusing to speak to us."

My father listened in disbelief. "Why wasn't I told of this last night when they came in?"

"My apologies, Dr. Ali, but you are leaving for America in two days. We didn't want to disturb you when you are preparing to return home."

"Why weren't these men dropped off at a military hospital?" My father asked sharply. "This is a civilian hospital. We have never had mujahideen at our hospital. We take care of those living in Keran and the surrounding villages, that's it."

But then he stood quietly for a moment. "As physicians we must assist anyone who comes into our hospital. We have taken the Hippocratic Oath," he said finally, "We cannot deny treatment to any person who requires medical care, especially emergency medical care. The ER physician and your team did the right thing Dr. Khan." Then he added, "I want to see their charts in my office immediately. Once I have reviewed them, I will come by with my own follow-up care. When any of the three men are well enough to talk, we need to document everything they tell us. When they are stable, I want them transferred out of here to another hospital."

Dr. Khan nodded and quickly walked away. My father took the stairs to his office. I went to the staff break room to make him his morning cup of coffee, but when I took it to his office it was empty.

I went to look for him in the intensive care unit, where there were four men with a variety of tubes and needles stuck in their flesh. One had had his arm amputated and another had lost a foot. They had been patched up by the ER physician, the on-call surgeon, and Dr. Khan fairly quickly, considering the circumstances and the nature of their injuries. Each of them had to have lost a significant amount of blood. I saw my father standing between two of the patients' beds, looking at their charts. I handed him his cup of coffee. Next to one of the beds was a tin plate, and on it were eight bloody bullets in a tin cup. If I unfocused my eyes, they could have been fruit pits. How strange that such small objects caused so much damage. My father saw me looking at them and said, "Dr. Khan and the staff did a terrific job. I think three of these men will live. One of the patients had three bullets in his body: in his left shoulder, stomach, and right leg. I don't know how he survived the wounds and the loss of blood. He is the only one who is keeping all of his limbs. The two other patients have each had a limb amputated. The patient with the head injury is likely brain dead. It could be days before we hear them talk and tell us what happened."

My father walked away and returned to his office. I sat down behind one of the nursing stations and asked Dr. Khan, "Do you need anything?"

"A break," he said. "I am going to get breakfast. If anything happens, come and get me from the staff break area." He left without waiting for me to answer.

I sat quietly, alternating staring at the unconscious patients and averting my gaze. After about thirty minutes the man with the missing foot opened his eyes. He looked around and saw his comrades, then let out a small whimper. He hadn't noticed me. With a look of resolve, he unplugged his tubes and tried to get off the bed! He fell to the floor. I ran towards him, picked him up with all my strength, and heaved him back onto the bed. He stared at me with dull surprise.

"I need to get back to my brothers. They need my help," he said.

Dr. Khan emerged in the door. He jumped in and helped me force the man back into his bed, then reattached the tubes. He looked at the man and said forcefully, "Your brothers want you to get better. You can't help them anymore. Your part in this war is over." The man had the most disappointed look on his face, and I wondered that this was the fact that most upset him, not his pain, nor the wreckage around him. He slumped, and a few moments later he was back asleep.

The staff doctors and nurses would be arriving soon for their morning shifts. Dr. Khan asked me to wait in the lobby and inform them as they entered that before they began their rounds, they were to first go to the staff break room for a meeting. When my job was done, I joined everyone there in the break room. The staff members were standing in a tense silence while my father and Dr. Khan explained the situation, some of them exchanging worried looks. After my father and Dr. Khan finished speaking, an internist named Dr. Hayat raised his hand. My father said, "Please speak freely, Dr. Hayat."

Dr. Hayat spoke directly and to the point. "Dr. Ali and Dr. Khan, with all due respect, it is my humble opinion that we should remove these men from our hospital immediately. What will happen if the Indians find out that we have *mujahideen* at our hospital? They have agents everywhere. Word will spread and when they find out, they could come after the hospital, maybe even the entire village."

Dr. Khan promptly answered, "No one knows they are here. You have nothing to worry about, Dr. Hayat. What do you expect us to do, just kick them out and put them in the street? Where are we supposed to send them?"

To my dismay, another doctor stood up and said, "I agree with Dr. Hayat. We need to get these men out of here."

"I don't believe we can kick them out," another physician said. "We will have a perception problem. What will the community think? The community gives a lot of money to the hospital. What will the donors think if we leave the freedom fighters to die?"

Soon everyone was voicing an opinion, some speaking respectfully, and others practically screaming. My father stuck his fingers in his mouth and whistled as loud as he could, a skill of his that had always impressed me, and everyone stopped and looked at him.

"We are a hospital and we are doctors," he said. "Our job is not to judge our patients. Our job is to treat them. It is our job to help them heal. It is our job to take care of their wounds and to ease their pain and suffering. We cannot and will not simply refuse these men treatment. It would surprise me if the Indians knew they were here and even if they did, they are not going to bomb our hospital or this village. We are in Azad Kashmir. We are free to do whatever it takes to help our people. I understand your concerns, but we are going to treat these men. When they are stable and we have located an alternative hospital to care for them, we will discharge them. But until then, they will stay."

Dr. Hayat tried to interject, "But Dr. Ali…I think we need…"

Before he could complete his sentence, my father looked at Dr. Hayat angrily and sternly said, "This meeting is over. There is nothing else left to talk about."

After the meeting, the staff spent their day like any other day at the hospital. I went to see Jawad.

When I told him about the situation with the young girl, he didn't seem fazed. "We have heard similar stories in the past from those crossing into Azad Kashmir," he said.

When I told him about the mujahideen being treated at the hospital, he matter-of-factly said, "This isn't the first time the hospital has treated mujahideen. They didn't know they were treating mujahideen because they would come as individual patients, and not in groups like they did last night."

His antipathy confused me. As I was leaving his hospital bed, Imani and Jawad's wife entered the room. I smiled at Imani, and she smiled back. I beckoned her to wait outside the door with me. She wore simple clothes and no makeup, but her face was as bright as an angel. "How are you doing?" I asked her.

"I'm okay," she said lightly, "But don't you have anything better to do than hanging out in Jawad's room? I thought you were working."

"I am, but I was waiting for you to arrive so that I could ask you a question," I said.

"And what question is that?"

I looked at her eyes and with tenderness asked, "Why did you do this to me?"

She was confused. "What did I do to you?"

I whispered so that only she could hear. "You killed my sleep. I can't sleep at night because I can't stop thinking about you."

She smiled and quietly said, "Hanzilah, stop it, my brother is right over there."

I desperately wanted to see her again. "When are we going to hang out?"

She gave an endearing look and said with a twinkle, "I don't think we will hang out anytime soon unless you get my dad's permission."

I quickly remarked, "Done. Where is he at?"

She laughed. "I don't know. You will have to find him."

"Well, let me go look for him and I'll be right back."

She shook her head with a laugh and said, "I hope you are lucky."

I sighed. "I hope so too."

As I walked away from Jawad's room and Imani's presence, my mind shifted toward more practical matters. Could I get engaged to Imani? We were both young, but getting engaged didn't mean getting married. I could finish college, and maybe in a few years we could get married. I knew it would be unusual to go into college engaged in the U.S., but I didn't care. I had never had serious feelings for anyone but Imani, and did not think that I ever would. Should I broach this subject with my father before he left for the States? All I knew was that I wanted to be with her for the rest of my life. I had been infatuated with her ever since I could remember, ever since we were children and I knew her only as Aliyah's friend and Jawad's sister.

I began walking toward my father's office, becoming increasingly nervous. My heart began racing. What would he say? He might say I was just a hormonal teenager with a crush and not take me seriously. He might laugh and brush me aside. His office door was closed. I stared at it for a few minutes. Then I knocked and he said, "Come on in."

My father was reading a chart. He motioned for me to sit down. My legs turned to Jell-o and I wondered if my father could notice them shaking. My palms were sweaty. I pushed my hands against my thighs to wipe the sweat and to stop my legs from moving. My father put his chart down on his desk, took off his glasses, and started to say something, but I didn't hear.

"Hanzilah, Hanzilah, did you hear what I said?"

I looked at him, took a deep breath and said, "I'm sorry, Dad, what did you say?"

"I said that the patient who was thought to be brain dead has died naturally. We didn't have to conduct the tests to determine whether his brain was still properly functioning and active. His organs began to fail, and he passed away naturally."

I stammered, "Oh, I'm sorry, Dad. What a terrible loss."

"Yes, we don't even know who to contact. We don't know who his family is. I hope one of his fellow warriors' wakes up and can tell us before we bury him tomorrow after the morning prayer." I was so skittish that I couldn't look him in the eyes. I looked at the floor and said, "Yeah, dad. I hope so too."

"Hanzilah, is something wrong?" He asked in a concerned voice.

Before I could answer him, he went on: "I know the past few days have been tough. Your friend Jawad's situation has been a difficult burden on you. Dealing with that young girl's family and now today seeing the mujahideen in our hospital fighting for their lives. It is a lot to take on, especially for someone your age. But son, this is the type of everyday things that a physician deals with. Now, cases in the States will be different. You won't be right next to a war zone. But as physicians, we are dealing with death on a constant basis, and you need to have the strength and resolve to handle it."

I said quietly, "Yeah, Dad, you're right. I have been troubled the past few days, mostly because of Jawad's situation. I should be upset about the case involving that young girl and the case with the mujahideen, but I can deal with that stuff."

I had lost the courage to tell my father about my feelings for Imani. I couldn't do it. What was I thinking? I stood up and turned to walk out of his office. Maybe I should talk to my mother instead. She was much easier to talk to. But as I was about to leave his office, something came over me. I turned back to face him and gasped, "Look, I know you think I'm upset about Jawad's situation and yeah, I am. That has been troubling me lately. But there is something else."

"What is it, son?" He wanted to give me the confidence to tell him what was on my mind. He knew I had been nervous. He said, "Listen, son, you can talk to me. You can tell me anything. I am your father. I'll always be your father no matter what."

My nerves were shot. "I know, Dad. Here is the thing…I ah…"

"Just tell me."

I spit out: "Look, Dad, I'm in love with Imani and I want to marry her. I know I'm young, and maybe I am too young to get married. But I am not too young to get engaged. I know what I want. I want her."

He was surprised. "You like Imani? Jawad's sister?"

"Yes," I answered with a surprisingly steady voice.

"Well, why do you like her so much? Explain it to me."

I took a breath. "Dad, every summer I came to Kashmir. I hung out with Jawad at his house, and Imani was always there. We would always talk. Never for long, just a few moments here and there. But she is amazing. She is funny, smart, beautiful, and I can't get her out of my mind. I constantly think about her, even when we're in the States. I sometimes can't go to sleep at night because I'm thinking about her."

"Hmm, I see. Are you sure that this is what you want?"

"Yes, it is," I said humbly.

"You want this right now?"

"Well, I don't want to get married right now. I am young and I know I have to go through college. I want to get engaged. I want to be free to talk to her and spend time with her."

I was surprised at how seriously he was taking me. "You are eighteen years old and about to start college," he said. "I can tell that you have thought about this matter greatly. You know this decision is going to change your life. You are young. Don't you want to experience this world? Enjoy college? Go to med school? Travel and see the world? Getting engaged and getting married at twenty-one, twenty-two is a tremendous responsibility." He paused and inquired, "How are you going to support her?"

I stayed composed and answered, "I can still do those things. Being with her doesn't mean I won't accomplish those goals. I can still go to college and attend med school."

He stood up and put his hand on my back. "Yes, you are right. You can still do these things. Engagement and marriage won't prevent that. But son, isn't it possible that watching your sister get married and being involved with the wedding has caused you to have these feelings? You are just going through a phase."

I could sense that my father was getting dismissive.

"I am not going through a phase," I said firmly, " I have thought about this for a long time, and I know what I want."

"Let me talk to your mother," he said, "I'll talk to her before I leave, and let's see what she says. If she is okay with it, then I am okay with it."

My chest felt light, a great burden had been lifted from my shoulders. I was elated. I ran out of his office, down the stairs, and out of the hospital. My first thought was that I wanted to see Imani and talk to her. I ran back up to Jawad's room, but no one was there. I asked one of the nurses, "Where is Jawad? Is he okay?"

"Dr. Khan approved his discharge," she told me. "He left with his wife and family about an hour ago."

His departure was bittersweet. I had enjoyed the good fortune of seeing Imani every day because she had been visiting Jawad regularly. I was happy that Jawad was well enough to leave, but saddened that Imani had left without me having the opportunity to tell her about my conversation with my father. I didn't know when I would be able to see her again, and I was growing impatient to be with her.

Chapter 2
VENGEANCE

July 22, 1993

THE NEXT MORNING I gave Jawad a toothbrush and several of my Kashmiri *shalwar kameez.* We got ready and ate the breakfast my mother prepared. It was a quiet breakfast.

I knew that if I said anything about leaving to join the mujahideen, my parents wouldn't let me go. If I said goodbye in any meaningful way, they would figure out that I was leaving. So after breakfast we grabbed our bags and left without saying a word. I ran out the door with my friends, and we walked briskly toward what remained of the main street of our village. The mujahideen who had come with Ali the previous day had set up camp there.

Briefly I stopped, turned my head, and looked back at our house, hoping to catch one last glance of Tamer or one of my parents. I saw my father standing outside, sitting on a chair drinking Earl Grey. He was looking right at me. I stopped for a second, looked back at him without smiling, and continued walking. I think he knew I was leaving.

The mujahideen were packing their things in their red 4 X 4 Toyota trucks. Ali told us to sit down and wait for him. He walked up to a mujahid wearing a thin beard and a *Pakol* hat. He was short and slightly plump, and he was wrapping a cloth around his black *shalwar kameez* when Ali approached him. Ali pointed at us, and the man looked over towards us inquisitively. When Ali was finished, the man had a smile on his face. They walked toward us in unison.

We stood up, and Ali introduced us. Ali pointed at the man and said, "This man is Yahya, one of our commanders."

Yahya smiled at us. "Ali tells me you want to join the mujahideen. We are part of the coalition of mujahideen forces fighting against the occupation. Our training camp is two hundred kilometers north of here. We have set up right next to *Chitta Katha Lake* in the *Shonter Valley*, and are there for the months of July and August. At the end of August, we leave for Jammu and Kashmir. We will give you everything you need to live, and we will train you to fight. We'll put you through a boot camp and teach you the basic tactics of guerilla warfare." He put out his hand and said, "Welcome, my brothers."

We each shook his hand, and the deal was closed. We were joining the fight for freedom. We sat in the trucks. They were quite spacious inside. Each truck had a specific person assigned to it, and only he could be the driver. Jawad and I sat in one truck, and Ali and Isa sat in another. Our driver had a magnificent weapon. I didn't know what it was called, but it looked like a light machine gun made of wood and metal. He placed it in a handle next to his seat. Jawad saw me looking at the weapon and said, "It's a Kalashnikov."

Yahya sat in the front passenger seat and said to the driver, "These are our new volunteers. Their names are Jawad and Hanzilah." The driver turned his head back, shook our hands, and said, "My name is Kaither. Welcome, brothers."

Kaither was light-skinned with a thick black beard. As we reached the top of the valley, I looked down at our village. It was the most beautiful place on earth to me. The lush greenery, the blue green water flowing through the river, surrounded by Chinar trees and mountains capped with white snow. Now the valley of Keran was full of debris and devastation. It was the last time I ever set eyes on Keran.

The roads of Kashmir are dangerous. There are no actual streets; you simply drive around on the single-lane dirt roads carved through the mountains. I didn't know how someone knew which direction they were headed. If a car came from the opposite direction, we would have to maneuver carefully around it. Some roads were so narrow that we had to reverse our car until there was enough room for the other car to pass. Most people drove very carefully on these roads. Kaither could not have cared less about the treacherous road conditions. He drove like a madman. He would speed up, brake, twist, turn, then speed up again. It was like riding a roller coaster, and my stomach was stuck in my throat for most of the drive. It occurred to me that we were going to die before we ever made it to the training camps. The other car behind us, with Isa and Ali, was maneuvering just as recklessly. At one point, I looked out and could see straight down into the valley below us. I saw a small riverbed clearly from over six thousand feet above sea level, and the terrifying beauty of it reminded me of when Dad had chastised Tamer and I for getting too near to the waterfall. One slip-up by Kaither and we would have tumbled into the valley and died.

Jawad didn't seem nervous or worried about Kaither's driving- He and Yahya had been making small talk throughout the drive. I composed myself and tried to focus on their conversation. I overheard Jawad asking Yahya, "Where did you get your training?"

"I trained in Kashmir with my fellow freedom fighters," Yahya replied. "Each person specializes in a task. I specialized in making bombs. I can make a bomb and detonate it from hundreds of yards away. I've placed bombs against the Indian forces in Jammu and Kashmir many times. Some were successful, others were not."

Jawad's interest was piqued. "Have you been to Srinagar?"

"Oh yes, I've seen Srinagar many times. It's the most beautiful city in Kashmir."

"Which part of Kashmir is more beautiful, the Azad side or the Jammu and Kashmir side?"

"Jammu and Kashmir is prettier than Azad Kashmir. The flowers, the landscape, the lakes, the rivers, and the animals are twice as many as they are in Azad Kashmir. Jammu and Kashmir is a sight to behold."

Jawad wasn't normally this talkative with people he had just met. He continued to pry. "Are you married?"

"I am married," Yahya replied coolly. "I spent a year with my bride, but I left because I felt a calling to the freedom movement. She has moved back in with her parents since I left."

"What about you, Kaither, are you married?" I asked the driver. Kaither shook his head. "I am married to the fight for freedom."

Yahya proudly said, "Kaither has been involved with the jihad since the eighties. He fought against the Soviets in Afghanistan."

Jawad was impressed. "Did you kill many Russians?"

"I fought in many battles. We killed as many Russians as we could."

"Why did you decide to join the Kashmir freedom movement?" asked Jawad.

Without turning around Kaither said, "Once the Russians left, the mujahideen fought against each other for control of Afghanistan. It became a civil war, not a fight for freedom. I decided to leave Afghanistan. When the fight for independence began in Jammu and Kashmir, I heard the brothers were looking for fighters, so I traveled into occupied Jammu and Kashmir and joined the Kashmiri freedom fighters."

As we continued driving through the valleys, I thought about my family. Would I ever see them again? I was supposed to be going to college, the best time in someone's life. Just a few weeks back I had given the valedictorian speech at my graduation, and now I was about to join a war. I didn't know how to fight. I had never even shot a weapon. I had barely held one, and that was just two days ago. All of a sudden, my decision to join the mujahideen seemed rash and foolish, even silly. It's not too late, I thought; we can turn back. I'm sure they will take me back to Keran if I ask them to.

But then I thought about Imani, and the mourning that would be awaiting me back in Keran. Imani was innocent, one of the sweetest people I had ever met. The Indian army attacked our village with no qualms about killing innocent people. It was because of them that Imani lay on her deathbed. By now she was probably dead. In fact, I was sure of it. I had seen death on her face at the makeshift clinic in *Abbaspur*. I remembered the faces of Jawad's family and his wife. I remembered holding the limbs of children and carrying them to burial. I thought of the innocent refugees whose bodies were blown to dust in their tents. I remembered the grim looks on the faces of the villagers as they buried their friends and relatives, and my doubts melted away. I had made the right decision. My people deserved to live a normal life. They deserved human rights. They deserved to see their children grow in peace. I was ready to die trying to give it to them. Looking at the other men in the truck, I felt a warmth in my chest, a sense of purpose, and I knew that I was in the right place. With my decision fully made, I faded into the most peaceful sleep of my life.

I felt a nudge against my shoulder: Jawad poking me. He pointed out the window and whispered, "Wake up; we're nearly at the camp. We should be arriving in about twenty minutes."

I nodded drowsily. It was dark. I must have slept for hours. I yawned, stretched, and asked, "What time is it?"

"It's ten at night."

I couldn't see anything through the window. The lights of the truck were not on. How in the world had Kaither been driving? I looked at him, and saw he had a weird mask-goggle-looking device strapped around his head. Jawad saw me looking and said, "He has night vision goggles on so he can drive without putting his car lights on and avoid being detected."

I was still in a daze, trying to wake up and come to my senses. I stared out the window. We were driving through a thick forest on a narrow, muddy road between trees. It was rough and bumpy, and we were moving slowly. Jawad looked at me expressionlessly and said, "You snore real loudly." If he had said something like that a few days ago, I would have laughed.

After a few minutes Yahya pulled out a small radio device and spoke into it, but I couldn't hear what he said because it was so loud in the car. Suddenly we stopped and our vehicle was surrounded by four men with Kalashnikovs and RPGs strapped to them. Kaither and Yahya pulled down their windows, and after one look at them, the men waved us through. We drove for another ten minutes, then were stopped by another group of four men with machine guns and small arms. Again, Kaither and Yahya rolled down their windows, and we were passed through. I gazed out Yahya's window, and the trees were no more. I could see moonlight hitting the grass floor, then realized quickly that it wasn't moonlight reflecting off grass but a large body of water surrounded by a small building and dozens of small tents. We drove a little further and parked next to several other trucks.

We got our meagerly packed bags out of the truck and Yahya said to Jawad and me, "Follow me." We followed him about three hundred yards through the tents. Small groups of men sat on the ground around small fires. Yahya indicated an empty tent near the edge of the camp and said, "This is where you guys will be for the next eight weeks while we train. I would go to sleep now, because your training begins at six a.m. tomorrow."

There was nothing in the tent but a couple of brown blankets. As we settled in, Ali and Isa appeared at the door to our tent. Isa slapped me on the back and sat between me and Jawad. "You guys made it. How was the ride over?"

"Hanzilah slept the whole way," Jawad replied. He looked over at Ali and asked, "How does the training work?"

Ali smiled. "The training is the hardest thing you will ever do. We will wake up early every day for the first few weeks and run, hike, camp, and learn to use basic weapons. In the last few weeks of training we each get specialized training. Finally, we are put in small groups and learn how to work together."

"What do you mean specialized?" I asked.

"We each get specific training for a specific skill. For instance, your specialty could be as a sniper." He could sense my nervousness. He paused momentarily and said, "I have asked to be part of your training group. It means starting over, but I want us to be together at the end when we are grouped into one small guerrilla group. Get some sleep. Tomorrow will be the toughest day of your life." I laid down on the floor of the tent with the coarse blanket over me, and listened to Jawad's breath until I drifted to sleep.

July 23, 1993

A lofty vision, gracious speech,

And a passionate soul—

These are the attributes

Of the leaders of all men

-Allama Iqbal

At 5:45 a.m., I heard the call for the morning prayer. But this time it was different. It wasn't the same call to prayer that was called in Keran and throughout Kashmir. There was a sentence added. I looked over to Jawad, who was struggling waking up from his deep slumber.

We stepped out of the tent. I yawned mightily and stretched myself. I glanced at the crisp lake, littered with boys cleansing themselves in preparation for prayer. Jawad and I went to the lake and washed ourselves. The water was cold and refreshing. As we cleansed ourselves, Jawad said to me, "You know, this lake is famous. I can't believe we're training here at *Chitta Katha Lake* and in the *Shonter Valley*." He pointed beyond the lake and said, "Look." It was still dark but I could see the outline of several enormous mountains. The lake was completely surrounded by mountains. "This area is frozen for most of the year. There are only a couple of months when the weather is decent. They must have chosen this site carefully. No one could ever guess there would be a training camp here."

There was a fairly large flat space spread with bedsheets to use as prayer mats beside the lake. As we walked to the prayer area, I quietly asked Jawad, "Why was the call to prayer different?"

Jawad whispered, "He added an extra sentence. The muezzin said prayer is better than sleep."

As we got into lines for the morning prayer, I stood next to Jawad. When the prayer was over, the sun began to rise and I could clearly see the valley, *Chitta Katha Lake*, and the surrounding mountains. The water was fresh and clear blue, and the picturesque mountaintops were covered in snow, although their lower slopes were green. I could see a group of red deer in the distance, wandering across one of the mountains. Jawad and I stood there, drinking in our wondrous surroundings.

Out of nowhere, Ali and Isa surprised us and tackled us to the ground. As we got up we were laughing. Even Jawad had a smile on his face. It was the first time I had seen his genuine smile since the attack.

"Go back to your tents and get ready," Ali advised. "The commanders will be coming out soon. We probably only have twenty minutes to eat and get ready."

Isa asked, "Where do we get food?"

"In ten minutes there will be tea and bread served in the area where we performed the morning prayer."

Jawad and I hurriedly returned to our tent, brushed our teeth, combed our hair, threw on some shoes, and ran back to the prayer area. Tea and bread with butter were being passed around. Looking around at the faces of the guys in the training camp with us, I saw that we were just a bunch of kids, none of us older than eighteen or nineteen.

Jawad and I sat down with Ali and Isa on a thin cloth laid out on the ground. A group of three boys sat next to us. They spoke to each other in English, with thick British accents. One of them jokingly said, "It's just like breakfast at me mum's."

Playing around with one another, they seemed like a merry group. I interrupted their conversation, offering my hand and saying, "My name is Hanzilah. Are you guys from England?" They didn't answer my question. They seemed taken aback to hear someone other than themselves speaking English in this remote place. Instead of answering, they looked at me strangely and one of them asked, "Are you from the United States?"

As Jawad, Isa, and Ali looked on I replied, "Yes, I am." One of them, who had fair skin, brown hair, and light brown eyes, said, "Yeah, we're from Birmingham, England." I raised my eyebrows in surprise and let out a laugh.

"You're really from Birmingham, England?"

A different member of their group answered, "Yes, we are really from Birmingham. He shook my hand, smiled, and said, "My name is Ammar. These are my best mates from Birmingham, Noor and Nick." Ammar was tall and dark-skinned, with curly black hair.

"These are my friends Ali, Isa, and Jawad," I said. "We're from Keran." We looked at one another cautiously. I tried to break the ice by asking, "Is your name really Nick?"

Nick chuckled. "No, my real name is Rashid, but everyone in my family called me Nickoo as a nickname. As I got older, my friends would hear my family calling me Nickoo, and Nickoo morphed into Nick."

Noor, who had long straight hair like a surfer, asked, "Which part of the States are you from?"

"You may not believe me, but I am from Birmingham, USA."

They looked at me in disbelief and collectively said "Bollocks!"

"Yeah, really, I am from Birmingham, USA," I said unabashedly. They laughed.

"Alright, I believe you," said Noor.

I asked, "Which part of Kashmir do you and your families hail from?"

"We're from Mirpur, the best part of Kashmir," Nick said slyly.

Jawad, Ali, and Isa understood English fairly well, but we had always spoken to each other in Kashmiri. I had never talked to them in English. Jawad did his best to join the conversation. In a thick Kashmiri accent he said, "Mirpur is nice, but the best part of Kashmir is Keran."

Nick retorted with a wide grin, "Mirpur's got the best food and the best girls in Kashmir."

We laughed hysterically among ourselves. Out of nowhere came a tall dark man with a pencil mustache, flanked by two men in black *shalwar kameez* carrying Kalashnikovs. Seeing us laughing, he stood over us and exclaimed, "Shut up!"

We were sitting cross-legged on the floor. Everyone turned quiet and looked nervously away from the man as he hovered over us, except for Jawad, who looked straight at him as he spoke. The man loomed over the entire group of trainees and screamed, "You won't be laughing for the next few weeks. What we are about to do is make you into men. The next few weeks will be the hardest days of your lives. During this time you will learn to follow orders, work as a unit, and trust one another. We start our training now! You idiots who were laughing, get up and stand up straight!"

We stood up. I strained to stand as straight as possible. The man stood in front of Isa and asked, "What is your name?"

Isa replied weakly, "My name is Isa, sir." He asked again, this time in a much louder tone: "What is your name?" Isa replied again, slightly louder, My name is Isa, sir."

"You are nothing. You don't even have the courage to say your name out loud so that everyone can hear it. Get down right now and give me twenty push-ups!"

Isa dropped to the floor and started doing pushups. I had never seen anyone boss him around before. The man stood over Isa and yelled, "What is your name?" As Isa performed the pushups, he screamed out, "My name is Isa!"

The commander walked over to Nick, the Brit, and glared at him. Nick stared back at him. He passed Nick and moved on to me. He stood right in front of me and asked in a loud voice, "What is your name?"

I didn't hesitate. I saw what Isa had gone through, and I screamed my name out as loud as I could: "My name is Hanzilah, sir!"

He stood there quietly pondering what to do or say to me. After a few moments of deliberation, he asked me, "Do you know who you are named after?"

I held his gaze. "Sir, my father told me that Hanzilah was the name of one of the companions of the Prophet Muhammad."

He was intrigued. "Is that all he told you about your namesake?"

Not knowing where this was headed and seeing how he had treated Isa, I just said, "Yes sir."

He looked around the entire group and asked, "Does anyone know the story of Hanzilah, the companion of the Prophet Muhammad?"

He waited to see if anyone would answer his question. No one raised his hand or spoke, either out of fear or ignorance. After a few moments he said, "No one knows? What a shame. Well then, I will tell you the story of Hanzilah."

"Muhammad and his companions were persecuted in their hometown of Mecca. Many of the early Muslims in Mecca were beaten, murdered, and oppressed in their own city. Muhammad and the early Muslims migrated to the city of Yathrib, an oasis town about two hundred miles east of Mecca, seeking refuge. Yathrib later on became named Medina, which means the Prophet's city."

"After migrating to Medina his former persecutors, his own tribesmen, of the city where he was raised and had been his home for over fifty-three years, came and attacked him and the early Muslims in the famous Battle of Badr. In this first battle, the Prophet and his companions, comprising only of a small force of three hundred and thirteen soldiers, defeated an army of one thousand enemy soldiers. His enemies suffered enormous casualties and were soundly defeated. It was a humiliating defeat.

"The Meccans came back the following year seeking revenge for their earlier defeat at Badr, leading to the Battle of Uhud. This time the Prophet and his army numbered about one thousand, and the enemy numbered three thousand. The Prophet and his commanders strategically placed a large number of archers to protect the rear of their army.

As the battle began, the Prophet's army was soundly defeating the Meccan army. As the battle waged on, the enemy began to retreat. When they retreated, the Muslim archers meant to be protecting the Army's rear gave up their positions so that they could collect the booty that the retreating army left behind. The cavalry of the Meccan forces saw that the rear was no longer being protected by the archers, and they took advantage of the failure of the archers to follow orders. In a vicious pincer movement, the Meccan cavalry collapsed on the Prophet's army, and assured victory turned into defeat. The army of the believers suffered many casualties; the losses were heavy. As the Meccan army was leaving, one of their commanders screamed out, 'We have avenged our loss in Badr and you have been defeated!' One of the Prophet's companions screamed out, 'We cannot lose! Our dead are in heaven, and your dead are burning in hell!'

"It was in this battle, the second battle, the Battle of Uhud, that your namesake's story takes place. Hanzilah was seventeen years old at the time. The day before the battle, he was married to a beautiful girl named Jamilah. His wedding night occurred the very night before the Battle of Uhud. The Prophet told him to celebrate his wedding. He asked Hanzilah to enjoy his honeymoon and refrain from joining the battle. Hanzilah was heartbroken by hearing this request and implored the Prophet to allow him to fight. The Prophet did not allow Hanzilah to participate in the first Battle of Badr because of his age, and this made Hanzilah even more determined to fight. The Prophet eventually conceded, telling him that on the morning after his wedding he could find out where the Muslim forces were meeting their enemies and join the army."

"Hanzilah and his bride Jamilah had a blissful wedding night. As he was leaving for battle his bride begged him not to go, for she had had a dream foreshadowing his death. Hanzilah refused and embraced his bride one more time before the battle. He joined the Muslim forces just in the nick of time, before the battle began. He fought valiantly during the battle. When the enemy had turned the battle with this vicious cavalry pincer movement a strong attack was made directly on the Prophet Muhammad's life, with the goal to kill him."

"Remember, the battle turned when the archers protecting the rear decided they cared more about wealth than they did about listening to orders. When the battle turned in favor of the Meccans, the enemy forces came very close to killing the Prophet Muhammad and even wounded him seriously. There were some warriors who came to the Prophet's personal defense during this targeted attack against the Prophet. One of his defenders was Hanzilah. He fought and refused to allow the Prophet to be killed. After the battle ended, Hanzilah's body was found amongst the dead. He had been martyred in battle. Hanzilah spent one night with his bride, then he made the ultimate sacrifice for his cause."

The commander looked at me with a straight face. "You are named after a great warrior, and you have a lot to live up to."

Then he moved away from me and continued harassing the new recruits. When he had finished his story, my mind turned to Imani. I wondered if she was still alive, or if she had passed by now. I wished I had been able to marry her and share one night of wedded bliss with her. I was here in this horrifying camp in part because of what the enemy had done to her. They had killed her, and I was going to avenge her death. I reminisced about our moments together and felt calm. I imagined her standing stoically beside me, taking my hand in hers as the commander screamed. Even in death, she gave me strength.

I noticed four other men arriving and standing next to the commander. He whispered some words to them, then told us to get into rows. Each row was given to one of the four men. Our row was appointed to a tall dark man with a mustache who wore a beret, a tight black t-shirt, and camouflage pants.

My friends and I were grouped with the British Kashmiris. The tall dark man didn't introduce himself or ask our names. He looked us over and in a deep voice said, "Follow me, and don't stop running until I tell you." He started jogging at a solid pace, and we followed. We ran away from the camp, along the shore of Chitta Katha Lake. The sight of the clear, extensive water and the purple wildflowers that dotted the bank calmed me. After some half of an hour, we then entered a trail and followed the man into the forests of the Shonter Valley. We ran through glorious trails of thick green vegetation for the next two hours, until the trails disappeared into a giant mountain, and we jogged up to its peak. When we got to the summit, we stopped. Everyone was breathing heavily except the man who had led us there. I slumped over with my hands on my knees and tried to catch my breath. I was exhausted, but also a little proud of myself — I never would have thought that I could be capable of such intense exertion. From the summit we could see everything: the lake, the waterfalls, the forest, and our training camp on the shore of the lake.

The man finally spoke to us. "We will be running back to the camp," he said. "But before we do, I would like to introduce myself. My name is Tariq. I will be your commander, and you will train under me for the next eight weeks. You will hate me before the end of these eight weeks, but what I teach you will keep you alive. We fight in occupied Jammu and Kashmir, a place you have never been to, a place where survival is key. You survive to attack, and you attack to live."

He paused to survey us one by one. I kept my face steady.

"In Jammu and Kashmir, the Indian forces will be hunting you. They will be seeking you out as you are seeking them out. We hit and run, we hit and run. We can't defeat them in pitched battles. We can't attack their bases directly. We weaken them with repeated stealth guerilla attacks. For every soldier of ours they kill, we must kill twenty of theirs. Do you understand?"

As Tariq was speaking, I looked over at Jawad. He stood upright and was listening intently. Isa and Ali were shoulder to shoulder. Ali was standing upright and appeared comfortable, because he had been through this training before. But Isa was leaning against him, gasping for air as much as I was.

The British Kashmiris were huddled together on the ground. They looked ready for afternoon tea and biscuits. After Tariq finished speaking, he walked up to them, stood over them, and said with great emotion, "Each guerrilla group is only as strong as its weakest soldier. We fight for one another, we are brothers, and no man gets left behind. But if you can't make it back to camp, then you can't make it in Jammu and Kashmir. Get up! Get up! Let's go!" He began running down the mountain. We looked at each other in bewilderment. Nick was perplexed. "We have to run again now?"

Tariq yelled, "Let's go! Come on, ladies!" Jawad was the first to start running behind Tariq, and the rest of us followed reluctantly.

The pace of our jog was faster on the way back. The trip down the mountain was much easier than the one up it, but about half an hour into our jog back, I was spent. My chest ached and my lungs burned from the thin Himalayan air. I worried that they might explode.

When we returned to camp, I bee-lined to our tent to lie down and fell asleep on the hard ground without even washing off. It couldn't have been more than a few minutes later when Isa opened the tent and woke me.

"Get up, Hanzilah, we don't have time to sleep," he said. "We have a quick lunch, then a class on weaponry."

I gave Isa a tired look, shrugged, and lay back down. I fell back asleep for another ten minutes, until, hearing the sound of boys chatting and the smell of food, I sprang up and joined the group for lunch. They were eating a simple dish of rice and chicken. I grabbed some food and sat down with the guys as we had sat together for breakfast.

Jawad raised his eyebrows at me, "You don't look so good. Are you ready to quit already, Hanzilah?"

I shook my head. "I didn't grow up in Kashmir like you. Running in this thin air is something else. You guys are used to it." I paused and glanced over at Nick. "How did you and your mates fare?"

Nick shrugged. "It was our first run. We're going to get stronger. You see that guy Tariq? Unbelievable, he didn't even break a sweat. He could have run for another eight hours and still not feel a thing."

I inhaled the food before me, and gulped down four large cups of water one after the other. When I was finished, I was ready to go back to my tent and sleep the day away.

Tariq approached us as we were finishing our meal and said, "Clean your plates and silverware." Jawad and Isa stood up and grabbed a couple of empty pitchers. They grabbed our silverware and walked to the shore of Chitta Katha Lake to clean it. The water was clean and pure, melted ice from the Himalayas, unfiltered and unpolluted, the best water I ever drank.

After Jawad and Isa cleaned the silverware, we sat in a circle around Tariq. Tariq took out the AK-47 he had carried on our run through the trails. He broke it down in terms of weight, range, uses, strengths, and weaknesses. He discussed its accuracy, the use of the sight, the magazine size, number of rounds. We sat there still weary from the run, learning from him the most mundane details possible about an assault rifle. The only thing we wanted to do was to go shoot the gun, and he was sitting there teaching us things that were going in one ear and out the other. As Tariq was going on about the AK-47, Nick abruptly said what we were all thinking: "Tariq, when are we going to shoot this thing?"

Tariq laughed. "The only thing you young guys want to do is shoot. You must learn the details of this weapon if you are going to be successful using it in battle. The information

I am giving you could save your life." He glanced over each of us and saw the excitement on our faces. He grinned and said, "Everyone get up and let's go shoot the damn thing."

We followed Tariq through some brush to a spacious meadow. There were targets set up throughout the field, with markers giving the distance to each target. The shortest target was twenty yards away, and the longest target was several hundred yards.

Tariq went into a small, locked, storage shed and came out with an AK-47 for each of us. I was surprised at how lightweight it was. It wasn't a very long gun either; it was shorter than a hunting rifle. Tariq showed us how to use the sight and asked us to practice aiming at the various targets. We stood there, pointing at targets and pulling empty triggers while he watched.

Tariq showed us how to load the weapon, and I thought that it couldn't be as easy as it was. You simply stuck a cartridge preloaded with bullets into the carbine. There was a safety and you pulled it back in order to shoot freely. I thought back to my fear only a few days ago when my father had handed me a gun, and winced at how childish it seemed to me already.

Nick inadvertently pulled the trigger, and a bunch of bullets hit the ground around him in an ear-cracking series of bangs. Tariq screamed, "You idiot! You are going to get us killed!" He grabbed the gun from Nick and pushed him aside. He looked at us in anger and said, "Don't shoot until I tell you! Keep your gun pointed at the ground at all times, with the safety on!"

After a few tense moments, Tariq calmed down and gave us a live demonstration. He hit the targets with ease, but without pride. He instructed us to load our guns and to aim carefully and shoot. The gun was awesome. It had only a small kickback, and the sight made it easy to aim. I had thought it was going to be much more difficult, but it was fairly simple to use: All I had to do was aim and fire. As we shot, Tariq came by each of us and gave pointers.

Nick sat watching the rest of us, looking ashamed. After about fifteen minutes, Tariq gave him a rifle, and he joined us in target practice.

To my pleasant surprise, we were hitting our targets consistently. I could hit the target about 350 yards away fairly easily. We cheered each other on, comparing one another's skill and accuracy. After about an hour and a half of target practice, Tariq showed us how to empty the gun, clean it, and put it back. That was my first experience of holding and using a powerful weapon. When I put the gun away, I felt tired.

When we returned to camp. Tariq had us sit in a circle, and observed our tired faces. Smirking, he said, "Gentlemen, this is the last session of your first day. In the mornings, we whip you up into shape. In the early afternoon, we learn and practice the weapons we will be using in the field of battle. From mid-afternoon until early evening, we learn and study guerilla military tactics. This will be your day-to-day routine for the next four weeks. Does anyone have any questions?"

Jawad raised his hand. "This training is for a full eight weeks, right? What do we do the last four weeks of camp?"

Tariq nodded his head. "During the last four weeks each of you will get specialized training for your particular skill in the guerilla unit. For instance, one of you will be chosen to specialize as a sniper, another to create explosive devices and incendiary devices. Another will be taught basic medical knowledge to treat injuries and provide pain management. Over the course of the next four weeks we will learn what you are each good at and figure out which area you will specialize in."

Jawad pointed at me. "Our medic is sitting right there."

Tariq looked at me dubiously. "Why do you say that?"

"Hanzilah's father is a famous doctor," Jawad told him (much to my chagrin). "He established the hospital in Keran, and Hanzilah worked at the hospital before it was destroyed by the Indians. He has basic medical knowledge already."

"Is your father Dr. Ali?" Tariq asked me.

I felt embarrassed. I got the same question everywhere I went. Would I ever escape my father's name? "Yes," I said. "My father is Dr. Ali. I did work at the hospital, but in a very limited capacity, helping with basic things. And only for a few weeks."

"Get up, Hanzilah, and walk with me," said Tariq. He grabbed me by the arm, and we walked away from the group towards the lake. He put his hand on my shoulder and looked at me sternly.

"You need to pack your things and go home. This life isn't for you. You don't need to be one of us. You need to go back and become a doctor. You can help the community in the same way your father has. We are here because winning this war is the only way we can live in peace. We can't escape to America like you and your family. We have no other choice. Go home, live your life, and make us proud."

I snapped. "Why do people keep telling me what to do? This is my life. I made this choice of my own free will.

I made this choice because those guys sitting there are my brothers. My village was attacked, and I want justice. No, Sir. I am not going back. This war is my war."

I turned away from Tariq and stomped back to the group. I sat down among my friends, ignoring their questioning looks. Tariq was still standing where I had left him, upright but with his hands on his hips, staring out at the lake. After a few moments, he rejoined us. I tensed, waiting for my punishment, but he did not look at me.

He sat down at the head of the circle and began lecturing about guerilla warfare tactics. "Gentlemen, guerilla warfare starts with selecting a target. Before we select a target, we have to gather intelligence. What I mean by that is that we hide in the shadows and monitor troop movements. We look for patterns and mistakes the Indian soldiers are making. We then select a stage for ambush. We have to pick a target that our small guerilla group can handle and carry out successfully, with maximum damage to the enemy and minimal damage to our team. We hit and run. It's that simple."

He glanced over to see if we were paying attention. "The typical strike pattern isn't what you think. We don't place two teams right across from each other and wait for a military caravan to strike. We don't shoot directly across from each other — that would be suicide. We would kill each other in friendly fire. Rather, we place our units tactically to strike, based on our intelligence. Do you understand?"

We listened closely as he went on about guerilla warfare strategy. "We don't attack every day. We hit in a nonsensical pattern in different geographic locations throughout occupied Kashmir. We look for out-of-place soldiers and military caravans. We camp and hide in the thick vegetation and mountains. Sometimes, we hide in plain sight."

Tariq spoke eloquently about how to kill and maim. The British Kashmiris asked a lot of questions while Tariq lectured on. Jawad, Isa, Ali, and I sat quietly and listened. When the lecture was over, Tariq told us we were done for the day.

We returned to our tents and horsed around until dinner, which was another serving of rice with chicken. I had a feeling variety in our food the next few weeks would be limited. After dinner, we cut some wood and got a fire going. Jawad managed to throw together a pot of Kashmiri tea, and we sat around the fire drinking it by the shore of Chitta Katha Lake. Other new recruits were doing the same, sitting in small groups beside a fire and chatting.

Tariq joined us, sitting down in front of our fire. "How did you learn about guerilla warfare?" I asked him.

"I learned it by fighting with the greatest guerilla warrior of the twentieth century," he said.

My curiosity was piqued. "Who is that?"

"He is known as the Lion of the Panjshir Valley. His real name is Ahmad Shah Massoud, and he defeated the Soviets in Afghanistan. Others try to take credit for winning the war against the Russians. Some say Hekmatayar won the war, and others say it was the ISI with the help of the CIA. But the undeniable truth is that it was Ahmad Shah Massoud. He fought the Russians when no one was fighting the Russians in Afghanistan. He started with nothing but a small group of fifteen men. They had nothing for weapons except one hundred-year-old British rifles. He and his small group of ragtag fighters would surprise the enemy and defeat them one by one. These small victories turned into large victories, and within a few short years this small group of men turned into a guerilla army with modern weaponry."

"How was he able to achieve that so quickly?" asked Jawad.

"He used his home field knowledge to his advantage against the Russians. He knew his land well. He and his family hailed from the Panjshir Valley, a mountainous area in northern Afghanistan. Not only did he fight the Russians during the war, but he built schools, set up clinics, and funded his soldiers, not with financial support from foreign governments, but by selling gems found in the Panjshir Valley such as lapis lazuli. I joined him in the mid-eighties and fought with him for three years."

I kept my eyes on the fire, listening to Tariq's story. Sitting among us, he seemed like a different man than he had today, like one of us.

"He was my teacher, my leader, and my mentor. I learned everything from him. Massoud and his forces were able to defeat the Russians with a tactical and methodical guerrilla campaign of nearly ten years. If the Afghans can beat the mighty Russians, then we Kashmiris can defeat the Indian army. We just started this war; it's only been a few years. Winning a guerrilla war requires patience, sacrifice, and determination. Massoud has showed us the path to victory."

I had never heard of this Massoud before, but if he could beat the Russians, surely we could beat the Indians.

As we sat around the fire and drank our Kashmiri tea that night, I felt a sense of faith grow inside of me. Before that moment, I had not truly believed that it could be possible. I had told myself that we could defeat the Indian army, but I hadn't truly believed. By the end of my first day, I felt sure that we could win freedom for our people.

August 20, 1993

It had been four weeks since we started our training. I had never accomplished and learned so much in such little time. Tariq didn't give us a break. He showed us tough love. The days had been long and hard, but in the evenings we would relax and get to know each other better.

By the end of four weeks, we could run for miles without getting tired in the thin air and light oxygen. We had become accurate shooters and could handle a variety of weapons. Our morale was high. We learned to see each other not only as friends but as brothers.

In the last four weeks, we were to each be taught a specific skill set and learn to work together as a team. Jawad was an amazing shot. He would spend the next four weeks learning how to be a long-distance sniper. I, like Jawad had predicted, was taught how to treat wounds and became the group's medic. Noor was trained in creating and setting up explosive devices. Ali became a specialist in the use of rocket-propelled grenades. Ammar and Isa were taught how to use small-range artillery. Nick was in charge of ammunition and communications.

I was instructed on how to amputate a torn limb, and given morphine and taught how to properly use it in managing pain. I learned how to use antibiotics and other types of medicine to treat a variety of ailments. I actually learned more medicine those last four weeks in the training camp than I had observing the physicians at my father's hospital in Keran. I wondered if my father would have been proud if he knew.

August 29, 1993

The last two weeks in the guerrilla camp were the hardest. We followed Tariq into the thickest brush and up the highest peaks, and walked for two days until we found a spot to set up camp and a security perimeter. We prepared as if we were in occupied Kashmir surrounded by the enemy. We practiced gathering intel, our communications, setting up and executing ambushes. We never knew what Tariq had planned for us. For instance, once, he set up a surprise attack on our perimeter in the middle of the night, and I never slept quite the same after. He showed us our weak spots.

Tariq gave us a metal device that looked like a small stove, with which we could light a fire without anyone seeing it. It was a really simple design, but it worked. You couldn't see that we had a fire going unless you got within fifteen yards of the metal stove. If the enemy got within fifteen yards of us, then we would be dead anyway.

One night in camp after we had set up our perimeter, Jawad and I sat together around our small covered fire. We hadn't talked much while we were at camp. We hung out every night at the end of the day's drills, but he rarely said anything to me directly. As a group, however, we sat, talked, and joked all together, never serious. The truth was that we were a bunch of kids. We were nervous, we were going into the lion's den, and some of us were not coming back alive. Perhaps none of us were coming back alive. Death seemed certain; it was a matter of how and when.

"Hanzilah" said Jawad, I have been ready for death since I was seven years old. I knew at the age of seven that I was going to die. My parents didn't want the doctors to tell me that I was sick and dying, but I knew back then that I wasn't going to make it past thirty. I have been ready for death my entire life. But you aren't. I am going to Jammu and Kashmir to fight and kill those who killed my wife and family. I want justice. Death is a certainty for me anyway. However, it's not for you. You can leave; it's not too late. Go live your life and be free."

When he said those words to me my body shook. I looked at the ground and brushed at the dirt with a small stick. I stared at my friend and said, "Death is a certainty for all of us. No, my friend. I am right where I am supposed to be. Isa, Ali, and you are my brothers, and I don't want to be anywhere else but here."

He gave me a curious look and said, "My sister really liked you. She told my parents that she wanted to marry you, right before the night they bombed Keran. She said that your father would be coming to propose. Is that true?"

I was stunned and didn't know what to say. All this time, he had known. He had known when we were burying his family. He had known when I was alone with her in that temporary tent clinic. He must have known his sister was the reason I had come to fight.

I nodded without looking up. Jawad looked at me seriously. "I would have been proud to call you my brother-in-law."

After a few moments of silence, he said, "Listen, Hanzilah, my sister is gone. In a few days we will be in occupied Kashmir, headed to our deaths. I would rather die fighting my enemy than die fighting this disease. But even though Imani is dead, you can live. Go and live. Forget about this place."

I stood, gazed at the waxing crescent moon, put my hand on his shoulder, and said, "I am not leaving. I am not a coward. I would rather die on the battlefield with you than live a life without Imani."

Ali, Isa, and the Brits walked over and joined Jawad and me as we sat around the stove fire. Nick looked back and forth between us and asked bluntly, "Why are you guys so serious and tense? You getting scared?"

"Not scared at all," Jawad replied. "Hanzilah and I were talking about Keran. I wonder if we will ever see it again."

Tariq joined us that evening. The past few days he had been off setting up some kind of surprise. But this night was different. For the first time in two weeks he sat and spoke to us. He gathered us now and said, "Gentlemen, you are ready. You are as ready as you are ever going to be. In a few days we will be crossing the Line of Control into Jammu and Kashmir. We will do exactly as we have done in the past two weeks, but the difference is that we will be doing it in occupied territory. We will engage the enemy, attack the enemy, kill them, and then escape to safety."

"Are we joining forces with another group?" I asked Tariq, "It's not just us, is it?"

"It's just us. We are a guerrilla group. There are other guerrilla groups like us operating in Jammu and Kashmir, so we won't be the only ones. But we won't be getting any bigger."

Our group consisted of eight people. It was Jawad, Isa, Ali, Noor, Nick, Ammar, me, and Tariq as our commander. What could eight people possibly do to the Indian military?

September 5, 1993

Where is the moving spirit of my life?
The thunder-bolt, the harvest of my life?
His place is in the solitude of the heart,
But I know not the place of the heart within.

-Allama Iqbal

It was 11:45 p.m., and we were sitting in the back of a fast-moving red Toyota 4X4 packed with guns, ammunition, grenades, medicine, food, and other supplies. Each of us carried some sixty pounds of gear. We were two miles from the Line of Control. Indian soldiers manned the entire Line with radar, night vision, tanks, and landmines. I had no idea how we were going to cross into Jammu and Kashmir without being killed on the spot.

In a unassuming valley, the truck came to a sudden stop. Tariq stood up and said, "Let's go. We get out here." We jumped out and grabbed our gear. The driver and Tariq's commander stepped out of the truck, embraced us, and wished us well. Then they left us.

Tariq could sense that we were frightened. It was real. It was happening. We were going straight toward the enemy. Jawad was calm and cool, as if he had done this a hundred times before. The rest of us were petrified.

"Follow me," Tariq said calmly. "I am going to get us into Jammu and Kashmir without any of us firing a single shot or seeing a single enemy soldier. We will be several miles in by morning prayer tomorrow."

We walked behind Tariq, as we had done so many times. It was dark, and I could see nothing. We walked along a trail for an hour, until we arrived at a small hut hidden among some trees. Inside were twenty Pakistani Army soldiers. Another large group was camped outside the building. When they saw Tariq, the soldiers approached and greeted him. He talked to them in hushed tones, then went inside.

Twenty minutes later Tariq came out. "At approximately 2:45 a.m., thirty minutes from now, a group of Pakistani soldiers four kilometers west of here will shoot artillery and heavy fire towards the Indian Army," he told us. "This attack will create a diversion, and that will be our opportunity to cross the Line of Control. Do you understand? The Line of Control is only seven hundred yards away. There is another small hut that you can't see. We need to get into it during the artillery firing. Do you understand? Follow me very closely, and don't make any noise. Don't even sneeze, do you understand?"

We nodded our heads.

We got in line and stood right behind one another, with Tariq in front. It was extremely quiet, too quiet. The Indian soldiers must see us; they must know we are coming. The only sound was the wind. Any decent sniper could kill us from this distance. They were going to pick us off one by one. We would be dead before we even got into Jammu and Kashmir. A feeling of failure came over me. I should have listened to everyone; I should have never left. But then I thought of Imani, and I swore I could see her standing right next to me wearing that same *shalwar kameez* that she had worn at my sister's wedding. I looked in her green eyes and she whispered, "Let's go." "

At exactly 2:45 a.m., we heard artillery being fired from a distance. After about four minutes of heavy fire from the Pakistani side, the Indian side shot back, giving us our chance. Tariq walked into the thick brush, and we followed directly behind him. We could feel the ground shake as we followed Tariq to certain death. Then suddenly Tariq disappeared into thin air, then Ammar, then Nick, then Isa, then Noor, then Ali, then Jawad, and then there I was, in a small, dark room surrounded by mud walls. It was quiet. Tariq looked at us and put his fingers to his lips. He knelt in the middle of the room, took out his pistol, and banged with it three times on the floor.

Beneath the dirt was wood. Someone knocked back three times, and Tariq moved out of the way. A man's head popped out of the opening, and he waved us inside and down a ladder into a hole about sixty feet deep. One by one we followed him, each of us slowly and quietly descending the ladder. At the bottom was another small room and another tunnel. Tariq glanced at each of us to make sure we were all accounted for. We followed the man into the tunnel. It was well lit and just large enough to walk through. There were small lights connected by one wire running the length of it. No one spoke. The air was thin, but our training in the Himalayas had prepared us well. We walked at a slow pace, and the ground above us shook from artillery fire. As we walked I thought about the stories I'd heard of veterans who suffered shell-shock and PTSD, preventing them from returning to a normal life. I did not think I would survive this war, in which case at least I wouldn't have to deal with the mental health consequences.

We walked for two hours behind the strange man without him speaking a word to us. Then the tunnel ended, and we stopped in another small room. Another ladder went up. Tariq glanced back again to make sure we were all present, then nodded to the man. The man climbed the ladder, but this time we didn't follow him. We stared at each other, dumbfounded. After a few minutes, the man came back down and whispered, "Let's go."

He went back up the ladder, Tariq followed him, and we followed Tariq. We climbed sixty feet, and I couldn't see anything; we were in complete darkness. Suddenly, we stepped up into what appeared to be a barn, complete with chickens, livestock, horses, and cattle. The man pulled the wood back over the hole of the tunnel, spread some hay over the cover, and placed several animals in the area where the tunnel was. He left the barn and closed the door behind him. We never learned anything about him, and we never saw him again.

Tariq looked at us and said in a hushed voice. "We are in Jammu and Kashmir. I told you I would get you here without firing a single bullet. It's six o'clock in the morning, and we can't leave this barn until nighttime." He led us into a small room where there were sheets and pillows. He took off his equipment and lay down comfortably on the floor. We followed suit. "No one leaves this room," he said softly "and no one makes a single noise until I say so. I am going to sleep, and I suggest you do the same."

Jawad was already falling asleep. Isa had created a nice little bed for himself out of hay. Ali was eating a cracker with a groggy look on his face. The Brits and I were a little bit more wide-eyed. My adrenaline had been flowing the past several hours, and I wasn't ready to go to sleep. I put my AK-47 next to me and sat against the wall. After about 45 minutes of sitting in silence, I made a small space to lie down on and quickly fell asleep, for the longest rest that I'd had in weeks.

September 6, 1993

But only a brief moment
is granted to the brave
one breath or two, whose wage is
the long nights of the grave.

-Allama Iqbal

It was 11:00 p.m., and we had spent the last fifteen hours cramped together in the small barn. As we quietly followed Tariq outside, I saw a couple of houses with their lights on. Large mountains loomed in the distance. Tariq pointed to the mountains and said, "Follow me."

The few people we passed in the village carried on their way without saying a word. We entered some brush and began walking a narrow hidden trail toward some of the highest peaks I had seen in the Himalayas. How were we going to get to the top before morning? How far were we into Jammu and Kashmir? How far was the Line of Control from where we were now? I had so many questions. But, like any soldier, I was following the chain of command, and right now the man in charge was Tariq. We followed our leader through the night and into the mountains. We hiked at a torrid pace — our training had prepared us well for this journey. The top of the mountain was covered in snow, but around the middle it was green. We came to a spot with heavy vegetation and large trees and Tariq said, "Stop. Let's set up camp here."

My watch read 3:30 a.m. We pitched a couple of tents and set up a smokeless fire. Tariq told Jawad and Ammar to set up a perimeter. While Jawad and Ammar covered us, we ate quickly. "We are going to rest here for a few hours," Tariq told us. "Jawad and Ammar will guard our perimeter for the first two hours, then Noor and Hanzilah will switch with them for two hours. Nick and Ali will take the last shift. Understood?"

We laid some blankets down in the tent. Tariq fell asleep quickly, and Nick, Ali, and Noor were snoring lightly within twenty minutes. But I couldn't sleep, knowing that in two short hours I was supposed to be up again.

I looked at my watch. It was 5:30, and I hadn't slept a wink. I woke up Noor and said, "Let's go." We put our jackets and shoes on and walked to where we were supposed to be stationed. "There is nothing going on, this place is quiet," Jawad reported.

The sun was coming up. It was cold, but bearable. The trees were large. I don't think anyone could spot us from a distance. We were in the middle of nowhere. The only action I saw that first morning was a family of red deer. In Kashmir we call them *hangul.* They are beautiful, majestic creatures. I thought about shooting one for food. I put my silencer on my pistol and took aim at one of the red deer, but then I remembered that my job was to watch the perimeter, not hunt. I shouldn't do anything without first getting permission. I put my pistol away. I waved at Noor and he waved back. We walked over to one another cautiously.

Noor said "Can you believe we are in Indian occupied Kashmir? I never thought I would make it this far."

"I didn't think we would make it this far either. I thought we would have died crossing the Line of Control."

Noor was shaking. It was a cold night. Noor's wavy hair was smothering his face. "How is life in Birmingham, UK?"

Noor smiled. "It's little Paki over there, we run that city. You got Paki restaurants, Paki grocery stores, and we even got Paki MPs. Most people work in the factories still. Living week to week."

"My Birmingham is nothing like that. There is very little diversity. It's the deep south, the people are polite, kind, and gracious."

I never asked any of the Brits why they came to Kashmir. I asked Noor "Why did you guys decide to join the fight?"

"We didn't come to fight. We came to volunteer with an NGO assisting refugees. But the stories the refugees told about life in Indian occupied Kashmir were full of horror. There was one young boy that we befriended from Srinagar. Every night he would wake up in the middle of the night and scream uncontrollably. There was a small bridge behind his house. Every night, he heard the screams of boys a few years older than him getting shot underneath the bridge behind his house by Indian soldiers. In the morning as he got up for school, he would see his neighbors carrying the bodies of the dead. Sometimes the corpses were mutilated. Can you imagine going to school every morning walking over a bridge to go to school that Indian soldiers used as a firing range?"

At 7:30 a.m. sharp, Nick and Ali came and replaced us. We walked back to the tent. Noor and I took off our shoes, laid them outside our tent, and crawled inside. As we lay down in our sleeping bags, I told Noor, "We are going to Srinagar and we will kill those murderers."

September 17, 1993

For the past week our team had been hiking continuously without even catching a glimpse of an Indian soldier. We had not yet passed through a village, and hadn't passed an Indian army base or seen another human being for seven days. The seven of us had begun to talk. Where exactly was Tariq taking us?

As we were hiking that morning, Noor asked Tariq, "Where are we headed?"

"We're going northeast."

Nick sarcastically remarked, "We know that. We can read a compass, thanks to you. But what are we looking for?"

Tariq shook his head. "You guys don't have any patience. We're headed toward a major Indian army base.

Our first mission is to monitor that base, gather intelligence, and then set up ambushes. We'll be there in a couple of days."

September 19, 1993

At two in the afternoon, we saw a paved road for the first time in two weeks. We positioned ourselves forty yards from the road, hidden in the brush, but we could see the road clearly. We huddled around Tariq as he looked at the map. He pointed to it and said, "This is it. We're where we need to be. We'll set up right here and monitor things."

For the next eight hours we watched. Our guns were aimed at the road, in case someone saw us. Ammar and Noor protected our rear. Tariq had repeatedly told us not to shoot unless we were attacked or he signaled for it. We sat there hidden, frozen, and full of trepidation.

It was 10:50 p.m. when we saw our first potential target, a small supply convoy. Initially there were no Indian soldiers, only a couple of small trucks with supplies in the back. Then two minutes later, right behind the convoy, was a jeep with two sharply dressed soldiers in the front and a couple of regularly dressed Indian soldiers in the back with machine guns. A few moments later, another small truck followed.

Tariq looked at us and smiled. We waited another three hours watching that road, but no other vehicles passed through.

September 22, 1993

We had been walking for days through the woods and the mountains. We always kept ourselves hidden, even from Kashmiri civilians. We stayed away from houses, farms, and villages. If we came near a village, we watched and monitored but kept a good distance so that we wouldn't endanger ourselves or the villagers. It was an eerie thing to watch people for hours.

For the past two days we had been watching a small village that looked a lot like Keran. Maybe a few hundred people lived there, in a valley surrounded by mountains. The village had a mosque and a well, and at the top of the valley was a small Indian army base. Based on our intelligence, we estimated the base to have approximately two hundred Indian soldiers within its high walls.

We were only thirty miles into Jammu and Kashmir, not far from the Line of Control. The base served primarily as a communications and supply base for the Indian army units protecting the Line of Control. We knew this because there were large towers surrounding the base without any guns on top of the towers, just light signals going on and off. Below the towers and on top of the high walls were some heavy guns, which were constantly manned. The base had a daunting vantage point. They could see into the entire village and spot an attack from far away, giving the Indian army a serious tactical advantage. It was not vulnerable to any kind of head-on attack, especially from a small guerrilla group like us.

We had identified two supply convoys going in and out daily. One left the base in the morning, and another returned in the evening. It was the same convoy we had spotted a few days earlier, about six miles back, that ran through the paved road at 10:50 p.m. This, it was decided, would be our first target.

September 24, 1993

We hold these truths to be self-evident,
that all men are created equal,

that they are endowed by their Creator with
certain unalienable Rights, that among these are
Life, Liberty and the pursuit of Happiness.

That to secure these rights, Governments
are instituted among Men,

deriving their just powers from the consent of the governed,

That whenever any Form of Government
becomes destructive of these ends, it is the Right
of the People to alter or to abolish it,

and to institute new Government,
laying its foundation on such

principles and organizing its powers in such form,

as to them shall seem most likely to effect
their Safety and Happiness.

- Thomas Jefferson,
United States Declaration of
Independence (US 1776)

We returned to the spot where we had first spotted the convoy on the paved road. We knew there were going to be four vehicles. Two supply trucks, a jeep with approximately four soldiers, and a final supply truck. There were eight of us. We calculated that from this distance, the response time of the Indian base would be approximately twenty-five minutes. We set up two explosive devices on the road for the first two supply trucks. Isa, Nick, Noor, and Tariq would then attack the supply trucks, just to make sure there were no soldiers traveling inside of them. We determined that we were going to set up one sniper for the jeep with the four Indian soldiers. The sniper was to shoot the driver so that the car would spin out of control, then Ali would spray gunfire on the remaining soldiers. Even though Jawad was the one trained to be a long-distance sniper, I was given the responsibility of being the sniper because if there were injuries, I could observe the attack and immediately help treat anyone in our group. The biggest responsibility of the attack fell on me. If I didn't shoot the driver in the head, the remaining Indian soldiers would be able to gather themselves and potentially attack us back.

Ammar and Jawad had the responsibility of taking out the fourth and final supply truck with rocket propelled grenades. We gave ourselves a total attack time of five minutes. Once those five minutes were up, we were to meet at a designated point about a mile south of the initial attack area, then head east into the interior of Jammu and Kashmir. We were not to stop traveling until sunrise.

It was 9:00 p.m.; the explosive devices were placed on the road for the first two supply trucks. I set up by myself in a spot where I would have a clean shot for about 25 yards of road. I hoped get two shots off. I was surrounded by thick vegetation; I had camouflaged myself well. Ali was set up closer to the road, but we positioned him so he wouldn't be in anyone's line of fire. I asked Ali through the radio if he could spot me, and he told me he couldn't. I had my rifle set up and was ready. I caressed the gun slowly and rested my finger on the trigger. I looked through my scope and silently practiced taking shots. I could feel my heart beating. My mind was nervous, but my hands were steady, ready to do the job.

I looked at my watch: 9:45. I had placed the radio near my head. Tariq spoke through it, asking, "Everyone okay? You guys ready?"

Jawad was the first to answer. "I'm ready," he said. We all followed suit and confirmed our resolve to execute the mission.

It was 10:00. Time was moving slowly. The radio came on; it was Nick: "Tariq, I have a question that has been bugging me this entire time."

Tariq said tersely, "What is it, Nick?" Nick was constantly prodding people, whether it be intentionally or not I couldn't always tell.

"How is it that a commander in the Kashmir Mujahideen wears a Rolex GMT Master? Is that watch real?"

Tariq laughed. "This watch is real. I bought it because a great revolutionary that I admire wore a Rolex GMT Master. His name was Che Guevara."

"Isn't that the guy whose picture is on those t-shirts?" Nick asked.

Tariq was surprised. "There are t-shirts with his picture?"

Nick responded, "Yeah, every bloke in bloody London wears his t-shirts," Nick told him. "I didn't know that guy was a freedom fighter."

"He wasn't just a freedom fighter; he was a revolutionary. I'll tell you more about him later. For now, we need to focus on the mission."

It was 10:30 when Jawad informed us on the radio, "They're coming. Estimated time of arrival is seven minutes."

I set my gun into position and waited.

I could see the lights of the two supply trucks. "All four vehicles are coming," Jawad said. The two supply trucks passed through, and a few moments later the jeep with the four Indian soldiers came into my vision. I had only five seconds to get a good shot after the explosive devices would go off. I was locked in on the driver, looking at his head but not his face. I took a deep breath and started to count in my head, "Five, four, three." Then I heard on the radio, "For Keran!" and the explosive devices went off. I pulled the trigger, I was on target, the driver's head popped backwards. The car went out of control. I heard two large booms, the RPGs from Jawad and Ammar. The sound of gunfire was everywhere. Ali ran straight towards the jeep, stepped right in its path and sprayed gunfire directly at the Indian soldiers. He looked around then ran in my direction. Suddenly, I saw Tariq walking in the middle of the road. He was holding a large bag, and his gun was at his side. Right behind him followed, Isa, Noor, and Nick, to inspect the ambush. I stood up and screamed, "Let's go!" They looked at their watches and ran towards me. Ali, Jawad, and Ammar started running down. We ran south.

The meeting place was a tree marked with a small symbol. When we got there, we were all breathing heavily.

Tariq looked at us and started saying our names: "Hanzilah, Ammar, Ali, Isa, Noor, Nick, Jawad."

"We are all here," Jawad replied.

"Is anyone hurt?

We shook our heads. "We're okay," said Noor.

Tariq put his hands on us to make sure and said, "Good. Now we have to move east and get away from here as fast as we can."

We hiked quickly through the trails. Even in the cold air, perspiration bubbled up onto my skin in droplets. We needed to get to a safe place before the sun came up.

Five hours had passed since the attack, and I was sweating like crazy. I needed a bath, I needed water, I needed to eat, to sleep. I was running on fumes; we all were. But when your life is at stake, you find the energy.

It was 5:00 in the morning when Tariq stopped us and said, "Let's set up camp. Hanzilah and Jawad, you guys are our first watch." Once the tent was pitched and the smokeless fire was set, Tariq took out the bag he was carrying and smirked, "I got us some food, boys." He took out bread, tomatoes, and onions. He cut up the tomatoes and onions and heated them up for about ten minutes. He gave us the bread and we dipped it into the tomato stew. We ate quickly. I took out my water canister and drank. The food tasted delicious, although that was mostly due to how famished I was.

Jawad and I set up on the perimeter as the rest of the group fell asleep. After about thirty minutes, I walked over and stood next to Jawad. We looked at each other but said nothing. I gave him my water canister; he took a sip and gave it back. Finally, Jawad said "I thought I would feel better if I killed the people who killed my family. But I feel nothing but emptiness. There is no justice in this world Hanzilah. I don't feel any better after killing those men. Do you?"

"No, I don't," I confessed. In truth, if I thought about it too much, I felt a little sick. A couple of months ago I was afraid to hold a gun, and now I had shot a man in the head.

"There is no justice in vengeance," I said, "If you were looking for justice, you won't find it here or anywhere. No matter what you do, your wife and family aren't coming back. But what we did tonight and what we are doing here is going to prevent those types of attacks from happening again. We are fighting for Kashmir, for its people, and for our freedom. Not revenge or justice."

Jawad stared at me. "Do you really believe that?"

I nodded my head. "Yes." I placed my hand on his shoulder. "We have to believe in what we are doing." After a brief pause, I remarked, "It is a strange thing to take a life. We killed people we didn't know. Maybe they were husbands, sons, fathers, or uncles. We don't know, but I am sure they meant something to their friends and families. We took those men away from their loved ones forever."

Jawad turned to me. "When the Indian army bombs our villages, they don't think the way you are thinking Hanzilah. Innocent civilians are collateral damage. But the men we killed aren't innocent; they are occupiers, murderers, and thieves. They volunteered to join the army of occupation. They stole our land, they kill our people, rape our women, and show no remorse. They call us the terrorists, but they are the real terrorists for violently oppressing us."

Jawad was as angry as ever, but I was full of regret and self-doubt.

"I was planning on going into a profession in which we delayed death," I said. "Now look at me: I bring death."

We didn't speak a word to each other for the next ten minutes as we stared at our surroundings. Then I moved to face him, hugged him, and said, "I love you like my brother," and walked back to my post.

An hour later, Jawad and I were relieved by Nick and Ammar. As we walked together back to our tent, Jawad held out his hand to shake mine, embraced me, and said, "I am happy you are with me."

As I lay down, I thought to myself: We aren't only fighting for Kashmir. We're fighting for each other.

September 30, 1993

We had been traveling east for six days. We dug ourselves in, took out our binoculars, and gazed down at a large valley bustling with people. Numerous neighborhoods surrounded a huge marketplace in the center of the valley. Military police roamed throughout. We could see them walking the streets in small groups, as well as a heavily armed police checkpoint at the entrance to the main market. We observed that every single vehicle entering the marketplace was searched by the military police. Tariq took us aside and said, "We are in a town called Uri. The Uri valley is the largest and most heavily populated valley near the Line of Control. The Line of Control is only eighteen kilometers away so we must tread cautiously as we enter Uri. There is a safe house in this valley for us to rest in for a few days."

Nick made a face. "You want us to walk into Uri, a valley full of Indian soldiers? They're going to kill us."

Tariq laughed and said, "They don't know who we are. It isn't as if they have pictures of us and are actively searching for us. We are going to dig a large hole and leave our equipment in it. We will change our clothes and wear traditional Kashmiri clothing. I have Indian ID cards for all of us."

"You have led us this far. We trust your judgment, Colonel," Said Ammar. In the past few days, we had stopped calling Tariq by his first name and called him Colonel. He really liked it. What he didn't know was that it was our way of making fun of him and lightening the mood.

We found a spot and dug a hole about five feet deep. We changed our clothes and put our equipment in the hole. We jammed a large piece of wood over our equipment so dirt wouldn't get in, then put dirt over the wood. When we were done, we layered the area with rocks and brush.

"We can't go into the valley together as a group," Tariq muttered. "That would look too suspicious." He took out his binoculars and said to Jawad, "You see that beige house to the southeast of the market, where there are three black motorcycles? That is our safe house." As Jawad looked through the binoculars, Tariq described to him how to get to the house.

"Nick and I are going there together," Tariq explained. "You watch us through the binoculars. When you see us in the safe house, wait thirty minutes. If in thirty minutes you don't see me step out of the house, then there's something wrong. You and the rest of the guys need to keep traveling further east until you get to Srinagar. If you see me walk out of the house within thirty minutes and walk around the house in a circle, that means everything is fine, and I want you to bring the rest of the guys in. Do you understand?"

Jawad nodded. Nick smiled as he was leaving and said, "I'll see you guys on the other side."

Tariq and Nick began walking into the village. We watched them walk right into the valley. I was nervous the entire time, but they walked right into Uri and disappeared from our sight. We couldn't see them any longer, but Jawad was watching their every step through the binoculars.

We waited patiently for Jawad to give us the signal. After about twenty-five minutes he said, "I see Tariq outside of the house. You guys ready?"

"It can't be that easy," Ammar said skeptically. "If we get stopped by the Indian army, what will we say?"

"All we have to do is follow the script," said Jawad. "If they ask who we are, just remember: we're cousins from Srinagar visiting our Uncle Aman in Uri."

We walked right into Uri, just as Nick and the Colonel had. It was a beautiful valley with a large highway. The river *Jehlum* flowed right through it. Around the river was some major construction, which looked to be the beginnings of a dam. The dam was incomplete, but it had already created a sizeable lake. We walked in a group, following Jawad, and no one stopped us or even noticed us. We looked like any other group of construction workers serving the dam. The military police were more concerned with the construction of the dam than they were with people walking through the valley.

We entered a neighborhood of about thirty houses. Each house was enclosed and surrounded by a fence made of brick and cement. Jawad approached a beige one and knocked on the door. A man came out and asked, "Who is it?"

Jawad answered, "We are friends of Aman." We heard the metal door handle slide, and the entry door opened. The man wore a grey Kashmiri velvet hat and had a serious face expression. "Come on in," he said.

In the living room sat Nick and Tariq, drinking Kashmiri tea and talking to a tall older man with grey hair and a mustache. The man stood up and said, "Welcome, everyone welcome. What can I get you to drink? Is tea good for everyone?"

We smiled and enthusiastically said, "Yes." Kashmiri tea sounded wonderful at that moment.

"This man is our friend. His name is Aman," Tariq told us. "Aman, these are my friends Jawad, Hanzilah, Ali, Ammar, Isa, and Noor."

"How have your travels been?" Aman asked.

Isa replied for us all. "They've been exhausting."

None of us had shaven in many days, and we looked disheveled and dirty. We could use some time to gather ourselves and relax. The caffeine in the tea had a real kick, and I could feel its energy and warmth seeping into me as I sipped it.

Tariq said, "My friends and I have really enjoyed the beauty of Kashmir as we have traveled through its wondrous mountains. A week ago, we took care of some business and are now looking for more opportunities."

Aman asked, "Where are you headed, my friends?"

Tariq put his tea down on the lamp table next to him and said, "We're headed away from here and plan to keep moving east."

"Be careful as you head east," said Aman. "The military enters the Line of Control through the highway that runs through Uri-National Highway 1A. This highway goes straight into northern India. It is the lifeblood of the Indian army. They have peppered NH1A with military checkpoints. It is extremely secure."

Jawad asked, "Why do they have such a high level of security for this highway?"

Aman smiled. "They have something to protect. You see the Indians are building a dam in Uri. It is a multi-billion-rupee project. They have a group of Swedish engineers designing and building it. They are bringing massive amounts of steel, cement, and engines into this place. Right now, there are over four thousand workers in Uri alone building this dam. It will take several years, but once the dam is completed, it is going to power the entire northwestern part of India, even Delhi. It's a massive project. They have to protect their investment, and that is why the highway is fortified. Avoid it as much as you can. There is another route to move east, but you have to go further north first, away from Uri, towards the more desolate parts of Kashmir."

Tariq smiled. "Thank you, Aman, for your advice and counsel. But most of all thank you for your generosity."

"Naturally I want to help my nephews traveling through our town. You can stay the night. My home is your home. There is a bedroom and a bathroom next to this living room. You may sleep in the bedroom, Tariq, and I will set up mattresses and blankets in this living room. I will have lunch and dinner served to you directly in the living room." He rose and left us to ourselves.

After Aman left the room, Isa yawned hugely and stretched his arms and legs. "I haven't sat on a couch in nearly four months," he said. "It feels so good. This tea is amazing. I am sick and tired of drinking that garbage tea you fools keep making with the different wild leaves and fruits that we find. All you idiots smell like garbage. I can't wait to take a regular shower and take a poop in a regular toilet. I am sick and tired of digging holes to take a poop in."

Ammar laughed hysterically and said, "Isa, you smell the worst of all of us. You're the first one who should take a bath."

We all broke out in laughter.

"I'm sick and tired of these onion dishes that the Colonel keeps cooking up," Ali joked. "All we've been eating is tomatoes and onions, potatoes and onions, chicken and onions. You don't have to put onions in every meal, Colonel."

We burst out laughing.

We had been so tense and serious for the past couple of months that these light moments were few and far between. We knew we were not going to be staying for long, but we desperately needed a good night's rest and some down time. We held on to our night of relaxation dearly.

October 1, 1993

After a hearty breakfast at the safe house, we returned to where we had left our equipment and supplies. Tariq got us together and said, "Gentlemen, we have to focus our attacks in this area. We are going to set up a small camp, and within a fifty-mile radius we're going to attack the supply trucks and the soldiers supporting this construction project."

I was surprised that Tariq was not heeding the advice of our host in *Uri*. I spoke up. "But Tariq, Aman said to avoid this area. It is littered with troops, military police, and support personnel. Shouldn't we keep moving east towards Srinagar and stick to our original plan?."

Tariq looked at me with irritation. "Don't question my strategy. Our job is to kill and ambush as many of the enemy as we can. They act like this land is theirs. They are spending billions on a project that is supposed to supply power to northwest India. Don't they know they should be getting ready to leave our land? They're stealing from the people of Kashmir by building this project to supply power to India. We will derail them. There are going to be soft targets throughout this National Highway 1A. We will follow the highway but keep our distance. The highway runs through the *Pir Panjal* range. As long as we stick to the mountains in this range, we can monitor the highway, set up ambushes, and retreat safely into the mountains."

I was unconvinced, but I nodded in assent.

The past couple of months training and fighting in Kashmir had taught me patience. We spent a lot of time waiting. It was not like the movies, where there's constant action. We couldn't move until nighttime, for fear of being detected. So we set up camp, kept ourselves hidden, and patiently waited until night.

At midnight, under cover of darkness, we made our move. There was a new moon, so we were working in almost complete darkness. We moved slowly and walked silently. After we passed the valley of *Uri*, we suddenly stopped. We had only been walking two hours. "I can't see anything," Tariq said, "and I don't want to inadvertently cross paths with the enemy. We have to stop and set up camp."

We had one pair of night vision goggles among us, but we each needed to be able to see our surroundings to travel securely. We went into the woods of the *Pir Panjal* range and set up camp. It was freezing that night. The weather reminded us that the harsh Himalayan winter was about to begin.

October 8, 1993

For seven days we had been heading southeast, following the NH1A. The highway was extremely active, with a constant flow of vehicles. The problem was that the vast majority were civilian vehicles. We needed to find a military target. We also had to find a spot where there was at least five miles distance between military checkpoints, in order to give ourselves time to attack and retreat back into the *Pir Panjal* range.

We thought about directly attacking a military checkpoint, but each checkpoint was well fortified, and they were prepared to attack back. Their weapons were already pointed at us. It was too risky. We had to find the right target.

Finally, we found a spot about sixteen miles southeast of *Uri*, with a good five-mile distance between checkpoints, and began observing this stretch of highway. For the next two days, we observed the flow of civilian and military vehicles. The military convoys were too large for us to risk attacking. We needed a smaller military convoy, or for the Indian military to make a mistake. Our patience finally bore fruit. One of the vehicles in a convoy of five armored vehicles fell behind. We saw our chance, but we didn't have much time to prepare.

Tariq gathered us and asked if we were ready to attack. We eagerly nodded and got into our positions. Ali, Nick, and I placed ourselves in the brush about thirty yards from the highway. Tariq and Noor were fifteen yards to the left of us. Jawad, Ammar, and Isa were twenty yards directly behind us and would provide us cover. The military car approached our section and came parallel with us. I replaced my sniper rifle with an AK-47. The truck was well protected by a gunner with a shielded glass protective cover surrounding him. Nick had an RPG strapped and ready to fire, and Ali and I had our fingers on the triggers of our AK-47s. Tariq came on the radio and started counting down the attack. He counted down to five, then four… then BOOM! Out of nowhere came a rain of gunfire sprayed toward us.

Someone, maybe the gunner, had seen us. He sprayed all over the brush. He was shooting directly at us, but in his haste he miscalculated our positions. Nick, Ali, and I fell to the ground for cover. We had placed ourselves behind a massive rock on the slope of the mountain. I took a quick shot at the gunner, but in the chaos, didn't hit him. I looked to my left where Jawad, Ammar, and Isa were stationed, and they had ducked for cover as well. Seven Indian soldiers came out of the truck and, using it as a shield, began firing at us. It was only a matter of time before the full might of the Indian army came down on us. We had to get out of there. If we stuck our heads up, it would be over. The heavy gunfire was limiting our ability to shoot back, but the Indians stopped shooting for a brief moment and, out of nowhere, Tariq quickly shot an RPG at the vehicle, hitting it directly, knocking it over and setting it on fire. Noor threw a grenade. The successive loud explosions caused confusion among the attacking soldiers.

We saw our chance. Nick, Ali and I started spraying gunfire on the Indians. Jawad, Isa, and Ammar were twenty yards to our right. They started firing their AKs directly at the vehicle and the soldiers. We could no longer see the Indian soldiers, and Tariq gave the signal to retreat. Nick, Ali, and I continued to shoot to provide cover as Tariq and Noor retreated back into the *Pir Panjal.* Then Jawad, Isa, and Ammar retreated. Nick, Ali, and I were stuck. If we stopped shooting, the Indians were going to shoot back at us. Nick and I both knew we were screwed if we didn't get out of there fast. As Nick sprayed the vehicle with gunfire, I rose, unleashed all four of my grenades, and tried to hurl them over the vehicle. A couple of the grenades hit the top of the truck, and a couple went over and exploded. This was our chance. We dashed into the mountains and back to our meeting point as fast as we could. When we were four hundred yards away, I could see about twenty Indian military vehicles arriving at the scene of the attack.

We caught up with Tariq and the group. They were waiting for us patiently and providing us cover just in case. We were all out of breath, but Jawad was heaving. Tariq put his hand on Jawad's back and calmly said, "We have to get out of here. We have to get as far away from this area as we can, as fast as we can. They are going to get their search dogs, and the dogs will bring them right to us. We don't have much time. I think there may be as little as thirty minutes before they catch up to us."

"We can run towards *Uri*," Noor proposed. "They won't expect us to go back towards the city."

Ammar shook his head. "That might work, but the search dogs can still follow our scent into *Uri*."

Ali asked, "What if we hijack a car and go further down towards Srinagar? How far is the next military checkpoint?"

"They're laid out in five-mile intervals," Tariq answered.

"Let's grab a car, drive three miles, look for a smaller road, and flee into the *Pir Panjal*," suggested Ali.

"Let's do it, we have to try something," Tariq finally said in exasperation.

We ran as fast as we could towards the highway. We waited for a vehicle, but there were none going into or out of *Uri*. After a few minutes I said, "This isn't going to work. Cars are not going to be able to get out of *Uri*, because we just destroyed that part of the road."

We frantically headed back into the *Pir Panjal* range. Then a miracle happened: It started to rain. Not drizzling, but pouring down violently. It was cold, but not cold enough for the rain to turn into snow. Maybe the rain would throw the dogs off our scent or stall the army from searching for us.

We were running as fast as we could into the *Pir Panjal*. Our training around the mountains of *Chitta Katha Lake* was proving invaluable, exactly as Tariq had told us it would. We continued running and hiking for the next five hours, deep into the *Pir Panjal* range in the cold, muddy rain. It was terribly exhausting, but we were relieved to be alive. As we ran I thought to myself: We were stupid. We should never have attacked in this area.

We traveled northeast against the range, hoping to come across a cave in the mountains so we could find safe shelter. Jawad pointed and said aloud, "Look. Up there is a cave about a hundred yards up the mountain."

"Yes, that looks like an opening," agreed Tariq. "Not sure if we can all fit in it, but let's head up there."

As we hiked further up the mountain, the areas below faded from sight in a thick, misty fog that had set in. I hoped the same fog was preventing the Indian army from finding us.

To our relief, the cave was large enough for all of us to fit in comfortably. "Let's rest here," said Tariq, "but only for a few hours. I want us to keep heading northeast. The further we get into the *Pir Panjal* range, and the further we are away from *Uri*, the better." We placed some rocks, shrubs, and branches in front of the cave. Ammar created a fire, and we huddled together. We were dripping wet and cold, but the fire felt good.

As we sat around the fire, Jawad calmly said to Tariq, "You can't put us in danger like that again. We have to be more selective with our targets. It was too risky to operate in an area swarming with military personnel."

Tariq nodded and said, "From now on we will be more careful." The Colonel then took out some tomatoes and said to everyone, "Take off your shirts."

We looked at one another. "Why?" I asked him.

"If they are searching for us, they must have search dogs with them," he answered. "If they have search dogs, then we need to throw them off our scent." He removed his shirt and said, "I'll show you." He cut the tomatoes into a few slices and rubbed tomato juice over himself until his skin was dripping wet.

Nick shrugged and said, "I guess we've got nothing to lose." He took off his shirt and took a tomato from the Colonel. What a strange sight we must have been, a bunch of guys with their shirts off, spreading tomato juice all over ourselves. The tomatoes were sticky.

I lay down against my jacket with my shirt off. The fire had warmed up the cave nicely. I dozed off.

In my dream that night, I saw myself leaving a hospital in medical scrubs. I got in my car and drove home. It was a traditional two-story red brick home, the kind you see in the nice neighborhoods of Alabama. I entered the home and walked through the foyer and into the living room. There she was. I saw Imani sitting on the couch, holding a baby in her arms. Her long brown hair was loose and her green eyes were shining. She smiled and said, "You are home. We've been waiting all day for you."

I felt a nudge. It was Jawad. "Wake up, wake up, Hanzilah! The Indians are only a few minutes away."

I dressed as quickly as I could and grabbed my equipment. Outside the cave, there was snow everywhere. It had been snowing all night, and it was still coming down.

We ran further up the mountain and found our party hiding right above our cave. The Colonel saw me and said, "Ammar was on guard duty, and he spotted the Indians about three miles south of here. It looks like there are about twelve to fifteen Indian soldiers, with three search dogs. We're going to ambush them. We left a couple of bombs inside the cave and a couple at the entrance. When they walk in, we'll blow up the cave and shoot the survivors. Noor is the trigger man."

Noor was holding a radio trigger in his hand. He smiled at me and said, "I got this."

Noor was the one who had received training on creating explosive devices that could be detonated from a distance. We set up and waited. I positioned myself against the cold, snowy ground right next to Jawad, hidden behind a tree and some large rocks. It was cold, and the snow was coming down steadily. Tariq said, "Don't attack until I give the signal or until the bombs in the cave go off."

We dug into the snow, camouflaged ourselves as best we could, and waited. I could see the Indian soldiers slowly approaching. The dogs were leading them directly to the cave. They were wearing camouflaged khaki. Many of them had the same tidy moustaches that the Pakistani soldiers wore. They were heavily armed. One of the leaders pointed in our direction and yelled, "This way!"

You could have heard them miles away. No wonder Ammar was able to identify them from such a distance. At this point they were only a couple hundred yards away. I counted fourteen soldiers and three dogs.

It was unnerving, waiting for them. My body was going numb from hiding in the snow. The dogs barked loudly and ran towards the cave. The same man pointed and shouted, "They're close by!"

The dogs stood at the cave entrance, waiting for their masters. All fourteen Indian soldiers were directly below us. The Colonel didn't signal anything, and Noor still hadn't detonated the bombs. I tensed.

The dogs' master said, "The scent ends here. They have to be in this cave." I couldn't believe that the tomatoes had worked.

One of the other soldiers said, "Let's throw some grenades into the cave, shoot freely, and kill everything in there."

A man that looked like their commander said, "No, we need to confirm they are there. Plus, the General said to capture them so we can gather intelligence."

A third soldier said, "Maybe they're sleeping. It's still early in the morning. I can smell food and smoke coming from the cave. I bet you they think they are safe up here in the mountains."

The Commander said, "I will take six of us into the cave. We will go in quietly and try to capture these guys. If we don't come out in five minutes, then the rest of you throw in your grenades and shoot into the cave at will. I will radio you to come in if it is safe. Do not shoot otherwise. Understood?"

The soldiers nodded. He pointed to six soldiers, and slowly they entered the cave.

Moments later, there were several large and devastating explosions both inside and outside the cave. Snow and rocks flew everywhere, one chunk of rock almost grazing my ear. I heard gunfire all around me as everybody started shooting. I could see nothing, but I began shooting blindly toward the cave. After a few minutes, the Colonel finally shouted, "Stop!"

Jawad kept shooting. Tariq again cried out, "Stop!"

We slowly got up out of the snow. We were safe; no one was hurt. We walked slowly toward the cave entrance. The cave was destroyed. Dead bodies and limbs were everywhere. The khaki camouflage clothing of the Indian soldiers was scattered. It appeared that all fourteen soldiers and three search dogs had been killed. I steeled myself. I had chosen this path knowing what it would entail. We rummaged through the area looking for guns, ammunition, grenades, and anything else we could possibly use later. Jawad said, "I found someone!" He was pointing his gun at an Indian soldier.

I ran over and checked his pulse. "He is alive. It looks like he is knocked out; I think he suffered a concussion."

Jawad looked over at the Colonel and asked, "Should I kill him?"

"No, not yet. Let's see if he can give us some information."

Noor said, "We don't have much time. We need to leave this area as soon as possible. I'm sure the Indians heard or maybe even saw the explosions. They will be here quickly."

The Indian soldier started moaning quietly. A few moments later he was conscious and staring at us in fear. The Colonel said, "Disarm him, tie his hands, and let's get out of here. I want three guns pointed at this guy at all times. Make sure he walks quickly with us and doesn't say a word."

He stood over the man, took his knife out, and put it against his neck. "We are leaving, and you are coming with us. You say a word or make one sudden move, and we will shoot you without hesitation. Do you understand?" The man nodded. Some blood was visible on his neck where the Colonel's knife had been.

As we left, Ammar, Noor, and Jawad aimed their guns at the man as we walked hurriedly away from the site of the attack. We continued moving as before, northeast, with the mountains and further into the *Pir Panjal* range, toward Srinagar.

We continued hiking deep into the night, until Jawad said loudly, "We need to stop and rest."

"I know," said the Colonel tiredly, "I have been looking for a cave for the past two hours and have been unable to spot a single cave. Has anyone seen a cave?"

In a quiet chorus we said, "No."

It was around one in the morning and we hadn't even taken a moment to stop and eat. It had been snowing lightly all day. We decided to set up camp around a group of large trees that should provide sufficient protection from the weather and some cover from any Indian troops searching for us. We cleared snow from the ground. There was nothing out here. It was a vast and beautiful emptiness of mountains, trees, and snow. Now the question became what to do with this Indian soldier we captured.

The man had not said a word the entire time we hiked through the *Pir Panjal* range. Ammar and Nick tied him to a tree. The Colonel took out his knife, went up to the man, and said, like a hero from an action movie, "We can do this the hard way, or we can do it the easy way."

The Indian soldier looked away from us and continued sitting quietly, saying nothing. The Colonel started beating him. He put snow on his face and let him sit there for five minutes with the snow covering his face. No one said anything to the Tariq, except for Isa. Isa took the Colonel to the side and whispered, "We can't torture this guy. We can't beat him up. It's not right. There are laws on how we are supposed to treat prisoners of war. I think it's called the Geneva Conventions or something."

I was standing right between the Colonel and Isa when he made that statement. The Colonel remarked, "When one of our soldiers is captured, they are not considered prisoners of war, they are considered terrorists. The Geneva Conventions are thrown out the window when they capture one of us. They will beat us, torture us, interrogate us, and they end it all with a bullet in our head."

Tariq took the snow off the man's face and started beating him again. It disturbed me to see someone I considered a friend being so merciless. I felt pity for the Indian. When Tariq had stopped beating him, I brought him a cup of tea, ignoring the angry looks from my friends.

The man smiled at me and took the tea.

"My name is Hanzlilah. What's yours?" I said.

"My name is Abdul."

I didn't believe him. "Really?" He nodded.

"Where are you from?"

"I am from New Delhi." I nodded and walked away from him. I looked over at Jawad, and Jawad was angry. He came up to me and said, in an angry tone, "This guy is fighting for them against us! Let's kill him and get it over with." I shook my head and said, "No, we can't do that."

Isa was the sole voice of reason. "We can't just beat this guy," he pleaded. "If he is a war criminal, aren't we supposed to have a trial? I don't understand what we're doing. We are violating the rules of war."

Tariq laughed. "We're supposed to have a trial? Who is the judge? If he is guilty, how do we punish him? We don't have a jail. My dear Isa, they don't give us trials, there is no innocent until proven guilty in occupied Kashmir. When they capture one of us, we are guilty. The only thing that the Indians concern themselves with is the form of torture and punishment."

I walked back to Abdul and asked him, "What's your rank, soldier?"

"I am only a simple private."

Tariq came forward and said, "You are a liar. What is your rank, soldier?"

He repeated, "I am a private." Tariq punched him violently in the gut. Abdul gasped for air. Tariq took out his knife and said, "I will slit your wrists and let you bleed out until you die. What rank are you?" Puffing for air, Abdul replied, "I'm telling you the truth. I'm only a private."

I pushed Tariq away and asked Abdul, "Which regiment are you a member of in the Indian army?" Gasping, he said, "I am a member of the Rajput regiment." Tariq and Jawad were talking between themselves, but I couldn't make out what they said. Tariq approached me and whispered, "According to our intelligence reports, it was the Rajput regiment that attacked Keran."

Jawad took his pistol out of his pocket and pointed the gun at the man. "I'm going to kill him."

Abdul started trembling. I pushed Jawad back and said, "No!" Jawad brushed me aside, pressed his gun against Abdul's chest, and asked angrily, "Were you part of the group that launched an attack into Keran on the Pakistani side of Kashmir?" Abdul replied with a straight face, "No, I was not. I am a simple private. I have never been to the Pakistani side of Kashmir. We man our stations and barracks at the Line of Control. I watch the Line of Control. That's my job."

I frowned. "If your job is to man the Line of Control, then why were you part of the army contingent searching for us?"

Abdul sat quietly. Jawad was angry and said, "This guy is no private. He is a liar. He has been telling us lies the entire time. His name is probably not even Abdul. No one with an Arabic name would be working for the Indians."

Jawad had his pistol in his hand waving it around, incensed and out of control. He had finally found someone he could take his vengeance out on. Abdul was a person who admitted that he was a member of the regiment that had killed his wife and family. I tried to intervene, but Jawad brushed me aside for the second time. He cocked his gun and shot Abdul in the stomach. I screamed out, "No, Jawad!"

But it was too late. I couldn't believe what he had done, to kill someone in cold blood. I never would have imagined Jawad capable of that. I rushed to Abdul. He was bleeding profusely. I grabbed some cloth and pressed it against his stomach, but Tariq grabbed me and forced me away. He screamed at me: "Hanzilah, you stay away from him, let him bleed out and die!"

Ali and Isa stood by silently. They knew why Jawad had shot this man. But Nick, Noor, and Ammar were shocked. What's wrong with you, Jawad?" asked Nick.

Jawad only stared at Abdul, silently watching him bleed to death.

I pulled Nick, Noor, and Ammar aside and began telling them the story of how Jawad's wife and family had been killed by an Indian military strike on Keran. They listened intently. It was the first time I had ever spoken about it to anyone. As I told the story, I became emotional. I didn't tell them about Imani. I only told them about the attack on Keran, how our village was destroyed, and how hundreds of innocent refugees and villagers, including women and children, had died as a result of a massive aerial strike. I told them how Jawad's entire family had died.

When I finished telling the story, Noor took out his knife, walked up to Abdul, and asked him, "Did you participate in the attack in Keran?" Abdul said nothing, but he was dying — he lacked the strength to say anything. Noor took out his pistol, pointed it at Abdul, and calmly said, "You killed my friend's wife and family." He then shot Abdul in the forehead and put him out of his misery.

October 29, 1993

Man is the star that brightens

Thy lonely, desolate world;

Will the eclipse of this star

Be a loss of Thine or mine?

-Allama Iqbal

We had been hiking for three weeks in the snow along the mountain range, staying as far as we could from any village. We assumed we were being hunted by the Indian army. We were following typical guerrilla strategy, but the Himalayan winter was crushing our fighting spirit. For the most part, our campaign was over until the winter ended. We needed to find a safe house until spring returned. Tariq told us there was a safe house in an area called *Baramulla*, a couple weeks journey away. Jawad's cough was bad, and he was struggling. The others thought he had a bad cold, and I couldn't betray Jawad by telling them the truth. He was getting weaker, and he was struggling to keep pace and vomiting several times a day. I knew he wouldn't admit that he was struggling. But it was obvious to everyone that he was in bad shape and needed medical care. If he didn't stop to rest and get some antibiotics, he was going to die. We set up camp that night, and I took Tariq aside and told him that Jawad was sick and would die if he didn't get treatment. I didn't tell him that it was cystic fibrosis. The Colonel understood. In fact, he knew we were all struggling and needed to rest and recover.

The following day, we came across a large tract of farmland: Hundreds upon hundreds of apple trees surrounding a small wooden farmhouse. We approached the house and knocked on the door. No one was there. We knocked again and waited, but no one came. Jawad was coughing horribly. He had a strong fever and sweat was coming down his forehead. He didn't say a word. He didn't make any excuses. He didn't even ask for help.

I couldn't wait any longer. I kicked the front door open and we were in. The house was small, but big enough for all of us. It was cozy and sparsely furnished. There were two bedrooms, and I made a bed for Jawad. He undressed, and I saw how bone thin he had become. He must have lost thirty or forty pounds in the past few weeks. The thin air in the *Pir Panjal* range had destroyed his lungs. I found some bed sheets and comforters and tucked him in. There was a fireplace with matches on the mantel, and I started a fire, feeling the warmth fill the room. I put my hand on Jawad's forehead; it was burning.

"I'll take care of you, don't worry," I said. He didn't respond and fell asleep quickly.

We got as comfortable as we could. We found deer meat in the kitchen. None of us had eaten meat since our time in the safe house in *Uri.*Tariq began preparing a meal for us. Evening fell, and Jawad still hadn't woken from his slumber. I took some drink and food to his room, woke him up, and fed him. He ate as much as he could, but as hard as he tried to hide it, I could tell he was dying. Jawad had packed antibiotics with him when we first started this journey. He had been taking them whenever he felt it was appropriate, but now he had run out, and my supply of antibiotics was empty as well. If we didn't get him medicine soon, his life would surely end within days.

As I nursed my friend, I heard the front door open and a man's voice: "Who are you people? What are you doing here?" I swore to myself. In the stress of caring for Jawad, I had forgotten that we weren't supposed to be here.

I peeked out of the bedroom to see a man pointing his rifle at us. Ammar, Noor, Isa, and Ali were pointing their guns at him.

Tariq stepped forward, "*Biahsaab*, my name is Tariq. We are travelers and friends from across the valley." He went up to the man and held out his hand. The man put his rifle down and shook Tariq's hand. "So you are travelers from across the valley?" he asked.

"Yes, we are travelers on a hunting expedition. Our friend is sick, and we needed to get him to safety. We saw this home and thought it was empty. We are not here to hurt anyone or steal anything. What is your name, *Biahsaab*?"

The man calmly answered, "My name is Faisal. This is my home, and you must leave. I can't have those from across the valley on hunting expeditions stay at my home."

Faisal was elderly, short, and bald, with a thin beard. He wore thick Kashmiri clothing, but I could see how slender he was. The sight of us must have been scary to him. We had thick, untrimmed beards, our hair had grown long, and we stank. The entire living space of his home was filled with our weapons. He had known who we were from the moment we walked in. We stood quietly and, after a few uncomfortable moments, Faisal asked, "Where is your sick friend?"

Jawad was sleeping when we came in. We watched as Faisal placed his hand on Jawad's forehead.

"It is my duty to help those from across the valley," he said. "This man, and all of you, can stay in my home until he gets better. But once he is better, you must leave."

I looked at Tariq and quietly asked him, "Can we trust this man?"

"I don't know, but we have no choice," he said.

Noor offered Faisal some tea and we asked him to sit with us. We sat together in a circle. I spoke first. "My name is Hanzilah," I said. "Our hunting expeditions have been successful. The animals we killed, their friends are upset with us for killing their friends and relatives."

Faisal nodded. "I once hunted these same animals. But now I live a life of peace. This land is my family's land. It has been passed down from generation to generation. My parents and their parents before them tilled this land and planted apple trees. We have grown apples for generations. My family does not live here anymore. I moved them to safety, into the interior of India, away from these valleys of hunting. They live in Uttar Pradesh and have become city folk. These days most people in these parts have moved their families into places where they can live in peace. We haven't seen peace in this land for years."

Tariq and Ammar placed a tray of cooked deer meat and stew into the center of our circle. We sat and ate together. We got to know Faisal by speaking in parables.

After dinner, I sat next to Faisal and asked him, "Is there a pharmacy nearby? I need some antibiotics for my sick friend."

"Yes, there is a village of a thousand people about five kilometers away, with a small pharmacy."

"Can you take me there?"

"Yes. We will leave together in the morning, and I will take you there. But no one else but you can come. Do you understand?"

We had some shaving supplies and scissors. I asked Ali to cut my hair. When the others saw, they too wanted their hair cut. I shaved my beard and cleaned my clothes using snow and soap, then set them beside the fire so they would be dry in the morning. When I looked in the mirror,

I almost looked like myself again, save the hardened quality of my face.

In the morning, Faisal and I stepped out of the house and walked to the village. The snow had stopped, and the sun was shining. The white snow was melting away, and you could see some greenery. Indian-occupied Kashmir was beautiful. As we walked, Faisal told me about his life and his family. I told him about mine, but I didn't tell him that I was originally from the USA. I told him about Keran, the hospital, the village, and how it had been destroyed. He told me how the Kashmiris of India had suffered above and beyond what had happened in Keran. He told me the stories of families torn apart, entire villages destroyed, how Indian soldiers used rape as a weapon and a form of control over Kashmiris. I had thought that most Kashmiris who sought refuge fled into Azad Kashmir, but now I learned that just as many, if not more, had gone to India for a life of peace.

We came upon a boat docked on a clean, blue river. "This is the Jhelum River," Faisal told me. "We are going to take this boat to the village. It will be much quicker."

We got into the boat, and he turned on the engine. We started going up the river, and about fifteen minutes later we were at the village dock. We tied up at the dock and walked into the village. The pharmacy was right in the middle of the village marketplace. The pharmacist prepared the prescription and, when it was time to pay, Faisal pushed my hand away and paid for the antibiotics himself. I pleaded with him to let me pay, but he refused. He said, "You are my guests and it is my honor to help."

We returned to the farmhouse as quickly as we could. Jawad was barely conscious. I gave him the antibiotics. He drank some warm tea and fell back asleep.

For the next week or so we stayed in Faisal's house. He was a kind man, and he treated us well. I kept looking after Jawad and would sleep next to him on the floor. I gave him as much liquids and food as I could, and I made sure he got his antibiotics on time.

I wished he would smile, just once, so that I knew he was getting better. That first week was tough, because I didn't know if he was going to make it.

But by the second week, Jawad was regaining his strength. The antibiotics were working and his body was starting to recover. I drew a warm bath for him. I heated as much water as I could and poured it into the simple metal tub in the tiled bathroom of Faisal's house. After the bath, Jawad immediately fell back asleep. When he woke, he smiled at me and said, "Hanzilah, you are the best doctor I have ever had, and I have had a lot of doctors."

"I am not a doctor and probably will never become one," I said.

"You will, I know it. You are going to save us all."

I shrugged, but was pleased.

We couldn't all keep staying at Faisal's farmhouse. He was taking a big risk sheltering us. Colonel Tariq suggested we scout the area and see if there was a cave or another place we could move to temporarily, while we waited for Jawad to get better. Once Jawad was better he could join us, and together we could continue traveling to the safe house in *Baramulla*.

It snowed briskly every day. The snow was now knee deep. After a few days of scouting, Ammar and Noor found a cave about three kilometers to the east. I helped them move into their temporary shelter and camp in the cave, then returned to care for Jawad. I was confident that in another week's time he would be strong enough to travel to *Baramulla*.

November 5, 1993

It was eight in the evening, and Jawad and I were eating dinner together in the living room with Faisal. Jawad was strong enough to move around in the house. He was still thin and coughing, but I was optimistic that he would recover. Suddenly, the radio crackled and we heard machine gun fire and explosions. We could hear the voices of our friends screaming. My heart went to my throat and I immediately grabbed my gear and weapons. Jawad did the same. I asked Jawad, "Are you sure you're ready to go out? I think it's better if you stay behind."

As he grabbed his weapons he said, "Shut up, Hanzilah." He put on his clothes as quickly as he could, and we left Faisal alone in the farmhouse.

We both ran through the snow, toward our friends' campsite. It took us thirty minutes to get there. We stopped about two hundred yards away. It was hard to see anything, and they had our group's only night vision goggles. We had to get closer. Jawad and I moved slowly and stealthily until we were no more than seventy yards from them. We knelt behind some thick brush. We could see everything. There were Ammar, Noor, Isa, Ali, Nick, and the Colonel on the ground, tied up and surrounded by twenty Indian soldiers pointing their guns at them.

A tall Indian soldier was screaming insults and asking them questions. "Are you the guerilla group that did the attack in *Uri* on the N1H1 Highway? Who do you work for? Which group are you a part of? Talk!"

No one said a word. One of the Indian soldiers grabbed Isa. He picked Isa up by the collar and began beating him with the butt of his machine gun. Isa cried out in pain. The commander took out his pistol, pointed it at Isa, and said, "If one of you doesn't start talking, this boy is dead!"

Isa's face was bloodied and bruised. I looked at Jawad and said, "What do we do?"

"I'll create a diversion. I'm going to move fifty yards west of here. I'll use my sniper first and hit what I can. When they figure out where I am, I'll start shooting with machine gun fire, and hopefully I will take out a good number of them. The ones I don't kill will start moving towards me. When they start to shift, you shoot them in the back and kill them. Do you understand?"

"Yes, but what if they get to you before I get to them?"

"Don't worry. Hanzilah, we have to do something right now or all of our friends are going to die. Remember, when I start shooting with the AK, that will be the signal to start your attack."

The Indian commander angrily said, "I am going to count to ten, and if one of you doesn't say something I shoot. He started counting. Isa closed his eyes, and I could see him silently moving his lips in prayer."

Before the man got to nine, Noor said, "We are Mujahideen from the Pakistani side of Kashmir."

"Who is your commander?"

Noor became quiet again. The Indian commander asked again, "Which one of you is the commander of this group?" No one said anything.

All of a sudden, a gunshot blasted out and a bullet hit one of the Indian soldiers in the forehead. Then the Commander who was asking questions went down, then the one who had beaten Isa. The other soldiers leaped to the ground. Confused, they didn't make a move. They were confused. Suddenly, a barrage of machine gun fire started raining down on them.

One of the Indian soldiers shouted, "It's coming from west of here."

The remaining soldiers put on their night vision goggles and began shooting in the direction of the gunfire. Jawad stopped. He couldn't shoot back, because they were shooting back at him with machine guns, seventeen against one. A handful of the Indian soldiers stood and moved toward Jawad, while the others continued to spray gunfire at him. This was my chance. I was close enough to kill them all. I aimed my gun at all of them and started ripping away. The men standing up were the first to go down. Before the Indian soldiers on the ground could turn toward me, I pounced on them and riddled their bodies with gunfire. It was over. They were all dead. I walked out of the shadows and Ammar, Noor, Isa, Ali, Nick, and the Colonel started whooping with joy. Ali said, "You saved us! I knew you would come for us!"

I untied Isa and said, "Go untie the rest of them."

Nick asked, "Who was the other guy shooting from the other direction?"

I replied, “That was Jawad.”

Isa exclaimed, “Jawad! Yeah Jawad!”

“Where is he?” asked Tariq.

Ammar screamed, “Jawad, come out! We’re safe!”

But there was no reply. As they were untying one another, I ran toward Jawad. It was hard to see in the dark. I could hear heavy breathing, and I followed the sound. I found him lying on the ground behind a large tree. As I knelt next to him I yelled out, “Jawad!”

He had been shot multiple times. I put my hand on his chest and could feel the warm blood oozing out of his body. He looked at me with unfocused eyes. “Are they safe?”

“Yes.”

I held him to my chest and he quietly said in my ear, “I am happy. When I meet my wife and family, I can meet them with honor.”

The blood was in his lungs. I looked at him with despair. He saw the look on my face, and he shook his head peacefully and said, “Don’t grieve for me. I won. I won.”

There was nothing I could do. Moments later, he passed away in my arms as the others were joining me. Jawad was dead, and I had let him die. Why hadn’t I shot sooner? Why had I waited for them to shoot back? I held my dead friend in my arms and screamed. Isa was the first to arrive. He looked at Jawad’s bloody body and knelt beside him wordlessly. The others arrived soon after and surrounded us. Tariq pulled me away from Jawad’s body and hugged me. He said some words that I don’t recall. He wouldn’t let go of me. He kept holding me tight, saying whatever words he thought would calm me down. I pushed him away and ran back to Jawad. Isa and Ali came up to me, and we embraced and consoled each other. We had lost our childhood friend.

The Colonel said, "I am sorry, but we don't have much time. The Indian army in all its might will be here soon. We need to leave right now."

"I am going to bury Jawad," I said. "You can leave if you want."

Ali said, "Let's bury our brother with honor and dignity. We can't leave him here this way."

We moved Jawad's body and began to dig at the spot where he had died. Nick, Ammar, Noor, and Isa joined us. We dug as quickly as we could. When the grave was deep enough, we picked up Jawad's body and placed him in the ground. I asked if I could lead the funeral prayer. The others stepped away, and I stood at the head of my friend's grave, raised my hands, and said in a teary voice, "God is great. All praise is due to God, the Lord of the worlds. He is the most gracious and the most merciful. He is the master of the Day of Judgment. Thee do we worship and thine aid we seek..."

I struggled with the words. I spoke as clearly as I could, and when it was time to say "God is great" out loud I said it through tears. The others behind me wept for Jawad as we recited the funeral prayer together. I couldn't stop staring at his body, but somehow I managed to complete the funeral prayer. As we pushed dirt into the grave, I thought how Jawad had possessed the courage and strength to bury his own family. I still don't know how he did it. When the funeral prayer was over, we all embraced. In less than twenty minutes, we had buried Jawad and performed his funeral prayer. We grabbed our things and did what we always did. We ran.

November 11, 1993

We arrived in *Baramulla* six days later. We had trekked a hundred kilometers through thick snow, and buried our gear outside of the district and walked in, exactly as we had walked into *Uri*. Our safe house in *Baramulla* was going to be our home until the winter ended. In the spring we would fight again. The safe house was small, but large enough to house us comfortably, and perfectly secluded outside of the main village. Had we not been missing Jawad, we would have had the time of our lives our first night there.

A few days later another small group of seven Mujahideen arrived as well, weary and half frozen. They had been fighting the Indians in and around Srinagar. Not a single one was from the free side of Kashmir. They knew their land well and used it to their distinct advantage against the Indian occupation forces.

The seven Kashmiris were named Farhan, Mujahid, Usman, Zain, Aziz, Ramiz, and Syed. Throughout that winter we got to know one another. It didn't take long for us to develop a bond. We were similar ages, with similar hopes. None of them wanted a war. They wanted to live in peace, but how could they with the conditions of occupation crushing their spirits? Members of their families had been taken out of their homes and placed in prisons. By now I knew too much to be surprised by the atrocities committed in Indian-occupied Kashmir, but hearing about them still saddened me. Farhan hadn't seen his father in seven years. He didn't know if he was dead or alive. By this point, he assumed he was dead. Zain's village had been attacked, and the survivors had either sought refuge in Azad Kashmir or migrated to more peaceful parts of Indian-occupied Kashmir. Mujahid was from Srinagar. He had been a college student when the revolution broke out. He described how the students in Srinagar had held peaceful, nonviolent protests in the late 1980s. They had stood outside government offices in Srinagar, demanding that a fair and just plebiscite be held. The response by the authorities to their peaceful protests was violence and murder. The peaceful protesters were shot at directly by the occupation forces with a hail of machine gun fire. Ramiz and Usman were the youngest in their group, but they looked the oldest. The toll of war was on their faces.

Farhan was their commander. They had been fighting the Indian army for three years. We had only been doing it a few months.

In the back of the safe house was a chicken coop. We had eggs and Kashmiri tea for breakfast every morning. When we wanted meat, we slaughtered a chicken. During the winter, a goat somehow got lost and found its way onto the land of the safe house in *Baramulla*. We ate goat meat for two weeks.

Farhan and his friends spoke often of their fellow Mujahideen who had lost their lives. When they spoke of them it was as if they were still alive here on earth.

Zain was the funniest in their group. He constantly told jokes. His jokes were not funny, but after he told one he would laugh very loudly in a weird, shrill voice.

After a while everyone would start laughing with him, even though they had no idea what he had said. His laugh was infectious, his jokes were dirty, and he cursed like a sailor. One night in February we were drinking Kashmiri tea before the fireplace. Snow was falling softly outside. Zain stood up in the center of the room, took off his shirt, and jumped on Farhan, rubbing his hairy chest all over Farhan's face. Farhan pushed him off. Farhan took off his shirt and grabbed Zain's head and pushed his head under his armpit, to make him smell it. The next thing you knew, we were all outside with our shirts off, throwing snow and wrestling.

Those three months stuck in that house with a bunch of rowdy guys were like being in a fraternity house in college. The more I thought about it, the more I realized that we were in fact in a fraternity. It was a brotherhood, but a deadly and dangerous one. Throughout those three winter months I thought often of Jawad, but mostly I thought and dreamt of Imani. I finally figured out what Jawad had meant when I was holding him at the end and he said, "I won. I won." He was the first person in history to beat cystic fibrosis. In the end, the disease didn't kill him, and he died on his own terms. Was that what winning was?

March 6, 1994

These melodious songs are not confined
To Time when rose and tulip bloom
Whatever the season of year be
"No god but He" must ring till doom.

-Allama Iqbal

The snow stopped falling, and the bright sun began melting the remainder of it away. We could see spots of grass coming out of the snow line. It was spring time, time for war. We had rested and recovered in the safe house in *Baramulla*. Of course, we had developed cabin fever within a few days of arrival, but there was nothing we could do. We had to wait. Now, we decided to join forces with Farhan's group and to head together to Srinagar, along the way doing our utmost to leave death and destruction for the occupying forces in our wake.

We left *Baramulla* in the middle of the night. I took a moment to gaze back at the village, a speckle of families in a reclusive spot at the top of the world.

The Kashmiri fighters led by Farhan never looked at a map. They led the way, and we followed. Prior to departing *Baramulla* we had planned a series of attacks in the area surrounding the highway toward Srinagar, the N1H1A. With our new Kashmiri friends' knowledge of the terrain, we felt it was the appropriate route to take.

Farhan and his team were able to gather intelligence from villagers who lived along the N1H1A. They had access to people and resources that we simply didn't. Our group had been afraid to walk into a village with our military hardware and weapons, because we feared attracting the occupying forces' attention. They, on the other hand, would walk into a village without fear and speak with members of the community to learn about the comings and goings of Indian soldiers on the N1H1A. The local police were even willing to point out Indian military groupings that we could attack.

Throughout that spring, we successfully ambushed the Indian occupying forces repeatedly, so much that it began to feel like a habit. Our small force united in effort was laying waste all along the N1H1A. The more successful we were, the greater the risks we took.

April 20, 1994

The new soldiers informed us of a large military base on the outskirts of Srinagar that had been charged with setting up checkpoints, investigating transport vehicles, and serving as a base for defense of the N1H1A into Srinagar. Farhan told us about a plan he and some other commanders had come up with to attack it. If we could place bombs on vehicles entering the base, we could remotely trigger them from a safe distance and depart without ever being seen. We could escape through the Jhelum River, and take the famous Kashmiri river boats into Srinagar and stay at a safe house in the capital. Now the question was how to get a truck laden with bombs onto the base without them knowing.

Ammar had the answer. We should dress up like Indian soldiers and create our own checkpoint. We would do an inspection, and during the inspection we would place bombs on the vehicles. Even if the vehicle was stopped at a real inspection prior to entering the military base, we could still blow it up and kill the soldiers manning the checkpoint or the entrance of the base.

Zain, for once being serious, told us that he had heard from a villager that at the beginning of each month a supply truck filled with flour and basmati rice was delivered to the base. During our false inspection, we could put simple fertilizer and incendiary devices into the bags. Farhan and his group would create a checkpoint and stop the supply truck. While they held up the truck, we would take out the basmati rice bags and flour bags and replace them with our bags filled with our bombs. Once the truck with our bombs was on the base we could blow it up through radio frequency. We had to be quick and efficient, but it could be done.

We went to work. We cleaned up the Indian uniforms from our previous ambushes, and filled rice and flour bags with an explosive concoction that Noor engineered. We were armed, ready to do damage, and unafraid of the consequences.

May 1, 1994

The first day of the month arrived, and it was time to carry out the mission. Unlike most of our other attacks, this one was to occur in broad daylight. We got word that the supply truck was on its way, approximately one hour away from the base. We had our escape route and our river boat ready.

Everyone got into place. Farhan and his group would be the ones manning the checkpoint. Our group was going to be there as well, but in the shadows. We had more than a hundred bags filled to the brim with explosives hidden with us in the spring vegetation.

The supply truck came into view. Farhan waved at it to stop, and the driver rolled down his window. "Where are you headed?" Farhan demanded.

The driver, a uniformed Indian soldier, said, "Who are you? I have never seen you before."

Zain came behind Farhan and pointed his gun. "Answer the Major's question."

The Indian soldier said "Okay, okay, sir. My name is Private Arpan Patel, and this is Private Minal Ullupi."

Farhan then asked, "Show me your military identification."

The two Indian soldiers gave Farhan their military IDs. Farhan looked at them and, while holding them in his hand, asked, "Which regiment do you belong to?"

Private Arpan responded, "We are in the Assam Regiment, 2nd Battalion."

Farhan nodded. "Isn't that Major General Bora's group?"

"Yes, that is correct," Private Arpan said. "Do you know Major General Bora?" Farhan matter-of-factly said, "I met him once in Srinagar. He is a tough general. He keeps everything close to his chest. What do you boys have in the truck? Do we need to open it up?"

"It's nothing, just some food," said Private Ullupi. "If we were carrying anything more than food, they wouldn't let us travel so lightly."

"I understand," Farhan said. "Private Arpal, do you have your written orders for this delivery?"

Private Arpal proceeded to hand him a set of papers. Farhan reviewed the paperwork. "I hate to do this to you boys," he said, "you seem like good soldiers. But I am under strict orders from Lieutenant General Ranbir Singh to inspect every vehicle. There has been some trouble around here."

Private Arpal shrugged and calmly said, "We know you're doing your job. It's important to be careful with security." He pulled his hand against a lever, and the back of the truck opened up. Farhan pointed to Zain and said, "Go check out the back." Zain walked toward the back of the truck and signaled to us. The back door of the truck was wide open. We made our move. It was exactly as the villager had said: lots of flour and basmati rice. We quickly pulled out as many bags as we could as Farhan talked to Private Arpan and Private Ullupi. He kept up the small talk, smiling and joking with them. Farhan was smooth. He could talk anyone up and keep the conversation interesting. He had an uncanny ability to get people to like him quickly.

They weren't even looking back as we unloaded the truck. After we had taken out enough bags, we loaded all 100 explosive-laden bags in the vehicle. It took no more than four or five minutes to make the switch. Zain walked back to Farhan and stuck his thumb up. Farhan smiled and said, "Well boys, looks like we are set." He handed them back their IDs and written orders. They slowly drove away from sight. We started toward our escape route and the river boat. We estimated that it would be another forty-five minutes before the truck arrived at the base.

We got into the boat and revved up the small engine. We worked our way to the middle of the river and slowly moved towards Srinagar. Colonel Tariq looked at his Rolex watch and said to Farhan, "It should be there in fifteen minutes."

No one said a word. We sat patiently on the boat and waited. Tariq looked at his watch and said, "Five minutes." We waited. Then Tariq announced, "Noor, it's time."

Noor pulled out his radio device. We all stood and stared in the direction of the base. Noor said, "Okay, boys, on my count: Three, two, one." The bomb went off and the earth shook. We could hear it from where we were. We cheered, but Farhan placed his fingers against his lips. We sat down again in the boat and headed toward Srinagar as fast as we could.

A few kilometers from Srinagar we docked our river boat, changed our clothes, and hid our military equipment in a small shed that we had scouted out. We separated ourselves into three groups onto three smaller boats. On one boat was fish. On another were vegetables and fruits. On the third boat, the one I was traveling on, were small tires for rickshaws and motorbikes. We slowly continued moving toward Srinagar. I had heard many amazing things about Srinagar from Farhan, Zain, and their group. They had raved to me about its beauty and lore, and my expectations were high. I was not disappointed. As we entered the city from the Jhelum River, the city became visible. Greenery was everywhere I looked, dotted with flowers so bright they almost glowed. A beautiful blue river traversed the city, and an enormous lake surrounded it. As we approached I took in floating houseboats, parks, Mughal architecture, British architecture, elegantly built houses, all surrounded by mountains in the visible distance. It was a sight to see. The river began to divide as we got closer, and we took a narrow path that broadened as we got further along. Moments later, we found ourselves on the massive lake. Seeing that I was in awe, Farhan, said, "This is Dal Lake. I fished on this lake throughout my childhood. My father would bring me here in the summer and we would fish for hours on a river boat."

Farhan spoke about his father frequently, who had been stolen from him by the Indian occupation forces.

Can you show me the city?" I asked.

"But of course, we shall have a grand time here. It's the middle of spring, and that, my friend, is the best time to visit Srinagar."

We docked the boats and unloaded our fish, fruits, vegetables, and tires. We walked a few hundred yards and arrived at our safe house. It was a quaint white bungalow right on Dal Lake. I laughed to myself. If I didn't think about it, I could almost pretend that we were on vacation.

May 2, 1994

Am I bound by space, or beyond space?

A world-observer or a world myself?

Let Him remain happy in His Infinitude,

But condescend to tell me where I am.

-Allama Iqbal

It was five in the morning when I heard the call to prayer pulsing through the city. I woke up and pulled myself out of the small bed of blankets I had constructed. The sun was rising. I walked outside and sat down on a chair on the small lawn of the safe house to watch the sun rise on Srinagar. It was breathtaking. There were two empty lawn chairs next to mine. I wished Imani were sitting right next to me watching the sunrise. She'd had a great love for beautiful things. I took a deep breath and began reflecting on the past few months. I thought about my family. I wondered if they thought I was dead. I wondered how my sister was doing in New York City with Khalid. I hoped Tamer was staying out of trouble. If I had never started this journey, I would have been taking my final exams for my freshman year of college right now. Life was going on without me, and I was headed closer and closer to death. I should have died long ago. Our group had been lucky. So far, only Jawad had passed away. That fact alone was a miracle considering how suddenly death comes in war.

Farhan and Ali stepped out of the house and sat in the lawn chairs next to me. Farhan brought out some coffee and toast. I hadn't drunk a cup of coffee in over a year. That first cup of brisk, black, strong caffeinated coffee felt like heaven on earth. It warmed me to my bones and woke me up inside. I could feel the caffeine rushing to my brain and making me more alert. Ali looked at me and said, "Nick, Ammar, and Noor want to go home. They want to go back to England." He paused and asked, "Hanzilah, do you want to go back to the States?"

Before I could answer, Farhan added, "All you guys should go back home. Ali, you and Isa should go back to Keran as well."

I shook my head. "Our mission isn't done. We set out to kick out the Indians from our land. We are nowhere closer to accomplishing that goal. If we stop now, everything we have done will have been in vain. Jawad's death would have been in vain. I can't stop. We have to keep fighting."

Tariq and Ammar joined us. Tariq said, "Hanzilah, it's time we went back. Our mission as a group is over."

I didn't say anything at first. I sat there quietly for a few tense moments. I changed the subject. "Farhan, you told me you would show me Srinagar."

"Of course," he said, "Let's go." He looked over at Ali and Ammar. "Do you care to join us?"

They nodded.

Farhan was true to his word. We left the safe house and started out for the city. The safe house had several bicycles. We got on them and pedaled out of the neighborhood and towards the city center. It was early in the morning, and the city's inhabitants were waking up and beginning their day. I saw young parents walking their children to school. A group of boys and girls our age dressed in school uniforms walked ahead of us, toward the northern part of Dal Lake. Farhan pointed to them and said, "They are students headed to Kashmir University. I can tell by their uniforms."

Farhan looked back at me. "Hanzilah, I have noticed that you read a book of poetry written by Allama Iqbal. The library at Kashmir University is named Allama Iqbal library."

I nodded. "That's interesting."

From our vantage we could see the campus of Kashmir University. I asked Farhan, "Can we go and check out the campus?"

"Sure, that's my school. I know that place like the back of my hand."

As we rode, Ali said, "I wonder what college is like. I was supposed to go to college and study textiles in Peshawar."

"You know as well as I," I said.

We stopped at the entrance to the university's sprawling campus. Students were rushing to class. Boys and girls were walking separately, but then mingled in large groups. There was a group of boys playing cricket right on campus. It all looked so normal. I wondered what my life would have been like if I had chosen that path, perhaps blissfully ignoring the conflict in my homeland.

"This area in Srinagar is called Hazratbal," said Farhan. "There is a beautiful mosque here called *Hazratbal Shrine*. It has a famous relic in the shrine."

"What relic?" Ali asked.

"They say they have a piece of hair that came from the Prophet Muhammad," Farhan said.

I asked skeptically, "How could his hair have survived that long, and how did it get here all the way from Arabia?"

Farhan shrugged his shoulders. "Who knows?" He paused briefly, then told us, "Last year a group of Mujahideen sought safety in the mosque and shrine after a gun fight with the Indian army. The mosque was stormed by Indian soldiers, and every single one of the Kashmiri Mujahideen died. We shouldn't go there because there is a lot of security surrounding Hazratbal shrine."

We headed back to Dal Lake and circled around it. It was gorgeous. The lake was full of small pointy boats called *shikaras*. Some people were fishing. Others were transporting people. One man had filled his shikara with flowers and was taking them to market.

From the lake we turned on a clean gravel road and headed toward the center of the city. There were checkpoints and Indian soldiers everywhere. It was strange to see so many armed Indian soldiers in such a tranquil place. I asked Farhan, "Why are there so many soldiers in such a peaceful city?"

He sighed. "This city isn't peaceful. There has been nothing but tragedy and war here."

The city center was surrounded by large government buildings and private commercial ones. Surrounding the government buildings and commercial plaza were hundreds, if not thousands, of soldiers. A large group of protesters was screaming and chanting, demanding freedom. They were brave people, screaming right at the hundreds of guns staring them down. I noticed many young children wandering around alone, some of them even working. We were sitting on our bicycles outside a small tea house watching the protests, when a round-faced boy of about ten came up to me and asked, "Do you want chai? Five rupees for some chai?"

Farhan smiled at the boy and said, "No, we don't want any, little man." He handed him a five-rupee note. The boy smiled back and put the money in his pocket. He walked away to try and sell to others. I asked Farhan, "Why are there so many little kids here working?"

He shook his head. "Hanzilah, many of these children are fatherless. Their fathers have died or are in prison or have simply disappeared. Their families and their mothers need money, so they work instead of going to school."

Ammar remarked, "Kashmir is the same everywhere. It is a land of beauty but its inhabitants are suffering. Why can't we be happy here?"

"Occupation," Farhan said grimly.

As we wandered Srinagar I saw people continuing to live their lives in the midst of war and occupation, families attempting to raise their children in spite of the obscene obstacles they faced. The markets were crammed with women shopping for their loved ones. I saw men and women biking or walking to work. I saw children playing cricket, exactly like I had with my friends during my summers in Keran. I saw teenage boys huddled in groups, gawking shamelessly at girls. We saw a group setting up a wedding tent on the lawns of a hotel. It looked nearly identical to my sister's wedding tent. Life went on.

As we were walking, Farhan pointed to a hill station and said. "That is *Hari Parbat*." I looked up at where he was pointing and saw a huge walled fort sitting at the top of a round hill.

"I've heard of it," I said, "A man who was a refugee in Keran told me about it. He and his family left that place to live in peace in Azad Kashmir. His five-year-old son was playing cricket with a flat tennis ball when I met him. They were a nice family. I am certain he and his children died during the Indian attack and bombing of Keran."

We walked back to the city center, where the protests continued. The same little boy came back to ask us again if we wanted chai. He had a big smile on his face. "Do you want chai?" He was hoping for another five rupees.

"What's your name?" I asked him.

He smiled wider. "My name is Ibrahim."

"How old are you?"

He took out his hands and started counting. He pulled one finger out for each number. As he was pulling his fingers out he said, "I am one, two, three, four, five, six, seven, eight, nine years old. I am nine years old." A nine-year-old boy was selling chai instead of going to school. I pulled out another five-rupee note and gave it to him. Ibrahim walked away happily.

We watched as the protesters continued yelling and screaming, demanding freedom. Suddenly and without warning, the Indian soldiers began firing in the air to disperse the crowd. As I watched, one of them aimed his gun at the protesters and began shooting directly into the crowd. A couple of other soldiers joined him shooting indiscriminately at the protesters and bystanders. Men and women ran in all directions, fleeing the gunfire. Ammar, Farhan, Ali, and I ran with them away from the city center. We stopped behind a large building. The crowd had dispersed, and the soldiers were holding their guns upright and walking around. At least twenty bodies lay bleeding on the concrete. Ambulance sirens could be heard in the distance. Farhan pointed to the area where we had been standing. A child's body lay near the coffee house. It was the little boy, Ibrahim, bleeding out on the concrete. My mind went blank with rage. I put my hands up to show that I was unarmed and ran toward him. I pointed to the little boy's body as the Indian soldiers looked on and screamed, "Don't shoot! I am going to help this little boy!"

Several of the soldiers pointed their guns at me, as I knelt beside Ibrahim. He had been shot in the forehead. He was dead when I got there. The Indian soldiers came up to me and pointed their guns. One of them said, "Turn around and go back. We will shoot you if you don't. Leave him here. The ambulance will take him to the hospital."

I put my arms up, turned my back to them, and walked back to Ammar, Ali, and Farhan. They were looking at me intently. Softly I said, "Ibrahim's dead."

As we walked back to our bicycles, I thought once again about how quickly and cruelly fate stepped in. Ibrahim had probably been having a great day, high on the money we had given him and what he could do with it. And then, in a second, his life had been taken from him, all because the Indians wanted to assert control.

Ali said, "I can't stop fighting. I won't stop fighting." I held out my hand to him. "Neither will I." Farhan stared at us and said, "We are going to come back tomorrow and kill them all."

We returned to the safe house on Dal Lake. As we entered Tariq asked me, "What happened in Srinagar? We heard they shot at the protesters." Nick came up and also asked, "What happened?"

Ammar told everyone what we had just experienced. Tariq interrupted. "We need to kill these murderers!" Noor, Nick, and Isa sat listening. Isa stood up and said, "I can't go home now. I have to keep fighting."

Ammar staunchly said to Nick and Noor, "I am not going home to the UK. I am going to continue with the war."

Noor and Nick both nodded in agreement. "We fight on."

And just like that, the wind changed again.

We started planning our attack. Farhan, Mujahid, Usman, Zain, Aziz, Ramiz, and Syed were familiar with Srinagar and broke down how it was laid out. They described the best ways to attack the Indian army in Srinagar. We spent the next four hours planning.

At the end of our strategy session, I spoke up. "Tomorrow many of us are going to die, perhaps all of us. I don't want anyone to feel that they have to participate in the attack. It's a suicide mission." I looked over at Ammar, Noor, and Nick. "You guys were headed home a few hours ago. You should go home to the UK and live your lives. I joined the fight knowing that I was going to die, and I'm okay with that."

Ammar stood and said, "We came here to fight for our homeland's freedom. I knew full and well that death was part of the risk. We have been risking our lives for the past year. We are not cowards."

"I am prepared for the worst," Noor affirmed.

"If tomorrow is to be our end, then let's kill as many of them as we can," said Nick.

"We can make it out of the city," Zain insisted, "We can escape after our attack, just follow the plan."

Tariq looked at us. "Death is not certain for any of us tomorrow. Remember, we fight to live."

May 4, 1994

Love is freedom and contentment,

Not at the mercy of kingly power.

-Allama Iqbal

All together there were fourteen of us. We split into two groups of seven. In my group were Farhan, Isa, Noor,

Ramiz, Zain, Ammar, and myself. The other group consisted of Nick, Ali, Tariq, and the rest of the occupied Kashmiris. Our plan was simple. We would come into the city center from two different directions. One group would attack from the north and the other would attack from the south simultaneously. We would further split each group of seven into a group of four and a group of three. Four of our group of seven would attack the Indian soldiers head on. Three would stay back and provide support from behind. The attack was to last no more than fifteen minutes. We would get as far as we could into the city center and kill as many Indian soldiers as we could. At the fourteen-minute mark, we were to place timed bombs as we retreated to our getaway vehicles. If we made it back to our vehicles, we would then flee the city.

It was 1:30 a.m. when we began our operation. The darkness was our ally. We got into two unmarked taxis. We were to drive as close as we could to the city center and our point of attack. We parked our taxi about three hundred yards from the closest Indian army checkpoint from the north. The city was empty. There was no one walking around, no one in the city except Indian soldiers. That was good, because it meant no innocent civilians would have to die. Tonight, it was between us and our enemy. Our group of seven stepped out of our taxi together and got into position behind a small building, facing a checkpoint about a hundred yards away. It was manned by ten Indian soldiers. We probably wouldn't even get past them. Farhan spoke into the radio and said, "I am ready to walk my dog." The Colonel, leading the group that would attack from the south, replied, "I am ready to walk my dog." We were set. The pieces were in play. At 2:00 a.m. we were going to attack. We waited for the clock to turn.

At 1:57 Farhan looked at his watch and said, "Three minutes."

My stomach gurgled, not from hunger but anxiety. I hadn't felt this nervous since our first mission, but then again, this would be our riskiest attack yet. It wasn't that I wanted to die, but I didn't know what I would do if I made it out alive other than keep fighting. That thought calmed me.

The group of four that were going to be leading the way for us was Farhan, Zain, Ammar, and myself. The three that would be providing cover would be Ramiz, Isa, and Noor. Farhan and I put our machine guns down. I gave my AK to Ammar, sticking my pistol in my back pocket and a grenade in my hand. I unleashed the pin but kept my finger pressed down on it so the timer wouldn't start. Farhan did the same. We walked toward the checkpoint. The soldiers stared at us. We were still a good fifty yards away when one of them said, "Put your hands up!" We obliged. The grenade was still in my hand, but it was dark and the Indian soldiers couldn't see it. We kept walking, holding our hands high. Three of the soldiers had their machine guns pointed right at us, while the other seven stared. The clock turned to two, and five shots rang out, hitting five different Indian soldiers. Farhan and I threw our grenades and leapt to the ground. I took out my pistol and started firing, not thinking, just moving. Behind me were Zain and Ammar, also shooting. Then, the gunfire subsided and I stopped. The Indians soldiers were all dead. We were all still alive. It was a miracle. Ammar and Zain came running behind us to pass off the AKs. We sprinted towards the city center. Ramiz, Isa, and Noor ran behind us. I could hear gunshots coming from the south — Tariq and his group attacking. Sirens started blazing throughout the city. Indian soldiers began amassing, hundreds of them streaming into the city center.

But they were confused, not knowing where the attacks were coming from. To our surprise, there were no more checkpoints. Instead a tank was lined up protecting the city center. The Indian soldiers saw us running and started shooting at us. A bullet hit Ammar in the thigh, and he fell to the floor. We were shooting aimlessly at the Indian soldiers, who were protected by the enormous tank. We had messed up. We were all down on the concrete, firing uselessly at the Indians. It was over. We had no choice but to retreat. Farhan screamed, "We have to get out of here! Let's place our bombs and get out of here!"

Ducking and running, Zain set the explosive devices on the ground and against the building walls. I rushed over to Ammar and pulled his bombs off of him, setting them as quickly as I could. Farhan, Ramiz, Noor, and Isa did their best to provide cover to Zain and me. Bullets flew flying back and forth. As I was placing a bomb against a wall, I felt a thud against my shoulder. The bullet went right through my shoulder blade painlessly. The adrenaline was flowing too hard for me to register the wound. Zain and I had placed the timed bombs successfully. As I retreated, I grabbed Ammar and we ran back together, him leaning heavily against me, both of us bleeding onto the pavement profusely. We ran back to the yellow taxi as fast as we could. Ramiz, Noor, and Isa gave us cover fire as we ran towards them. The tank turned, took aim, and shot a massive missile right at us.

BOOM.

It hit a wall directly behind us. I was sure they were not going to miss again. A bullet hit me in the back with debilitating force and as I hit the ground, I heard our bombs go off in another series of booms. Smoke and concrete were everywhere. Farhan grabbed me up and the four of us kept running toward Ramiz, Isa, and Noor as they gave us cover. As we ran, a bullet hit Ramiz straight in the forehead. Noor and Isa tried to pick him up, but, Farhan urged them forward. He was gone. The six of us remaining kept running as fast as we could towards our yellow taxi. I felt another bullet in my thigh and let myself fall.

"Go on," I said, "I'm done. It's okay."

Farhan screamed, "No!" He scooped me up and ran. In his arms, I felt almost like a child being carried to bed. I could hear the chaos behind us, but as Farhan ran, his feet pounding against the pavement began to feel like a boat on a river, and the deafening noise blurred into the background. I faded into unconsciousness.

May 7, 1994

I was lying in bed. I looked up and a strange man I had never seen before was looking right at me. He whispered softly, "You have lost a lot of blood." He pointed to an IV drip. I looked to the right. Ammar was lying on a bed next to me. He was sleeping and had an IV drip connected to him as well. "We're still here", I thought with mild surprise. Instantly, I passed out.

May 9, 1994

I woke up. Farhan and Isa were sitting in some metal chairs next to my bed. Isa smiled. "You're awake," he said. I was in massive pain. My shoulder was stinging, my lower back burned and my right leg felt numb. My head was foggy, whether from the pain or the medication I didn't know.

Farhan looked at me reassuringly and said, "You're going to make it. You're going to be fine."

The same man from before came back and said, "You need to eat."

Ammar was still lying in the bed next to mine.

Farhan saw me looking at Ammar. "Ammar is going to make it. He lost a lot of blood. But he will be fine. He has been more worried about you than about himself."

Isa put his hand on my forehead and said, "You are going to live. Just keep fighting."

I could barely speak. In a broken voice I asked, "Where is Tariq? Where is Ali? Where is Nick? What about their group?"

Farhan looked at Isa, then back at me and whispered, "They are martyrs. They died fighting courageously against our enemy. They attacked straight into the city center and killed over forty Indian soldiers." I felt a burning from behind my eyes, but I was too broken to cry. My friends were dead. Tariq, Ali, and Nick were dead. Out of the four of us that had joined, Isa and I were the only ones remaining.

I gathered myself and asked Farhan, "What about our group?"

"We all made it except for Ramiz. He died during the gunfight giving us cover to escape. Other than you and Ammar, the rest of us made it out with some minor injuries."

"When I get better I will return to fight, " I said solemnly. "so I can avenge my brothers."

Farhan looked at me with sad eyes and said, "This war is over for you Hanzilah." Then, the tears came, rolling down my face in a feverish stream, and I wept myself back to sleep.

May 25, 1994

It had been two weeks since the attack, and I was starting to recover. I could get up, stand, and walk around the room for about five minutes before the pain became too much. Ammar was doing much better than me. He had lost a lot of blood, but he had only suffered a flesh wound in his thigh. I had been shot in multiple areas throughout my body. I learned that the strange man who kept reappearing to treat and nurse me was Doctor Shafiq. He had taken the bullets out of my body. He treated me with antibiotics and gave me plenty of fluids and blood to keep me alive. Considering the limited tools at his disposal, he had managed to treat my injuries successfully. We were in a place called *Khiram*, a hundred kilometers from Srinagar. Ammar and I were staying in the basement of the Grand Mosque in *Khiram*. The basement of the mosque had a small clinic where they treated the Mujahideen for the injuries they sustained during the war. There were a couple of other rooms with other fighters who were recovering as well. During the next few weeks I would pray at the mosque for the daily prayers. I would walk around it and try to give myself the physical therapy that I needed to recover.

It was an ornate mosque with blue and white tiles and a simple but large white dome. Dr. Shafiq and his small staff of volunteers took care of me and Ammar. Isa, Noor, Zain, and Farhan stayed at a safe house not far from the mosque and visited us daily to keep our spirits up.

June 15, 1994

Isa and Noor were sitting with Ammar and me on the lawn outside the Grand Mosque in *Khiram*. We hadn't spoken a word in five minutes when Isa said, "Let's go home."

"What home?" I responded flatly. "Isa, they destroyed everything."

Isa calmly said, "We can rebuild it."

I stood and said, "I can't go back home. There is nothing for me there."

Isa was adamant. "If you can't go back to Keran, then Hanzilah, you need to go back to the States." He then pleaded in a soft tone: "Go live your life. We did what we set out to do. We fought for Keran. We fought for Kashmir. We brought justice to our enemies."

"What about Kashmir's independence? We haven't won the war. We can't stop now."

"We aren't going to stop," Noor answered calmly. "The war for freedom will continue. You can't fight anymore. Ammar can't fight anymore. You both are injured. It's time to go home Hanzilah."

I muttered, "Summer is the time to fight. This is the fighting season. It would be cowardly for us to leave now, and I am not a coward. Why don't we wait to leave until the end of the summer?"

"Because right now is our chance to leave," said Noor. "There is a train that departs daily from Jammu to New Delhi via Amritsar. Once we are in New Delhi we will be safe. From there we can easily head south to the coast of India. Farhan told us that it is fishing season, and it's easy to travel using a fisherman's boat from the Indian coast to the Pakistani coast."

I was confused. "Why not go back through the Line of Control?"

"If we go back toward the Line of Control and enter through Pakistan we would most certainly be caught," Isa explained. "The way that Noor described is the way to go home safely. We could be in Karachi in a week's time."

Ammar got up, patted me on the shoulder, and said, "Hanzilah, put your pride aside. It's time to go home."

July 1, 1994

It was early in the morning when Isa, Noor, Ammar, Farhan, and I walked into the Jammu train station from different directions and at different times. We went to separate ticketing lines and purchased our individual tickets to New Delhi. We sat in two train cars in different rows. We didn't acknowledge one another, the safe thing to do. We had a twelve-hour train ride, with nearly six hundred kilometers to travel.

I sat on the same train car as Isa, separated by only a few rows. I watched him as the train noisily began to roll out of the station. He kept his gaze on the window, but his posture seemed content somehow, ready to be home. I stared out the window for the next hour as we traveled through Jammu. I didn't realize how large it was until we were leaving it. After about an hour I ordered some chai and opened a magazine I found on the floor to read. It was *Time*, and in it was an article about the Kashmiri diaspora's role in the movement. One of the peaceful Kashmiri activists living in the United States was asked about the civil war. "Our struggle is not a civil war," he told the journalist. "How can we secede from what we never acceded to in the first place?" He sounded a lot like my Uncle Riaz.

I put the magazine back where I had found it. The conductor announced, "We are now in Himachal Pradesh."

We had departed Jammu and Kashmir. I turned my head and looked one last time as it was floating away from sight, but I couldn't tell where the Indian-occupied land ended and Azad Kashmir began. When I looked back, I saw nothing. That's what I felt, a grave emptiness and void. I looked over at Isa, and he was sound asleep, looking much more peaceful than I felt. For the past year, anger had fueled me, been my life. Now what was I to do with all this anger?

Nearly a year had passed since the attack on Keran. It had been a year since I lost Imani, and I still thought about her constantly. It had been six months since Jawad had died, and I missed him every day. At least I wouldn't have to tell any of his family members about how he died sacrificing his life for us. There was no one to tell.

My friends had died, and I was lucky to be alive. I truly had thought that I would die in this war. I felt almost ashamed for surviving. How in the world had I made it out of there alive? It had never been my intention.

I didn't think I would have to face my father again when I left Keran a year ago, but now there was a chance we would be reunited shortly, if we made it safely back into Pakistan. Should I call him when we got to New Delhi? To call my parents and let them know I was okay was the right thing to do. But I didn't have the courage to face them after the way I had left. I didn't think I had a future beyond the war. Now what?

It was early in the evening when the train arrived in New Delhi. We walked out of our train cars continuing not to acknowledge one another. Masses upon masses of people scurried about. I had not seen so many people in one place in my entire life. We left the station and walked towards the area where the rickshaws were located. We just needed a place where there was enough noise for us to talk and meet with one another. The rickshaws were loud, and the masses of people everywhere gave us the cover we needed to meet and plot our escape.

Isa and I had been walking with one another. We both stopped in front of the rickshaws. We acknowledged each other and smiled. Isa said, "I can't believe we're in Delhi."

"I can't either."

Ammar, Noor, and Farhan joined us a few moments later. "It can't be this easy," Noor said.

"They don't know who we are. India has got seven hundred million people." Ammar replied unworriedly.

"We made it, mates," said Noor.

Farhan smacked Noor lightly on the back of the head and said, "We are not even close." Farhan paused, looked at each of us and said, "Follow me."

For the next thirty minutes we followed him through the enormous city until we stopped in front of a restaurant called the United Coffee House. We walked in. It was a prim and proper restaurant, the kind you might see in an Indian movie. I observed several German-speaking tourists congregating. The hostess arrived and Farhan spoke to her in Hindi. When we sat down Farhan said, "This place has the finest food, and I think we deserve a nice, well-cooked meal."

After we ordered drinks, Noor was the first to speak. "Isa, what do you plan to do when you get back home?" he asked.

Isa fiddled with his straw. "I plan to go back to Keran and visit my family. I'll start from there and see where things take me."

"Do you think you will return to fight?" asked Ammar.

"I don't know."

I looked over at Ammar and Noor. "Are you guys headed straight back to the UK, or planning to spend some time in Mirpur before you return?"

"We're going to the UK, and I don't think we will come back, at least not for a while," Noor said.

Ammar said, "I want a normal life. I want to be a kid for a while."

"I think I'm going to go back home and enroll in uni," said Noor. "I want to experience college life."

Ammar poked fun at Noor. "Noor just wants to go to uni so he can hang out with this Paki girl that he has got a crush on."

"That is a bunch of bollocks," said Noor.

Ammar grinned. "If you aren't going to try to hang out with her, then maybe I'll enroll in uni and give her a call."

"Stay out of it, Ammar." We all laughed.

Farhan looked over at me and asked, "Hanzilah, what are you going to do?"

I took a deep breath before I answered. “I don’t know, but I can’t go back to Keran.”

Isa looked at me in surprise. “Why not?”

“There is nothing for me there,” I murmured.

“Come back with me. You can stay at my home for as long as you need to,” Isa offered.

I shook my head. “I can’t go back to Keran. I will go to my uncle’s house in Lahore and stay there a while. That is, if my family takes me back.”

We shared a delicious meal together that night, splurging for our first time eating out in a year. I think my friends were relieved to have survived the war. I, on the other hand, felt nothing that night but emptiness. What had this year been for, if we were leaving without winning our freedom? Was all this killing nothing more than venting our anger? What had we accomplished? I was overwhelmed with disappointment and a sinking feeling of hopelessness. Farhan noticed and came and sat next to me. “Is everything all right?”

“I don’t understand what we accomplished,” I admitted to him. “We’re leaving our brothers behind.”

Farhan said to me soothingly, “Hanzilah, we will take the shackles of occupation off Kashmir. You should take consolation that you were a part of that process. Now is the time for you to go and live. What did Tariq say to you before the attack? He told you we fight to live. We fought, and now you must go and live.”

I didn’t say a word. I stared at my friends’ faces around that restaurant table. I realized I was happy for them. They had fought, and now they were going to live.

After the meal ended, we walked together back to the train station. We split up again and individually purchased our tickets for Ahmedabad, capital of the state of Gujarat. I followed a few steps behind Isa as we entered the same car and took our seats. As we sat and waited for the train to start moving, the seats of our car began to fill up. A young lady and her husband sat down across the aisle from me. They were giggling and smiling at each other. They looked like newlyweds, their lives moving forward full of hope. The loud clangs of the train distracted me from my brooding. As the train started to move, I closed my eyes and fell asleep. A few hours later I woke up and stared out the dark window. The moon wasn't full but it was bright. I could clearly see the land we were passing through: a vast barren desert. We were in Rajasthan. The young couple was sleeping as well. The girl had her head against her husband's shoulder. The man had his hand on top of her hand, rested on her thigh. I stared out the window at the desert of Rajasthan. I took a deep breath and fell back asleep.

When I woke up again, the heat and glare of the sun shone through the window and on my face. I looked back at Isa. He was awake and nodded at me. The young couple was still sleeping comfortably. The train announcer said loudly through the intercom, "We will be arriving in Ahmedabad in fifteen minutes. Please get ready to depart the train upon arrival."

The young couple woke up, and I turned toward the window. The land had changed. No more desert. I saw farmhouses, cattle, goats, and crops. I could see the city in the distance. As we entered Ahmedabad the city was waking up. The train came to a slow stop.

I followed Isa off the train. We walked to the rickshaw station and waited for the others. When they arrived together, Farhan said, "We have one hour until the next train. I suggest we go back to the station and buy our tickets for a place called *Dwarka*."

Noor asked Farhan, "How far is *Dwarka* from here?"

"It's about four hundred and forty kilometers from Ahmedabad."

"Is there another train after that?" I asked.

"No more trains. *Dwarka* is right on the Indian ocean," Farhan said, to our relief.

We walked back to the train station together, purchased our tickets for *Dwarka*, and sat down in the empty train.

When we finally stepped off the train at *Dwarka*, we could smell the ocean. Ammar, Noor, and Farhan were waiting for us at the rickshaw station. Farhan hailed two rickshaws. It was searing hot. I sweated profusely in the rickshaw, squeezed in so close to Isa that I couldn't tell his perspiration from my own.

After about twenty minutes, we arrived at *Bet Dwarka*. Hundreds of fishing boats were lodged at piers there. We followed Farhan to the beach next to a pier. He pointed to the beach sand and said, "Get comfortable; we wait here."

Noor asked, "How long are we waiting here?"

"Until nighttime."

I put my bag down and stuck my feet and body into the sand. The sand felt cool against my body. I lay there for about an hour, just thinking: about how to approach my family upon our return, whether I would always feel as close to my fellow mujahedeen as I was now, of what the families of my fallen brothers would feel upon hearing of their death. When my thoughts grew too heavy for my mind, I got up and walked toward the Indian Ocean. It was blue, but not a clear blue. I walked into the ocean and got about knee high into the brisk water. The waves were flowing gently. Ammar walked up behind me and asked, "Have you ever seen the ocean before?"

"Yeah, I've seen the Atlantic Ocean and gone fishing in the Florida Keys with my father," I told him.

"What about you?" I asked.

"This is my first time."

I was surprised. "Isn't England an island? How come you've never seen the ocean?"

"It never crossed my mind. The ocean is beautiful, now that I see it for the first time. I think I'll visit when I get back to the UK," he said softly.

I nodded. "I think we should travel as much as we can. The world is so big."

"We have that opportunity now," he said, "Surviving what we went through gives us an opportunity to do whatever we wish."

I wanted to say that he was right. But I didn't. I was at a crossroads and terribly confused. "Ammar, we have to stay in touch. This cannot be the last time I see you guys." Ammar gave me a big hug and said, "We will always be brothers."

Isa and Noor walked up to us, and we all stared out into the Indian Ocean. For the first time, I felt free.

It was breathtaking watching the sun set on the ocean as we sat on that warm beach. Night came, and Farhan still hadn't returned. We were still waiting exactly where he had told us to wait. Finally, we saw him and another man walking toward us from a distance.

Farhan acknowledged us as they approached and said to the man, "These are my fellow fishermen. We caught many fish in the north. These fishermen are my brothers."

"Then they are my brothers," the man responded.

We shook hands and exchanged pleasantries. Farhan calmly said to us, "Brothers, let's go."

We picked up our bags and followed Farhan and the man. After walking on the beach for thirty minutes, we came to a pier with four boats tied to it. We followed Farhan and the man onto the boat docked at the very end of the pier.

A strong breeze blew, ruffling our hair. Ammar's long wavy mane flew wildly over his face. The man revved the boat engine and steered us to the open ocean. Noor and Isa became seasick. Their faces turned yellow and soon enough they began to vomit. They were in bad shape as we made our way toward Pakistan. I got up and went to the man who was taking us there and stood next to him as he steered the boat. "Where are you from?" I asked him in English.

"I am from *Dwarka*."

"What do you do for work in India?"

"Fishing," he said as he pointed to ten barrels on the boat.

I walked over to the barrels and opened one of them. The smell of fish surged into my nose. I looked for a second at all of the dead fish, piled on top of one another, their eyes unseeing. I walked back to the man and sat down next to him. We stared out into the ocean together silently for a few moments. Then I asked him, "Are you married?"

He smiled. "Yes, and I have five kids."

"Your wife gave you five kids?" I echoed. "You have a very nice wife." He smiled back and laughed.

"My friends are getting seasick and have been vomiting," I told him politely. "I am worried they might get dehydrated. Is there anything we can do?"

"I will slow the boat down," he said. He did, and it came to a complete stop on the ocean floor. He went to a small chest and took out some ginger. "Eat this ginger," he told Noor and Isa. "It will help the seasickness."

The boys grabbed the pieces of ginger and began chewing it. The boat was calm on the water. After about twenty minutes, they began to look less pale. The man turned the engine back on, and we started our push west towards Pakistan.

The boat was small and cramped, and it was impossible to relax. The engine was too loud to sleep. Everyone, including Farhan, looked uncomfortable. The only man who seemed at ease was the man captaining the ship. The sun began to rise, and after nearly six hours on the boat we finally saw land: a small mangrove island. More mangrove islands came into view, and I could see the city of Karachi in the distance. I was relieved. I wanted to step off that boat as soon as possible. We didn't head directly toward the city, but instead into this dense area of islands.

The man navigated through the mangroves and cut a path through the water to a small pier. He docked, and we were all relieved to be finally back on land. Just in time for me – I had started succumbing to the seasickness. The mangroves were thick, but a clear path had been cut through them. We followed the man, and after half an hour we were out of the mangroves and staring at a paved road. Farhan and the man stopped right in front of the road. Farhan smiled at us kindly. "This is where we say goodbye," he said.

We said our goodbyes to the nameless fisherman who had brought us to Pakistan, and then it was time to say goodbye to Farhan. His job was done. As I was embracing him I said, "Thank you for saving my life. I will always pray for you."

"We are brothers," he replied. "There is no need to say thank you to your brother. Don't pray for me. Just pray for Kashmir and our people."

Ammar, Noor, and Isa embraced Farhan and said their heartfelt goodbyes to him. Part of me wanted to cry. Farhan had literally saved me. We had been through hell and back together, and now we were saying goodbye with no means to stay in touch. He turned around and headed back to the boat. We watched him disappear back into the thick mangroves. I never saw him again.

We were about twenty kilometers outside of Karachi. We stood on the road, waiting for a taxi or rickshaw to pass. It wasn't long before a taxi came. It was a small Suzuki Mehran yellow taxi, big enough to fit us uncomfortably. Noor told the driver in Urdu, "Take us to Cantt."

We drove through the city of Karachi for thirty minutes until we got to the upper-middle-class neighborhood of *Cannt*. Noor and Ammar stepped out of the taxi in front of an old two-story house. It was time to say goodbye to them. Isa and I embraced our brothers. We had started this journey together. They lost their childhood friend, Nick. We had lost our childhood friends, Jawad and Ali. It was harder to say goodbye to Noor and Ammar then it had been to let go of Jawad, Ali, Nick, and Tariq, because this time it was by choice. As I hugged Ammar goodbye, I told him, "I will come visit you in Birmingham, UK but only if you promise to come to Birmingham, USA."

Ammar patted my back. "You can count on it," he said.

I hugged Noor. "You saved me so many times. I wouldn't be alive if it wasn't for you."

"I will miss you dearly my friend," he replied.

It took only a few minutes for the driver to take us from there to the train station. We quickly bought our tickets and ran to make the daily train to Lahore. The train was revving its engine for departure when we got on to one of the train cars. For the first time in our travels from India to Pakistan, we sat next to each other in a train car. It was packed with people.

The train looked a lot like the trains we had traveled on in India. It was going to be a long ride, eighteen hours to Lahore. Along a brief portion of the route, the Indian-Pakistan border was easily visible. Just like in India, there were a lot of farms and farming villages along our route through Pakistan. We came to a place that was entirely desert, just like Rajasthan. We then entered the Punjab. The Punjab was lush and green — the power of the Indus and its tributaries was omnipresent.

Isa and I didn't talk much during our train ride. There wasn't much to say. We had spent a year together. I knew everything about him and he knew everything about me. Our shared experiences were things we didn't want to remember or reminisce about. It hurt too much to talk about what we had been through and the friends we lost.

We were silent companions on that ride, but I think it made us closer.

By the time we arrived in Lahore it would be early in the morning and still dark. I had only one place to go, and that was my Chacha Riaz's home. I didn't know what to expect. I hoped he would take me in and treat me the same as he had treated me all my life.

The train finally arrived into the Lahore train station at 3:00 a.m., and we stepped down and found taxis and rickshaws waiting outside. It was time to say goodbye. I was headed to the neighborhood called *Defence*. Isa was going to another part of Lahore called *Baghbanpura*. He would stay with his cousin there for a few days, then travel home to Keran. He was the only one who was going to return to the place where our journey had begun a year ago. I was overcome with grief as we embraced, all that we had lost crashing down on me. My body shook and I held back tears. "I love you like my brother," I told him.

"I love you like my brother," he said, hugging me tightly.

Finally, he let go and we walked to our separate rickshaws. Before he got into his rickshaw, I called to him, "Isa, we fought so we could live. Go and live, my brother."

"I will if you do the same, Hanzilah," he said.

He got into his rickshaw and it sped away towards *Baghbanpura*. "Take me to *Defence*," I told my driver.

Forty-five minutes later, I pulled up in front of my uncle's home. It was four o'clock in the morning. I rang the doorbell to no response. I rang again. No response. I rang a third time and saw a light come on the second floor. A man walked out onto the balcony. It was my uncle. "Who's there?" he called.

"Chacha Riaz, it's me, Hanzilah!"

"Hanzilah! Is it really you?"

"Yes, it's me!"

I saw him run back inside. The lights came on, and I heard him running to the gate. He slid the door open. I was facing my uncle. It was strange, his face looked the same as I remembered it, although I felt like an eternity had passed since us seeing each other. He grabbed me, hugged me, and said, "Allah, thank you! Allah, thank you! My nephew is here."

He hugged me and began weeping. "You're alive!" he exclaimed. "You're alive! Welcome! Welcome!" He held me, and I let myself be embraced in his warm hug. My aunt came out and asked tiredly, "What is going on?"

"It's Hanzilah," said my Uncle, "He is alive!"

My aunt was in shock. "Is it really Hanzilah? Oh my God. I can't believe it!" She came up to me and put her hand on my head in the way that all older Pakistani women do with male relatives.

My uncle grabbed my bag, took me by the hand, and pulled me into the house. He didn't want to let me go. He kept holding my hand as we sat in the living room. He said to my aunt, "Bring my nephew something to drink and some food." Then, still clutching my hand, he said to me, "Get up." He led me by the hand to the telephone and started dialing. Someone picked up, and my uncle said excitedly, "Karim! Hanzilah is in my house!" He gave the phone to me, and I put it to my ear. My father's voice was on the other end, saying, "Hanzilah, is that you? Is that really you?"

With tears in my eyes I said, "Yes, Dad, it's me. I am here in Chacha Riaz's house."

"Are you okay? Are you hurt?"

"I'm okay. I'm fine."

My mom came on the line. "Hanzilah, my son! Speak to me." My voice cracking, I said, "Mom, I love you. I'm back. I'm here with Chacha Riaz." It was so strange to hear my parents voices, warmer and more solid than in my memory.

My uncle held me by the hand the entire time. He wasn't letting me go. I spoke to my parents for the next thirty minutes, reassuring them that I was okay. I gave the phone back to my uncle, and my father spoke to him for a few more minutes. Then my uncle and I sat back down in the living room, as he continued holding my hand. He stared at me and said, "Thank God you came back. We missed you so much. We thought the worst. We thought you were dead. Tell me everything."

Then, shaking me to my core, the kitchen door opened, and a girl walked out of the kitchen holding a shiny silver tray with food and a bottle of Coke. It was Imani.

At first I thought I was seeing things, but there she was. She looked beautiful. I stood up and said, "Imani?

She stared at me and gave a weak smile. "Welcome home, Hanzilah," she said quietly.

She sat down next to me and my uncle. He said, "Imani moved here with us after the attack in Keran. She came to Lahore to get treatment. We decided to adopt her. She lives with us, and she is studying at Lahore College."

I stared at her. There she was. She was alive, but not the same. That quietly joyous spirit was gone. Softly she asked me, "Where is Jawad?"

I had not thought that I would ever have to tell his family what had happened. I was seeing the girl I loved for the first time in a year, and the first thing I had to tell her was how her brother, her sole remaining relative, had died. For the next three hours I told them everything. I started from the very beginning. I told them how we had trained for two months with the mujahideen. How we infiltrated into occupied Kashmir. About my brothers Ammar, Noor, Nick, Isa, Ali, Tariq, Farhan, Zain, and the other Kashmiris we joined. About Jawad and how he had died saving us. Imani wept when I told her about Jawad. I told her what had happened in Srinagar, about the little boy Ibrahim and the innocent protesters who had been murdered. About our attack in Srinagar and how I miraculously survived. How I was treated for my wounds, and how I returned to Pakistan by sea. My uncle listened patiently, taking it all in. Imani was in bad shape. She could not stop weeping. She got up and left without a word. I watched her go upstairs. My uncle stayed beside me. He said, "I love you Hanzilah. We all love you. But I need to know the truth. Please don't lie to me. Are you planning to leave us again and go back?"

I shook my head, this time certain that my time with the mujahideen was over. "No," I promised him.

Chapter 3
PEACE

July 13, 1994

I WAS EATING brunch in my uncle's home. I had not seen Imani since the first night I arrived. She would wake up early and go to college, and when she came back, she went into her room and stayed there. She didn't even want to look at me. I wanted to talk to her, needed to talk to her, but I didn't know where to begin. How do you start a conversation with someone who was at the brink of death and survived? Who, when she did survive, discovered that her family was dead and her brother was gone? My uncle had taken her into his home, and I knew she felt strange in this enormous city. Her life in Lahore was entirely different from the village life of Keran and must have been strange to her. It was strange even to me. All the people she had known were gone. Her family and friends were gone. Her village was destroyed.

Struck with determination, I walked out of my uncle's home and toward the neighborhood market of *Defence.* There I found a rickshaw driver and asked him to take me to Lahore College. Its gates were closed, manned by security officers who let in only students. It was a woman's college, so there was no way I was going to get in. I waited patiently outside. There was a large group of boys in gray pants and red jackets standing outside the gates of the college. I guess I wasn't the only twenty-year-old chasing a girl.

I struck up a conversation with one of them. "Do you know what time the college opens the gates?" I asked.

He looked at his watch and said, "In about ten minutes."

"Where do you and these boys go to school?"

"Government College." I smiled. That was where my uncle taught.

The gates opened, and a flood of girls emerged. The boys in blazers began handing out pieces of paper with their phone numbers on them, trying to give them to every pretty girl they could. The odd thing was the way they tried to impress the girls by speaking in English. Those teenage boys repeated the same phrase over and over: "Please take my phone number. Please call me."

I was laughing inside, but I supposed I was no different than them. I too was chasing a girl who didn't want to talk to me. I kept looking for Imani, but I couldn't see her in the crowd. Finally I caught sight of her walking across the green lawn of the campus alone. I began to worry that she might try to avoid me, so I stood to one side of the gate and waited. Finally, she walked out of the gate and headed toward one of the many waiting rickshaws. I walked behind her and loudly said, "Imani."

Startled, she looked back at me. She stopped and waited, a slight frown on her face. I could feel my heart beating. I was nervous. I didn't know what I was going to say to her. I hadn't thought I would get this far. She was wearing the white *shalwar kameez* school uniform of the college. Her hair was flowing in the wind, and those big green eyes stared right into my soul.

I stood next to her for a few moments, stumbling around, as she looked on. Finally I said "Hello."

"How are you, Hanzilah?" she asked levelly.

I smiled back at her, happy that she had actually spoken to me.

"When I am with you I do very well, but when I am without you, I suffer," I whispered. "I am sorry. I am so sorry. Please forgive me."

She sighed and looked away. "There is nothing to forgive you for," she said softly.

I owed her at least a hundred different apologies, and she let them all go. "How do you like Lahore?" I asked.

"It's so big and full of people."

"Have you seen the city yet?"

"No. I go to school and come straight home."

I smiled and said, "Let's see it together." I took her books, and we walked together into the city of Lahore. We walked for about twenty minutes until we came across a nice-looking restaurant. "Are you hungry?" I asked her.

She said nothing. I said, "Let's go inside and get something to eat."

We walked in and sat down. We talked, and slowly she began to feel more comfortable with me. Still, she was more inhibited than she once was, more protective of herself. What had I expected? How do you go through what she went through and come out the same person? I myself wasn't the same person. As we talked, I realized how different I had become. The events of the past year had changed us both. But they had not changed how I felt about her.

We left the restaurant and as we stepped out I asked her, "Have you ever seen *Badshahi Mosque*? I hear it's beautiful. I hear it's the second largest mosque in the world. Would you like to see it?"

She smiled at me for the first time. "Yes, why not. Let's go."

I called a rickshaw and said to the driver, "Take us to *Badshahi Mosque*." We got into the rickshaw together and she sat beside me. She kept her eyes on the window, and I watched her slender tan fingers rested stilly in her lap. I wanted to take her hand, but I restrained myself.

We arrived in front of an enormous building. Beside it was an ornate white and gold temple, and behind that was the *Badshahi Mosque*. The buildings in this area of Lahore were beautiful and wondrous. We were surrounded by Mughal, British, and Sikh architecture all in one setting. We walked towards the enormous Mughal compound and stood in front of its enormous gate. Walking toward the lawn just outside the fort, we came upon two police officers in front of a mausoleum. I asked Imani, "Who is buried here?"

She didn't know. There was a sign: "This is the Mausoleum of Muhammad Iqbal, also known as Allama Iqbal, the National Poet of Pakistan." The words settled into my body. The man whose poetry I had been reading, which had given me a measure of peace and tranquility throughout the horrific violence of war, was lying before me. I stood in front of his grave, said a prayer, and gave thanks to him as Imani watched. I imagined him as a young man like me. She must have thought I was being odd. But when I finished, I said to her, "One day I will tell you about what this man did for me."

We walked to the Sikh temple, called *Gurdwara Dera Sahib*. It was white and gold. A Sikh holy man named Guru Arjun Dev had been martyred at this site. The people of that faith had built this building to honor him four hundred years ago.

We finally came to the *Badshahi Mosque*. We walked across its enormous brick lawn and headed toward its white-domed prayer area. It was surrounded by tall minarets. We walked past a small museum with holy relics. As we exited the mosque I stopped right in front of the doors and gently took Imani's fingers in my hand.

I looked in her green eyes and said, "Every day I thought of you. It was you who kept me alive out there. I love you. Nothing has changed. But I want to see that twinkle in your eye again. I know you have lost too much, and I know that you are suffering but I want you to be happy again someday. Please give me the chance to make you happy. I love you and I want to marry you. I'll take you to the States and you can start fresh from what has happened here. Will you marry me?"

She said nothing for several moments. She stared right at me. She paused and I became nervous. Then she said, "Yes, but you first have to get permission from my new father."

"You mean my Chacha Riaz?"

"Yes, he is my father now." She laughed a little bit and I felt a deep warmth rising inside of me. Maybe a version of the future I had always planned on could still happen.

July 14, 1994

It was 2:00 a.m. when Chacha Riaz and I drove to Lahore International Airport. My parents and Tamer were coming to see me. They had taken the first possible flight when they heard I was in Lahore. My uncle and I went to the VIP lounge and waited there.

The door swung open and my family rushed toward me. My mother got to me first and cried, "Oh son, I am so happy to see you!" She began feeling me everywhere, making sure I hadn't lost any body parts. Tears of joy flowed down her cheeks.

Tamer hugged me next. He had grown at least five inches in the past year. "I thought I would never see you again," he said.

"I am happy to see you too, little man," I told him.

My father was watching me. I was afraid to look at him. He hugged me last, and as we embraced he whispered, "I love you, son. Don't ever forget that."

"I'm sorry. I am so sorry for what I put you through. Please forgive me," I said.

That afternoon, as we sat together drinking tea in my uncle's home, Imani walked in. My mother and father went to greet her, and she sat down with us. I couldn't take my eyes off her. After about an hour of small talk, she got up and went to her room.

My father and I went into the guest bedroom and talked. I told him everything I had gone through over the past year. He didn't say a word or ask any questions as I spoke. He listened patiently. He told me again that he and my mom loved me very much. "I don't care about the past. I care about the future. I want you to come home with us," he said.

"I'll come home, but only on one condition," I said.

"What's your condition?"

"I won't leave this country without Imani with me as my wife."

"I will agree to this condition, but only on the condition that you never go back to Keran or any other part of Kashmir again," he countered.

I didn't hesitate. "I will never go back."

He left the room and walked out, leaving me alone. A few moments later he brought my uncle in and asked his brother, "Hanzilah wants to marry your daughter Imani. Will you bless us with your permission?"

My uncle looked only mildly surprised. "If she says yes," he said happily, "Then you have my permission."

August 25, 1994

Completion of your Love is what I desire

Look at my sincerity what little I desire

- Allama Iqbal

I was sitting at the wedding altar waiting for my bride to arrive. It was a small humble wedding. My sister had arrived from the States to attend the wedding, and my parents and Tamer were present, as well as Isa. My uncle and aunt and their four boys were there, but the rest of the guests were unfamiliar to me, mostly. Imani's classmates from Lahore College were present. I didn't care about the wedding ceremony; I just wanted Imani. The drums and music began and some young children, along with Imani's classmates, entered the marriage hall. There she was, walking with my uncle into the marriage hall. She looked beautiful in her wedding dress, her brown hair parted in the middle, her see-through veil was on her head, long hair flowing past her shoulders. She was stunning. She came to the wedding altar and sat next to me. My father sat to my left, and Chacha Riaz sat to Imani's right. The maulana was sitting between us and he started reciting the same words that had been recited at my sister's wedding a year ago. He asked me if I accepted Imani as my wife. "Yes, I accept her as my wife," I said with as much certainty and sincerity as I could muster. He then asked Imani if she accepted me as her husband. "I accept him as my husband," she answered.

And just like that, the marriage ceremony was done. My father and many others came to embrace and congratulate us. For the next two and a half hours food was eaten, pictures were taken, and there was dancing. I don't remember any of it except for the actual ceremony, when I promised myself to her and she to me. That was the only thing worth remembering.

When it was time to leave, Imani and I got into a car decorated with flowers. The driver took us to the Pearl Continental Hotel, where my father had rented a marriage suite for the first week of our married life.

We walked into the hotel and up to our suite. I opened the door and carried her in. It was a magnificent hotel room, decked out with all the amenities. The bed was littered with rose petals I had sprinkled there earlier in the day. I carefully set my bride on the bed, knelt and took her hand, looked her in the eyes steadily, and placed on her wrist a diamond bracelet. She smiled and said, "It's pretty."

"You are so beautiful when you smile," I whispered. "I am going to make you smile as much as I can."

August 10, 1995

May God acquaint you with some gale

Your tides no stir at all exhale

Respite from books you do not get,

But Book Revealed too soon forget.

-Allama Iqbal

In the year since we got married, Imani and I had found solace in one another. The bubbly girl I knew before slowly returned. Some days were harder than others, but together we worked through the pain of all that we both had experienced. The anger that had fueled me had been erased and replaced with gentle affection and the promise of a normal, peaceful life with my loving wife. Slowly, she began to open up to me little by little, and I to her. I told her of my time with the mujahideen, and she shared with me the horribly lonely year she'd had after the bombing of Keran. We leaned on each other.

Imani and I had been in the States for four months. I started my freshman year at Stanford. I had reapplied and been readmitted. Imani and I would live in the family dorms for the next four years, as I pursued my degree in biochemistry, a popular major for pre-med students. She enrolled at San Jose State to complete her bachelor's degree, and learned to like the California lifestyle, although we both missed Kashmir.

March 13, 2002

It was my third year of medical school at the University of Alabama, my favorite year because the focus was on clinical rotations at the hospital. I had recently finished a rotation in the Emergency Department. I discovered that I really enjoyed emergency medicine and decided to apply for medical residency in that specialty. I left the hospital at 6 p.m. and headed home. As I walked into the apartment my six-year-old son, Jawad, came running to me screaming, "Baba's home!"

I knelt, picked up my son, and carried him into the living room, where a pregnant Imani was sitting on the couch, her hands on her belly. If it was another boy, we planned to name him Ali. I put little Jawad down on the carpet, and kissed Imani on her forehead and belly. We sat together, and caught up on our day while Jawad played with toy soldiers. We had dinner as a family, and after we put Jawad to sleep, Imani prepared some traditional Kashmiri tea. We sat outside on our apartment balcony and stared into the night. "Is everything okay?" she asked me. "You seem a little distant tonight."

I looked at my beautiful wife and said, "Everything is not okay. It's better than that. Everything is wonderful."

She smiled back at me. "Everything is wonderful."

October 8, 2005

I was sound asleep in our bed when the phone rang. It was my father, crying. He was trying to speak but couldn't get the words out. I quickly asked, "Dad, what's wrong?"

He calmed down and said, "There has been a massive earthquake in Kashmir. They are saying 100,000 people have died. The children were in school when the earthquake occurred. The schools collapsed on top of them. Thousands of our children are dead. Entire villages are gone. They are saying the entire city of *Muzzafarabad* is in rubble. Our hospital in Keran has been destroyed. I am leaving for Kashmir immediately."

"Dad, I'll go with you."

"No, son. We agreed you would never go back."

"Dad, please, let me go. I just want to help. You have to let me help you."

"You can come, but you can't come with me to Keran."

I hung up and turned on the television. CNN was showing terrifying images of Kashmir. The structures that my father and others had worked so hard to rebuild were crumbled, with who knew how many civilians underneath.

October 14, 2005

I landed at Islamabad International Airport with my father. We got our luggage and found a taxi driver willing to drive us to Kashmir. I had contacted a relief agency, and I was meeting up with a group of volunteers in *Muzzafarabad.* Dad would continue to Keran. It had been eleven years since I last set foot in Kashmir. I didn't know what to expect. The images and news reports had been very explicit in their descriptions of the damage, but to see it in person would be something else. We drove through Murree and up toward the Himalaya. As we entered Kashmir, we saw nothing but rubble, dust, and death where villages had been. Aid workers, trucks, food, supplies, and people were scattered about as we crossed from one valley to another. The response by the Pakistani government and the world to the earthquake had been rapid.

Helicopters flew back and forth across the valleys. Construction vehicles picked up cement and moved them from one place to the next. Aid workers sifted through the rubble looking for survivors. It looked eerily similar to the sight I had witnessed twelve years earlier in Keran. At *Muzzafarabad*, we found devastation everywhere. The commercial areas were gone. The buildings throughout the city were on top of each other. Beautiful houses that used to buttress out of the mountains were nothing but shattered cement. As we came into what had been the city center, I looked up to the Governor's house, and it was in shambles.

"The Governor and his wife are dead," my father told me.

I thought about the Governor, who had given me the gift of Allama Iqbal's poetry, along with advice that I leaned on whenever I came to a crossroads in my life. After a few silent moments I said to my father, "That man saved my life."

"He saved a lot of people's lives," my father said with sadness in his voice.

We found the headquarters of the relief agency that I was going to be volunteering with. As I stepped out of the taxi my dad said, "I will be back here in three weeks' time to pick you up." I looked at my father. He was growing older, and he looked it, but on his face was the same stoic determination that I had always admired, and I took solace in it.

I nodded my head. "I'll be right here, I promise."

October 21, 2005

My relief agency has been working in conjunction with the United Nations and the U.S. military. For the past week I've been working primarily in *Muzzafarabad*, where the most damage has occurred. I'm working in a makeshift hospital that the relief agency has set up. Even two weeks after the earthquake, we continue to find adults and children who are still alive beneath the rubble. I've been treating twenty to thirty survivors daily.

The survivors have varying degrees of injuries, but in most cases, they have breathing issues, are malnourished, and have suffered minor cuts and bruises. Luckily, that's all very treatable. Many times, a parent or relative will walk into the hospital and find that the child or person they thought was dead is still alive. Those are the good days. But in so many other cases there is no surviving relative, parent, or spouse. The survivor has to move on, knowing they are the only person in their family to survive the earthquake. It makes me think of Imani, who is waiting back home, not wanting to bear witness to further destruction. Many

Pakistanis and Kashmiris have begun lining up to adopt the surviving parentless children, and when I told Imani about this over the phone, she said, "Praise God that there are more people like Riaz"

I want to travel into one of the devastated valleys and help directly at the front lines. With a group of relief workers, I ride in a truck toward a small village forty kilometers from *Muzzafarabad*, right on the Jhelum River. As we enter the valley, we can see about ten structures that appear to have been small homes, totally wiped out. No one has been here yet, according to the manifests. We start going through the rubble, picking up cement blocks, and screaming at the top of our lungs to see if there is anyone still alive here. We have a handful of search dogs going through the rubble. With the help of the dogs we are able to pull out many bodies from the debris, though none of them alive. As I sift through the rubble, I hear a faint sound. "There's someone alive down here!" I say.

A handful of volunteers come forward, and we pull out as much of the debris as we can. There is a little girl stuck behind a wall. We use a sledgehammer to push through the wall, carved out a large hole, and pull her out. She has dark matted hair and closed eyes. She looks the same age as Ibrahim, the boy I saw be murdered in Srinagar. I put my fingers to her tiny wrist and can feel a pulse. She's weak but alive.

I feel her arms and legs for broken bones, and amazingly, find none. We radio a relief helicopter to come immediately. When the girl awakes, I pour water into her mouth. She swallows it urgently, looking at me with wide eyes. I hold her in my arms while we wait, as if she is my own child. She doesn't say a word.

"It's going to be okay. It's going to be okay," I say over and over again until the words lose meaning. Twenty minutes later, a helicopter comes and some medics whisk her away.

After they take the little girl, I need a moment to collect myself. I walk towards the massive Jhelum River, sit, and gaze across it. I'm overcome with sadness and hopelessness. Is this land cursed? I love Kashmir so deeply that it hurts me, and it feels like nothing I do can save it. Why, in this spectacular land, is there so much pain and suffering? What did my people do to deserve sixty years of war and now this massive tragedy? There is no more anger in my heart, only grief and sadness. I say a small prayer and ask God once again to give our people and this land peace. I stand and gaze into the middle of the river.

The water ripples, and as I watch, a bottle-nosed beast springs up from beneath it with a happy whistle, oblivious to my presence. I watch its head sticking out of the water as it continues downstream. All that I can do is laugh to myself and wave.

Jawad was telling the truth. There are dolphins in these rivers.

This story is a work of fiction based on actual events.

As of 2014, 70,000 Kashmiris have died and 8,000 have disappeared. Sexual assault has been used as a weapon of occupation by Indian soldiers. Indian soldiers have utilized torture and human rights abuses are condoned by the Indian government. In 2019, the Indian government in violation of its own constitution scrapped article 370, and revoked the limited autonomy of Kashmir. The people of Indian occupied Kashmir now live in the world's largest open-air prison.

Kashmir remains occupied.

ACKNOWLEDGMENTS

In the nineteen nineties, I traveled to Azad Kashmir. I visited Muzaffarabad and the nearby valleys. During my trip, I met with the refugees fleeing the horrors of occupation. For many years, I thought about these refugees and the people of Kashmir, they are the inspiration of this novel.

This novel is a work of fiction based on actual events that occurred in Kashmir. But it is a work of fiction, nonetheless.

Names, incidents, locations, characters, and the timing of events are based on my imagination and are used fictitiously. Any resemblance is merely coincidental.

There are so many people I would like to thank, but first and foremost, I would like to thank my spouse who supported my creative spirit. I would also like to thank Samir, Lucy, and Ethan for reading the manuscript and assisting me.

Made in the USA
Las Vegas, NV
31 October 2021